Her Ladyship's Ring

P. J. MacLayne

Her Ladyship's Ring
Copyright
© 2015 by P.J. MacLayne

Her Ladyship's Ring is a work of fiction. All names, characters, events and places found in this book are either from the author's imagination or used fictitiously. Any similarity to persons live or dead, actual events, locations, or organizations is entirely coincidental and not intended by the author.

ISBN-13: 978-0-9985014-3-7

Published in the United States of America.

Acknowledgments

Many thanks to Cornelia Amari for her continued support and encouragement

Also to my cover artist, K.M. Guth, for putting up with my inexpert suggestions

And to Amy at Author E.M. S. for her invaluable expertise.

*To my Uncle Loren,
who allowed me to spend hours in his jewelry shop
while he fixed watches.*

horizon. "But I don't think you're going to get much done tonight."

He was right, unfortunately. But I could at least tackle a couple before it got colder and darker. I knew where I wanted to start. "I won't get any done if we stand here all night." I said as I grabbed the bottle of window cleaner and headed for the front door. Luke picked up the newspapers and the boys trailed behind me.

The window seat under the bay window on the south side of the house seemed the perfect spot to sit and read or contemplate the summer blooms in the garden. At least, that was my vision. All the windows overlooked at the moment were bare bushes and a few remaining traces of the last snowfall. Even though they still had the original single pane glass, I didn't plan on replacing them.

I broke into song as I sprayed down the left-side window with an extra-thick coating of cleaner and went to work. To reach the very top, I had to stand on my tippy-toes and stretch. As the layers of dust and grime rolled off and the last few rays of sunlight streamed in the spot I'd cleaned, I smiled.

Then screamed and hit the floor when the window on the right-hand side shattered, covering me with broken glass.

Freddie—Detective Thomason—sat beside me in the ambulance parked in the driveway while the paramedics cleaned the cuts on my face and hands. Luckily, my arms and torso had been covered by my jacket. "Once we find the bullet," he said, his face grim, "We'll have a better idea of what's going on. Probably a kid who got a new gun for Christmas and couldn't wait to try it out. Happens every year, but normally they're shooting birds, not houses." He leaned across the gap and carefully plucked a fragment of glass from my sleeve.

I winced as the paramedic swiped a medicated pad across my cheek. "You're sure it was random?" I asked.

"There's no reason for anyone to be after you anymore, right?"

Not since the stolen necklace, a present from Jake, was anonymously returned to the Museum of Fine Jewelry. "No." At least, I hoped not.

A policeman I didn't recognize—and I knew most of the town's cops—shoved his way past Luke and Joe, anxiously hovering at the back door of the ambulance. "Detective, can I speak to you privately please?" he asked.

Freddie nodded and climbed out of the ambulance. I watched with interest as he and the officer walked towards the porch. The officer, one of those people who used their hands to talk, waved them wildly in the air. The flashlight he held created a miniature laser show as he moved it about. But my attention was diverted when the paramedic discovered another ding on my face and applied the medication that stung worse than the original cut.

"Are any of those cuts going to leave a scar?" Luke asked from the peanut gallery.

"They shouldn't." The paramedic cupped my chin in his palm and moved my head back and forth, studying his handiwork. He pushed a strand of long brown hair that had escaped from my bun away from my face. "Not as long as she keeps them clean and they don't get infected."

One more thing for me to worry about. I tried to remember which cheek James Bond's scar was on. Or were female PI's supposed to be flawless? If so, I'd never qualify. My glasses were enough to eliminate me.

It didn't take long until Freddie came back. "How long were you here before the shot was fired?" he asked. He seemed tired as he climbed back into the ambulance and stood opposite me, bending so his head wouldn't scrape the roof of the ambulance.

"Maybe fifteen minutes."

"And Luke and Joe were with you the whole time?"

"Well, no." With Freddie back into cop mode, not friend mode, I got nervous. "I drove up ten minutes or so before them." I glanced at the boys, and Joe shrugged.

"Did you go into the house while you were waiting?"

"No." I felt the heat in my cheeks. "I thought I saw something moving upstairs, and decided to wait outside for them. It was probably just the reflection of a bird on the window, but I didn't want to take any unnecessary chances. Besides, they were bringing the cleaning equipment."

"Did you hear the shot? Was there more than one?"

What the hell? "No, I didn't, I was singing."

"Badly," muttered Luke.

"Off-key," added Joe.

I never claimed to be good.

"But we didn't hear it either," Luke said, defending me.

Sirens wailed in the distance, and Freddie cocked his head as if to judge how far away they were. "I don't know how you get yourself in these situations, Harmony," he said.

"What's going on?"

Freddie stared out the back door of the ambulance. "The shot may not have been totally random."

There was no gust of wind, so why was I suddenly shivering? "What?" I sputtered.

"Officer Sloan located the body of an unknown male in the back yard. Until the coroner takes a look, we won't be able to identify the exact cause of death. However, based on Sloan's initial observations, it appears to be a gunshot."

❋ ❋ ❋

Later that evening, most of my best friends showed up at my place to make sure I was safe, reminding me I needed to buy more chairs. Not that I had room for them. Although the apartment took up the entire third floor of Luke and Joe's Victorian, it was only four rooms. Five, if you counted the bathroom. Or three, if you counted the dining area and living room as one room, because no wall separated the two areas.

Freddie and Sarah claimed the loveseat, and Freddie, as usual, had his arm draped over Sarah's shoulders, twirling a lock of her long brown hair between his fingers. Luke had dragged chairs from my kitchen table to the front room, one for himself and one for Janine. I had the place of honor in my new-to-me recliner. Joe sat on the floor near the front door, his revolver handy, acting as my bodyguard. The two bottles of wine on my coffee table—one red, one white—were untouched. None of us felt like drinking.

We didn't feel like talking either. We'd covered the weather, the latest Steelers' win, and Joyce McAllister's new baby, but we all knew what wasn't being discussed. I couldn't even work up the nerve to tease Janine about her new short and sassy haircut. The news channel was covering some celebrity gossip but it was just background noise. Finally, I couldn't take it anymore.

"How long will it take to ID the victim?" I tried

to sound professional and detached, but I don't think it worked.

Freddie grunted. "Unless his prints match someone in the crime database, he might never be identified. No wallet, no tattoos, clothing that can be bought anywhere. We might catch a break and find someone by his description reported missing, but there's no guarantee he has anyone who cares enough to file a report."

The information didn't help lighten the mood any. I shuddered and pulled the afghan wrapped around my shoulders tighter.

"Can you imagine dying and having no one miss you?" Sarah said softly, voicing my thoughts.

A long silence followed her statement.

"There's a lot we don't know yet," Freddie said. "Until we get the coroner's report, we can't be sure if he was killed at the house, or killed somewhere else and dumped there. The caliber of bullet that killed him may be different than the one recovered in the house. Officer Sloan is trying to run down a lead about one of the boys in the neighborhood showing off a new rifle and accidentally pulling the trigger."

"How long until you get the report?" I asked.

"Possibly tomorrow, might take a couple of days." Freddie grimaced. "If the coroner recovers a bullet, the State Police will want to analyze it, and that will take at least a couple more days."

Joe shifted, stretching his legs. "We can clean out the spare bedroom real fast and you can stay downstairs with us, Harmony. At least for a few days."

I blew him a kiss. "Thanks for the offer but I'll be fine here."

"Maybe you should put in an alarm system," Sarah suggested.

"Or Piper can stay with me for a few days." I grinned. Piper, Luke and Joe's dog, was fiercely protective of his people, and I was one of them. Unfortunately, his breath stank.

"As long as you keep your doors locked, vary your schedule, and keep aware of your surroundings, you should be fine," Freddie said. "You know the drill. You won't be able to work on the house for a few days anyway. Not until the investigation has wrapped up."

It's not like there was a schedule for the remodeling, and Luke had already boarded up the broken window. My research on the role of women in the Revolutionary War for one of the authors in the writers' cooperative would provide enough of a distraction to keep my mind occupied. With a winter storm predicted to move in within a few days, I'd be happy staying home and curling up with my laptop and a cup of hot tea. I made a mental note to check my supply of tea before I went grocery shopping.

❊ ❊ ❊

The wine glasses still graced the coffee table when I made my way to the kitchen and turned on the coffee pot. Sleep had been hard to come by, and

I needed more of a kick start than my favorite mint tea would supply. So much for my effort to cut back on caffeine. Despite the brave face I'd put on for my friends, the all-too familiar prickle of worry kept me from sleeping soundly.

As I waited for the coffee to brew, I put away the glasses and returned the chairs to the kitchen table. With my first cup in my hand, I settled into the loveseat and tucked my feet under me, ready to face the day. I'd venture downstairs to retrieve my newspaper after I woke up a bit more.

The footsteps on the outside stairs broke my temporary sense of contentment. Like a phone call in the middle of the night, anyone coming by this early in the morning could only be bringing bad news.

Freddie's advice rang in my head as I headed to the door, and I peered through the peephole as my visitor's fist struck the door. Pale blue eyes looked back at me. I grinned, and threw the door open.

"Still hacking into the police computer system, Eli?" I asked.

He answered by pulling me close and pressing his lips to mine.

"Actually, no," Eli said a few minutes later as he handed me my newspaper. "It was on the news last night." He grinned. "I didn't hack the system until afterward."

At least he wasn't bugging my place anymore. "So you caught a red-eye and flew right up."

"Something like that."

"I'm glad you did." I stroked his unshaven cheek. "It wouldn't be the same without you. So why don't you come in and close the door? The coffee is fresh."

We settled into the loveseat, cups in hand, and the coffee carafe on the table. "Are you sure you're all right?" Eli asked, eyeing the cuts on my cheek.

"Better now," I answered as I snuggled closer, the heat of his firm body more comforting than the warmth of the coffee. "I can't figure out who I ticked off this time. You don't have a wife you haven't told me about, do you?"

He laughed. "No wife, no ex-wife. You're the only serious relationship I've had in five years." He hesitated and ran his fingers through the tendrils of hair that had escaped from my bun while I slept. "We are serious, aren't we?"

It was too easy. "You may be serious, but I'm still playing the field. Hank from the bowling alley asked me out last week. And your friend Lando wants to know if I plan to share a room with him for the ComicCon."

Eli tensed, and I took pity on him, turning so we were face to face, and punched him lightly on his upper arm. "Yes, we're serious. I turned Hank down, and told Lando I wasn't sure if I wanted to go to San Diego. I mean, I let you in and I haven't even showered yet. That sounds serious to me." I leaned in and kissed him.

He sat up and put his coffee cup down on the table and then took mine and set it down as well.

He put his arms around me and tugged so I was half on top of him. With one hand behind my head, he returned the kiss.

His hand strayed down to my neck, and he pushed the collar of my robe over my right shoulder. His lips followed where my skin tingled from his touch. My own fingers caressed his chest in unspoken encouragement.

I should have known better. I was so involved that I didn't hear the footsteps on the stairs, and we were both startled by a pounding on the door. Eli groaned as I pulled away from him and stood.

"Are you expecting anyone?" he asked.

"No." But my apartment seemed to be a magnet for activity these days, instead of the quiet sanctuary it used to be.

"I'll answer it." He swung his feet off the couch, stood, and pulled his gun from its shoulder holster in one smooth movement.

Chapter 2

A few swift strides, a quick peek through the peephole, and Eli smiled, returning the gun to its hidden spot underneath his suit jacket.

"I suppose you want me to let Merrilee in," he said.

Merrilee was my blond friend with a supermodel body. But it wasn't a holiday, so she should be at work, not knocking on my door.

"Of course." I adjusted my collar and ran my fingers through my hair in a feeble attempt to restore it to some illusion of neatness.

Eli flung the door open. "Long time no see," he said, grinning at Merrilee's astonished expression.

"Aren't you supposed to be at work?" I strolled over and tucked my arm into Eli's. I'd clue him in later to the experiment. How long would it take for her to spread the rumor that he'd spent the night? And who would be the first to ask me about it? If she was paying attention, she'd notice that he was completely dressed while I was in my old flannel nightgown. "You want coffee?"

"Teacher duty day," she said, nodding, and I went into the kitchen to get her a cup. Eli followed and opened the cupboard door, giving him an excuse to lean close and huskily whisper in my ear, "One of these days, we will do this."

"I'm looking forward to it," I whispered back.

Yeah, that whole incident described our love life. Missed opportunities and interruptions. Someone always coming by my place at the wrong time. Hell, the night we went to his hotel to be alone he got an urgent call from work and I fell asleep before he got off the computer. With him living in Florida, he couldn't drop by anytime he wanted.

Merrilee only stayed for half an hour before leaving for work, muttering something about meetings. Eli got a call before she left so I headed for the shower after closing the door behind her. By the time I got done, he had his laptop set up on the kitchen table and was busy typing. I put on another pot of coffee, and turned on my own laptop. It would be a good day to work from home.

By mid-morning, his suit coat and holster had come off. The coat hung on the back of the chair and his gun lay on the table within easy reach. Not that I expected any trouble, but he obviously wasn't letting his guard down. My searches for information on the sex lives of the pioneers on the Oregon Trail were fruitless. All I found was porn. My author would need to use her imagination for the book, unless I could wade through the garbage and find real facts. Sex sells, but I sometimes wished the authors group I do research for would find something else to write about.

About the time I finally found a scholarly paper with solid information, I felt a soft touch on my shoulder. "Ready for a break?" Eli asked.

"Sounds like a plan." I bookmarked the site before putting the laptop on the coffee table. "What did you have in mind?"

"It's freezing outside, but I need to stretch my legs. How about a walk around the block?"

It wasn't *that* cold, but then, he was a Floridian. He left his suit coat on the chair in the kitchen, but re-holstered his pistol and strapped it on. I grabbed our jackets from the coat tree by the front door. I'd picked it up from my favorite thrift shop. A nice cherry red, it didn't match any of my other furniture, but I'd always wanted one.

As we walked down the steps, he zippered his coat. I grinned, and although the wind was blowing, left mine open. As we walked towards the street, I fell in step beside him. Without looking, he reached out and took my hand. We strolled a few blocks without talking. Avoiding the puddles and cracks in the sidewalk meant that once in a while we had to let go. Each time, once the obstacle was cleared, we joined hands again. It reminded me of being in high school, but I liked it.

After we'd walked six blocks or so, he suddenly

stopped. "I can see why you love this place, Harmony," he said.

I heard the unspoken "but." Not wanting him to say the rest, I interrupted. "You think it's cold now, stick around for a few days. There's a front moving in and the temperatures are supposed to dip into the negatives.

Eli zippered his coat up a little farther.

"Then you add in the wind chill," I added with a wicked smile.

"Come back to Florida with me," he said. "Spend a week or two."

It wasn't the first time he'd asked. He reached out, pushed a stray lock of hair away from my face and let his hand rest on my cheek.

I melted.

The squeal of tires broke the moment. Eli shoved me behind him, and in the next moment, reached for his gun. I stifled a giggle when he swore as he realized he couldn't reach it with his coat fastened.

"Get a room," called a familiar voice.

"Hey, Joe," I said.

"Welcome back, Eli," Joe pulled his car to the curb. "Harmony didn't mention you were coming."

I smirked and Eli groaned quietly. "Last minute decision," he said.

"We'll expect the two of you for supper tonight." Joe waved and drove off without waiting for an answer.

"We'll have no privacy tonight either, will we?" Eli frowned and shook his head.

"Unless I lock my door, unplug the phone, and turn off the lights."

"And the minute you didn't answer the door, a representative from the police department would knock it down, trying to make sure you were okay."

Although it was flattering to know how many people cared about me, at times it was inconvenient.

In silence, we turned around and retraced our steps, heading back to my place.

Freddie must have read our minds, because he pulled up in his Mustang as we walked up the sidewalk to my steps. From the serious look on his face, he was on official business. We waited for him as he got out of his car. He nodded at us before closing his door.

"I heard you were in town, Hennessey," he said.

Eli sighed. "Got in this morning."

"Staying long?" Freddie asked.

"Only a day or two. Don't know how much of this weather I can handle."

Freddie and I exchanged amused glances. "What's up?" I asked.

"I wanted to update you on yesterday's incident," he answered, with a lop-sided smile. "But perhaps we should take pity on the Southern boy and go inside." Thank heavens, he was in a happy mood which should mean good news.

We tromped up the steps and I headed to my

kitchen to start another pot of coffee, my cut-back-on-caffeine resolution forgotten. Then I took my place on the loveseat next to Eli. "Have you figured out who shot the window yet?" I asked.

"No, but we determined that the blast that broke the window was from a shotgun."

"Pellets?" Eli asked.

Freddie nodded. "Explains why the glass shattered so badly. A bullet from a rifle likely would have punched a solitary hole in the window, but left it otherwise intact. That means it was from a different gun than the one used to kill the victim. We don't have the results back on its make, but we can rule out a shotgun based on the wound."

"So are you back to your theory about a dumb kid testing out the gun he got for Christmas?" I asked.

"Yes. Still trying to track down the lead we got yesterday."

The coffeemaker beeped and I jumped up to bring out the pot and the cups. "How long until I can get back to work?"

"Don't rush it. We've got the back yard marked off as a crime scene. Someone from the department will let you know when we've finished processing the area."

I felt bad that I couldn't go back right away. At least people would be nearby to keep the house company.

"Why are you in such a hurry to get back to the house?" Eli asked after Freddie had left. I was washing the dirty dishes; he was drying them and putting them back in the cupboard.

"I have a connection to it, and don't want it to be lonely," I confessed. "Alone all these years, and it has such potential. Can't you imagine what it will be like all fixed up? And hopefully a young couple will buy it and fill it up with kids and cats and dogs."

Eli grinned as he put down the towel and wrapped his arms around me. "You know how they make kids, right?"

"Maybe you should show me," I answered, my voice a breathy whisper.

And his cell phone rang. He pulled it from his pocket, glanced at it, cursed, and answered. "What's up, John? I asked you not to call me unless it was an emergency." Eli sent me an apologetic look, shrugged his shoulders, tucked his left hand into his right armpit, and started rocking from his heels to his toes and back. I recognized the signs. This would be a long call.

I had listened to his side of calls before and understood little of them. When he talked programming, it wasn't the English language he used. So I left him to take care of business while I put together sandwiches for lunch. Nothing fancy, because I hadn't expected company. Just the basic baloney, lettuce and tomato on wheat bread. Eli liked mayonnaise and mustard on his, and I added sweet pickle relish to mine.

He didn't even notice when I set his in front of him. By now he'd resumed his seat at the kitchen table and was typing away on his keyboard. I shoved the sandwich closer to him, and he looked up, smiled, mouthed "thank you," and went back to work.

Seated across from him, I devoured my own. Then I returned to my easy chair, fired up my laptop, and went back to my research.

Two pages of my notepad were filled with notes, and I'd gotten everything I could from the site. But the researcher had linked to several other papers that looked promising. As I typed the first of them into the search bar a loud "God damn it, John, why didn't you say that an hour ago!" came from the kitchen.

I turned to see if there was anything I could do to help in time to see Eli slam the lid of his laptop closed.

"I'll be there," he snarled into his phone then forcefully slammed it down on the table. "One day with my lady," he said softly. "That's all I asked for." He glanced up as I walked over, stood by him, and ran my fingers across the top of his head. He grabbed my hand, pulled it down to his lips and gently kissed it. "I have to go. There's an emergency at work and I'm the only one who can handle it."

"I guessed that."

"I want to invite you to come with me. But from the sound of it, I won't be getting any sleep for a few days, let alone have time to spend with you."

There didn't seem to be anything I could say to help, so I rubbed his back. Sensing the tension in his muscles, I pushed harder.

Eli leaned forward and rested his head in his arms on the top of the table. "You don't know how good that feels."

I moved behind him and massaged his shoulders. He let out a loud sigh. "I don't want to leave," he said, his voice muffled. "Especially if I get more of this."

"You can't put off going back for one day?"

He sighed again. "No, but promise me we can pick up where we leave off when I come back." He straightened up, I leaned over to give him a hug and he put his hands on my arms. "And I will be back, Harmony, I promise you."

It wasn't until several hours after he'd left that my mind finally processed what he'd said. And then, despite the emptiness of my apartment, I smiled.

He'd called me "his lady."

Chapter 3

The predicted storm swept through Oak Grove, dumping six inches of snow in one night. A thick layer coated the yard around the old house and the footprints of the glass repair men mingled with the trail of a cottontail rabbit. Now that the police had finished their work and weren't tramping around the oversized lot, I guess the resident wildlife felt safe to come out of hiding.

The new window didn't blend in as well as I wanted, but I didn't want to replace all the glass panes right away. Besides, I hoped that after I finished cleaning the remaining originals the difference would be less noticeable. The addition of white lacy curtains should complete the camouflage.

They'd replaced the broken window on the second floor too, but I was in no hurry to inspect their work. In fact, I was planning on asking Joe to handle that duty. The room still gave me nightmares.

A loud squeak from the front door interrupted

my contemplation of the yard and I twirled around, but it was only Joe carrying in his tools.

"Thought I'd fix the doors on the kitchen cabinets," he said. "Have you decided on the knobs you want to use?"

I'd been unable to find any documentation on the original hardware. "I'll let you pick," I told him. "You have good taste." If it was left up to me, I'd end up with odds and ends found at thrift shops, and the house deserved better than that.

Joe grinned. From the glint in his eye, he'd already picked out the knobs and handles he wanted.

"Before you run off to the hardware store, will you check the window they replaced on the second floor?"

The look on Joe's face turned to one of concern. "You've haven't gone upstairs once since you bought the house."

Shit, he'd noticed. How was I going to talk my way out of this one?

He didn't give me the chance. "Now. You are going upstairs. I'll go with you," he said sternly.

"Naw, I'm good. I want to get these windows cleaned before it gets dark."

Joe grabbed my arm. "You can't avoid it forever, Harmony." His voice softened. "You might as well get it over with."

It wasn't logical for me to buy the house and then never go into the room where Eli and I had been held captive. I sighed, and nodded. "Let's do it."

Joe stuck close behind me as we climbed the stairs. There was no reason for my stomach to be doing flip-flops or my knees to wobble. I hadn't been this nervous when now ex-cop, Clearmont, stuck a gun to my back. The adrenalin kicked in so fast that day I never had the chance to be scared.

I paused at the top of the stairs to examine the bannister. One of the spindles was missing, and another cracked. "Are we going to have to replace all the rods?" I asked. "We'll never find any pre-made ones to match these."

"I've got a friend who should be able to make some," Joe answered. "They won't be a perfect match, but they'll be close enough to work. There's a couple closer to the bottom I want to replace too."

He destroyed my plan to return to the first floor and do an inventory of the spindles. Pretending it didn't bother me, I climbed the last two steps to the second floor and turned to the left. Just ahead loomed the open doorway to the empty bedroom.

"Do you want me to go first?" Joe asked from behind me.

The idea was tempting, but I needed to do this on my own. "No. Thanks," I gritted my teeth and started down the hallway.

I stopped in the doorway and scanned the room. There were no lingering traces of my imprisonment. The new pane in the window sparkled in the sunlight, and not a shard of broken glass remained on the floor. Someone had cleaned the room and I didn't spot a scrap of rope, or wrappings from the medical equipment they'd used on Eli, or dried blood anywhere. It was just an ordinary, empty room.

"Thanks, Joe," I said, turning to him with a brilliant smile. "I needed this. Did you do the cleaning?"

"Me and Luke."

"You painted too." I remembered the walls being a dirty yellow-white, as if a heavy smoker occupied the room sometime in the past. Now they were a pale blue, the color of my bedroom at home. Based on the slight, lingering odor of fresh paint, they'd completed the job recently.

"Just a leftover can from the basement," Joe explained. "We bought too much when we painted your place."

Smart guys. Having the room a familiar color erased the last bits of my anxiety. "It looks good. I owe you."

I made a trip to the third floor while Joe headed to the hardware store. The back yard was still taped off with police security tape, but from the third floor I'd be able to get an overview of the area. Curiosity about the spot where the body was found finally got to me.

Disappointment barely describes how I felt. There wasn't anything to mark the exact location.

The snow had concealed the proverbial chalk marks, if there were any to start with. Lots of little plastic flags of various colors decorated the ground, but I wasn't able to discern any pattern to them. I needed to ask Freddie what each color meant.

As I stared out the window, I caught a glimpse of movement in the shrubbery at the edge of the yard. Freddie had warned me about the possibility of curiosity seekers, and I reached for my cell phone to call him. Or maybe one of the investigators had returned, so I waited for a moment before dialing. When the resident cottontail bunny bounced its way from one bush to another, I grinned and relaxed.

I turned and noticed the closet door hung from one hinge, and the door knob had punched a hole in the wall. The damage was new, and I assumed that it happened during the search for the missing necklace. I wondered how many other unplanned repairs needed done. Without a notebook to start a written list, my less than perfect memory would have to do for now.

The last room I surveyed was the small room at the end of the hallway, the one I visualized as a home office. There was no obvious damage, but I opened the closet door just to check. Tucked away in the corner, I almost missed it. A neatly rolled-up sleeping bag.

Funny, I didn't remember seeing it there the last time I'd been in the room. The cops had been up here since then, but no one else that I knew about.

So where would a sleeping bag have come from?

Of course I checked it out.

I hauled the bag out into the light and unfolded it. It was just an ordinary green sleeping bag that could have been picked up at a dozen different stores. The tag had been cut off, but I didn't find that unusual. I always removed the tags from my blankets because I hated when they scratched my feet in the middle of the night.

It didn't look like something a homeless person would leave behind. It was too new, too clean. Nothing else in the room indicated anyone had been there. With the recent police activity around the house, I didn't see how someone could have gotten in without being seen. And the front door had shown no sign of being broken into. I needed to check the kitchen door to make sure it was still intact.

As I debated what to do, I absentmindedly started to fold the bag. Should I put it back where I'd found it or haul it downstairs? I raised it high in the air as I shook out the wrinkles, and a familiar scent wafted by my nose. It was the essence of the seashore on a foggy summer day.

In shock, I dropped the bag and sank down next to it, overwhelmed by the memories flooding my brain.

It smelled like Jake.

Jake always wore the same aftershave, Amber Bay, a specialty brand not sold everywhere. I knew because I tried to buy him some from the local stores and no one carried it. It wasn't sold on-line either, so I ended up giving him a tie instead.

But how would a blanket smelling like Amber Bay end up at the house? Granted, Jake wasn't the only man who wore that aftershave, but I'd never run into anyone else in Oak Grove who did.

The downstairs windows didn't just sparkle when I finished cleaning them, they *gleamed*. Any spots I saw were smears on my glasses. I rubbed harder and longer than necessary as thoughts frantically swirled through my mind. Counting and recounting the weeks since Jake had gone to prison, I kept coming up with the same answer. Another six months until his release date. But no one had said anything about him escaping, and there had been no news reports about it either. I couldn't believe Freddie would forget to mention something that important, even if he was dealing with a murder.

The idea that the body was Jake's crossed my mind. More than once. But Freddie had seen the victim, and surely he would have recognized Jake. So, thankfully, I discarded that theory.

Perhaps Freddie had gone back to his old habits of hiding information from me, to "protect" me.

The meager "hacking" skills I had wouldn't get me into Oak Grove's police computer system. Eli could, but I wasn't going to call him and ask. He didn't need to worry about his cousin based only on my over-active imagination.

Maybe the Oak Grove grapevine had heard something. Girls' night out was the perfect opportunity to tap into the news.

❋ ❋ ❋

"Is Freddie dropping by tonight?" I asked Sarah as we settled into our habitual booth. The Pink Flamingo was busier than usual, but Al, the manager, remembered to put a reserved sign on the table for us. He joked we should call him "Big Daddy Al" but no one ever did. Still, he appreciated our long-running tradition of spending Wednesday evenings supporting his business.

Al was big on tradition. He still had the same faded pink plastic flamingos in the front window that had been there for years. Of course, they'd been bright pink when he first put them on display.

The rest of the place was starting to show its age as well. The booths in the restaurant portion were an avocado green, popular in the sixties. Al kept patching them when the vinyl tore, but they were overdue for replacement. And the bar, where we liked to hold court, wasn't much better. Although smoking was no longer allowed, too many years of smokers had permanently stained the ceiling an odd shade of pale brown. Some days I swore I could still smell stale cigarette smoke.

Sarah giggled. "No. He claimed he had work stuff to take care of. I think he just wanted time to sit around in his underwear and veg out watching TV."

I tried hard not to visualize the scene. Freddie wasn't bad looking, but I'd rather see Eli in his underwear—or better yet, with nothing on.

"Earth to Harmony," Sarah laughed, startling me out of my daydream.

"What?"

"You were thinking about Eli, weren't you?"

Heat rose in my cheeks.

"Anyway," she continued, giving me a break and not teasing me any further, "I said Merrilee is bringing a friend tonight. A new teacher at the school."

"Oh?" I quirked one eyebrow. "A new friend, eh?" Merrilee's "friends" changed with the seasons. It was almost spring and time for her to find a new lover.

Sarah shrugged. "Not like that. She's a substitute filling in for the rest of the year and is having a hard time adjusting. Merrilee wants to make her feel welcome."

"I think we can help with that. Did you get the friend's name?"

"No, Merrilee got another call and we had to hang up."

As always, I kept my eye on the front door. "Well, there they are now, so we should know in a minute."

First impressions count for something, as much as I hate to admit it. And the lady with Merrilee made a good first impression. She was tall, with black hair in a cute pixie cut, a golden brown complexion, and an athletic build. I was still trying to guess what sport she played by the way she moved when they arrived at our booth.

"Hey guys, this is Lorelei Booker," Merrilee said, sliding into the booth next to Sarah.

Lorelei hesitated at the end of the table for a heartbeat, so I smiled at her, patted the seat beside me and said "Hi. Nice to meet you. I'm Harmony. Have a seat."

She smiled slightly and sat beside me. Sarah reached her hand out across the table and said "I'm Sarah. And Janine should be here anytime now."

"Please call me Lori." She shot a glance across the table as she shook Sarah's hand. "Merrilee thinks Lorelei is such a cool name she refuses to use my nickname."

The waitress came to get our drink orders, and we ordered Janine's standard light beer for her so it would be waiting when she arrived. Lori earned points for ordering a local brewery's wheat beer. I decided to be adventurous and try out the new IPA Al had added to his stock.

"What grade do you teach?" I asked Lori, filling in the dead space while waiting for the waitress to deliver our drinks.

"Usually grade school, but when the district offered me this long-term opportunity in the middle school, I jumped on it. One of the teachers will be out for the rest of the year on maternity leave." She waited while the beers were served and took a deep swallow of hers before continuing. "Now I'm wondering if I made a mistake. The kids say Mrs. Watson was some kind of super teacher, and I don't think I can fill her shoes."

"Don't try," Merrilee said. "Mrs. Watson is a good teacher, but you must be too or the school wouldn't have asked you to take over. So don't be Mrs. Watson. Be yourself. Sure, the kids will need to get used to you, but you'll be fine. Just give it some time."

Merrilee can be an airhead sometimes, but when it comes to teaching, she knows her stuff. Lori nodded, but I'm not sure she was convinced. She rubbed her neck, pushing aside her shirt collar, and I caught a glimpse of a scar. "I keep telling myself that," Lori said. "But I can't quite make myself believe it."

"How long have you been teaching?" I asked.

She paused before she answered. "About a year now."

She looked to be around my age, so either she was younger than she looked, or she wasn't telling us everything. Lord knows, there's nothing wrong with switching careers, and I didn't understand her hesitation to share. For some odd reason, I didn't trust people the way I used to. It might have to do with being kidnapped twice last fall. Still, I made the swift decision not to push the issue. There were other ways to get the missing information. When I was ready to dig, the entire internet would be at my fingertips.

The late but timely arrival of Janine drew the limelight away from Lori—or Lorelei, as Merrilee insisted on calling her. For once, Oak Grove's gossip network had nothing to solve the puzzle of the sleeping bag I'd found. I dropped Jake's name into the conversation at *least* once, but none of the girls picked up on it. Time for a different approach.

❋ ❋ ❋

Friday afternoon, I buried myself behind a stack of books at my favorite table in the library. Busy deciphering a map in an old atlas, I didn't hear him until a quiet cough broke my concentration.

"Hey," Freddie said, from his position across the table from me.

"Hey yourself. What brings you here?" A quick scan of Freddie's face told me he was on duty. He wore a certain solemn look that was as much his "uniform" as his ill-fitting suits.

"Mind if I have a seat?"

I shoved aside a pile of books so we could see each other. "Your taxes pay for this place too."

Actually, city taxes paid for only the basic expenses of the library. Back in Oak Grove's glory days, a large trust fund had been established to support its operation. The city paid for heating and electricity, while the foundation paid salaries and bought the books. Thanks to the Board of Directors' shrewd management of those funds, the library was in good shape far into the future. Being one of the original Carnegie libraries didn't hurt either, because groups interested in preserving historical buildings donated the money that kept it in tip-top condition.

Freddie grinned as he took the chair opposite from mine. "The city ought to charge you rent as much time as you spend here. Might help to solve the ongoing budget crisis." The truth was, I donated more money anonymously to the library than it would have cost me to rent an office, but only a few people knew that.

I snorted. "The way to fix that is to fire a couple of city commissioners who spend more money decorating their offices than the city spends on fixing potholes. But you didn't come here to talk politics, did you?"

"No." After glancing around, Freddie leaned forward in his chair. "I came to let you know they identified the body found over at the old house. His fingerprints were on file with the state."

"Oh?" I asked, trying to sound casual while my stomach churned. *Please don't let it be anyone I know.*

"He was a pawnbroker out of Cleveland. Had a small chain of stores throughout northern Ohio. Initial information says he wasn't very good at it and was on the verge of having to shut most of them down."

He still hadn't told me the guy's name.

Freddie lowered his voice. "They're still looking for his next of kin to notify them of his death. And this is confidential, you can't tell anyone. Not yet."

He leaned in closer. "Guy's name was Calib Booker. Calib with an 'I'."

This can't be a coincidence. "Booker, you said?" I asked.

"Yes. Why?"

The words rushed out. "I met someone with that name the other day. A new teacher at the middle school. She came with Merrilee to the Flamingo." I took a breath. "We missed you, by the way."

The frown on his face deepened. "What was her name?"

"Lori—Lorelei—Booker."

He pushed his chair back and stood. "It isn't the name of the victim's ex-wife, but it's a lead worth checking out. Thanks, Harmony."

I didn't even wait until he walked out the front doors before I opened a new window on my browser. *Let's see what I can find out about you, Mr. Calib with an 'I' Booker, may your soul rest in peace.*

Chapter 4

I ignored the reminder set on my laptop to tell me to go home—twice. Even the glares of Janine at the front desk didn't faze me. Ten different windows of my browser were open, and there were more links to explore. Mr. Calib Booker was an interesting man, although not necessarily a nice one.

The list of people with reasons to wish him dead grew longer with each new link. Well, almost. I doubted he'd done anything to upset anyone at the twenty-fifth anniversary celebration of the founding of the Baptist church he attended, and where he was a deacon. The majority of other articles made it seem like he didn't live up to his professed beliefs.

There was a chance he hadn't known the painting the little old lady brought in to sell was worth fifteen times what he gave her for it. When he bought the houses where an international corporation planned to build a mall? Sheer luck, because there was no proof anyone leaked the plans to him. The fact he gave the people who owned them less than the houses were appraised for, then sold them for ten times the amount was just good business.

The employees who claimed he cheated them on their pay and forced them to work unpaid overtime? Just disgruntled ex-employees who couldn't be trusted. The claims he beat his ex-wife and put her in the hospital? The ravings of an alcoholic who fell down a flight of stairs after getting blind drunk.

One article speculated he'd been the front for a crime organization, but the police couldn't prove it. The only thing they ever pinned on him was a series of unpaid parking tickets. And he'd fought those, claiming in court the city changed the parking zone behind one of his stores. Without ever having met him, I didn't like the guy.

"The library's closing, Harmony," Janine quietly said from behind me. "Time for you to go home."

I nodded, proud of myself for not jerking so she wouldn't see she'd startled me. "Yeah, I'm done here anyway," I closed the laptop's lid, stretched and pushed back my chair. "I'll put away the books tomorrow, if that's all right. Don't do it for me."

"Tomorrow's Saturday. Don't make a special trip in to take care of these." She smiled. "I'll put them behind the desk and let the volunteers deal with them. We've got a couple of newbies coming in and it'll be good training."

"High schoolers?" I asked.

"Yep. Wanting hours for their class project. They'll probably spend more time gossiping than working. If I'm lucky, there'll be a good one in the batch."

I started to object. Back in high school, I'd been one of those volunteers, just like Janine. In fact, that's how we met. Her arched eyebrows clued me into the fact that she was kidding.

"You almost got me." I smiled as I shook my head.

"Which shows me how tired you are. Now get out of here and don't do any more work tonight."

Good advice, and I should've listened. Instead, after eating my supper of leftover crock-pot beef stew, I plugged in my laptop and picked up where I'd left off, curious about Calib's family, and why the police were having trouble locating them. Of course, the ex-wife might not want to be found, and I wouldn't blame her. But how about parents, or siblings, or children?

When my favorite genealogy websites turned up nothing, I resorted to less reputable sources. There are companies who claim they can locate anyone, and for a small added fee, will give you their phone number and criminal history. Of course, some of that information is gathered from phone books, but, once in a while, they provide a useful tidbit of knowledge.

Not this time. The five different phone numbers I collected for him wouldn't do a bit of good. It's not like I planned on calling him. The man was dead.

Sometime after midnight, as I was getting ready for bed, the rather obvious thought finally struck me. I should call those numbers and see who answered.

More of the plan came to me as I tossed and turned, unable to find a comfortable position. I needed to buy one of those throwaway phones so the calls couldn't be traced back to me. Somewhere, I still had the one Eli gave me last fall, but I didn't want to use it. I wanted to save it for emergencies. Buying one locally didn't sound like a good idea either. Someone would see me and ask questions I'd rather not answer, and Oak Grove was small enough that the "news" might get picked up by the rumor mill.

Oak Grove was one of those "rust belt" cities, fallen on hard times when the steel mills moved overseas. When the jobs disappeared, so did the half of the population. The downtown area had more than its share of empty storefronts and the mall near the edge of town wasn't full. Not being a fan of the big box stores, my choices were limited.

A trip to Pittsburgh sounded like a fun way to spend my Saturday.

As I'd reached the on-ramp to the interstate I'd changed my destination. Instead of heading south to Pittsburgh, I made a last-second decision to go to Cleveland. I could buy a "burner" phone just as easily there, and make a side trip to one of the pawn shops owned by Booker. If word of his death hadn't leaked out, they should still be open. I would stop along the way, find the address in the phone book, and let the GPS app on my phone guide me to it. Maybe the trip would give me a different perspective of the man.

The clerk, a balding middle-aged white guy, didn't look up from his cell phone even when I sneezed twice. Once he'd asked me if I was pawning something or paying for something I'd pawned and I said no, I no longer interested him. Unlike Gary who owned the pawn shop in Oak Grove, he wasn't the talkative type.

Not knowing what kind of neighborhood his "flagship" store was located in worried me. Dolores wasn't built for undercover work. Though I wasn't doing anything illegal, I didn't want anyone to find out what I was up to.

A quick glance out the front window of the pawn shop as I pretended to browse the shop's slim section of books assured me she'd be all right. The shop was at the edge of a middle-class suburb of Cleveland, and most of the other clients were better dressed than me. None of them, however, had a nicer car.

Abandoning the books, I navigated a path through the cluttered displays to the jewelry counter. The number of wedding rings on display made me sad as I speculated how many of them were pawned or sold after a divorce. One ring caught my eye—it reminded me of my grandmother's ring, stored under lock and key in my safe deposit box. I cleared my throat to get the attention of the heavy-set clerk. "Can I take a look at this?"

He reluctantly put down his phone, picked up a set of keys, and sauntered over. "Whadya want to see?"

"This ring." I pointed through the glass. "Third from the top."

With a grunt, he unlocked the case, picked up the ring and set it on the glass top. As if handling a long-lost artifact, I picked the ring up to examine it. I also stole a glance at the clerk's nametag. Eric.

More than a simple gold ring, the engravings on the outside were an intertwining of two delicate ropes. They looked like Celtic knots. Any markings on the inside were gone. Someone, probably a woman based on the size, had worn this ring for years.

"Any idea on the history of the ring, Eric?" I asked. Make it personal, so he'd be more willing to bargain.

Eric smelled a potential sale and became talkative. "It's been in stock for a couple of years. If I remember, we got it from one of our regular suppliers. And the supplier hasn't been around lately, so I got no way to ask him. I'm surprised the boss hasn't melted it down for the gold content. Can't tell you much more than that." He eyed my ringless left hand. "Why doncha try it on?"

He didn't have to ask twice, but I slipped the gold band on my right hand, not my left. It fit as if custom made.

"Looks good on you," he said. "You oughta buy it. I can come down on the price a little."

The tag showed a price of one hundred-fifty dollars. I pulled the ring off and handed it back to him. "Let's see what else you have." Oh, I intended to buy it, but Gary had taught me a thing or two about bargaining.

Twenty minutes and five rings later, I sighed loudly. "I don't know. They're all very nice, but they just aren't 'speaking' to me if you know what I mean."

From the look on his face, he didn't, but he didn't want to tell me that. "So which is your favorite?"

I took my time studying the selection again. "I like the setting on the ring with the pink stone. What did you call it? Kunzite? But pink is so not my color." I sighed again. "And I like the first one, but it's a little on the plain side."

"I can come down ten bucks on that one."

"Only ten?" I shook my head. "You'll have to do better than that."

He could feel the sale slipping through his fingers. "One thirty-five."

"Tell you what, Eric, one-fifteen and we have a deal." I'd have to re-arrange my budget to cover it, but I really wanted that ring.

The clerk shook his head. "I can't discount it that far without getting approval from Mr. Booker."

"Mr. Booker?" I asked, pretending I didn't know who that was.

"The owner. The guy up on the wall." He gestured to a picture hanging behind him. "And he's been unavailable for the past few days. Guess he went on a trip and forgot to tell us. Wouldn't be the first time."

A trip straight to hell, I thought to myself. "Well then, I'll come back another time."

He didn't like that answer. "Look, things have been slow and Mr. Booker hasn't been happy. I'll give it to you for one-thirty."

I had him right where I wanted him. I chewed on my bottom lip. "Can I see the ring again?" After he gave it to me, I held it up to the light and pretended to study it, but I was really examining the photo on the wall of a pudgy man wearing a white shirt, black suit coat, and tie. His attempt at a smile looked more like a sneer. I was glad I'd never met him.

"I like it," I said eventually. "I'm just not sure I like it a hundred-thirty dollars' worth. You don't know anything about its history? Something that makes it special?" The ring called to me. If he could give me a clue as to why, it would be worth the extra few bucks.

When he shook his head, I handed the ring back to him and turned to leave. "Sorry to have wasted your time."

"Wait! You said one-fifteen?"

"Yeah."

"Don't tell anyone, we'll split it at one-twenty-two and it's yours."

At this point, Gary would have advised me to go for the kill and get the price lowered even further. But I felt sorry for the clerk. I suspected he might be out of a job once news of Booker's death got out. "I'll take it," He held out his hand and we shook on the deal.

He watched me climb into Dolores. Was he calculating how much she was worth? With a smile, I pulled out into the street and headed home with the ring and my new phone on the seat beside me. If he'd noticed her first, he wouldn't have offered me the bargain basement price. I got away lucky. Again.

My personal distaste for telemarketers who called on nights and weekends meant I wouldn't start my calls until Monday. But that was okay, since I'd missed my normal Saturday cleaning, there was plenty to keep me occupied. Instead of doing my chores to music, I tuned into the twenty-four hour news channel from Pittsburgh. If there were any breaking developments in the Booker case, they'd be the first ones to carry it.

I took time to call Eli too. Somewhere along the way, I decided I wasn't going to sit and wait for him to call me. If I was lucky and he was free, we'd talk. And my lucky streak held.

"Has it warmed up?" he asked.

"We made it above freezing two days in a row." And the sound of his voice made me feel warmer. "How's your weather?"

"We're having a cold snap. It got below seventy last night. I needed my jacket when I went to the store this morning."

"Wimp," I chortled. "How's your mom doing?" She'd fallen, he'd told me in a text.

"She's fine. Twisted her ankle, that's all. It'll be sore for a few days, but hasn't stopped her from her normal activities." He laughed. "She's a little upset she won't be able to go skydiving for a few months."

I wasn't sure if he was joking or not. "Your mother skydives?" I asked, amazed.

He laughed again. "No, although she told me she wants to for her seventy-fifth birthday. That gives me a few years to talk her out of it."

"I'd like to meet her."

Eli's voice softened. "You have a standing invitation to come to Florida. Just give me enough of a warning so I can throw away all the old pizza boxes." I could imagine the twinkle in his eyes.

I didn't tell him I'd already plotted the route to his doorstep and saved it on my phone. "One of these days," I said. "But not this week. I'm swamped. I need to raise my rates for research or start turning people down. I wish I knew whom to thank for my popularity." I had my suspicions, but knew he'd never admit it.

"I'm glad things are going well. How's the house restoration?"

"Pretty much at a standstill until the electricians get in there and do their magic."

He cleared his throat. "Any word on the dead guy?"

"Not officially. Besides," I teased, "I figured you knew everything the local cops found out."

"I've been too busy to keep up with it."

"Well, unnamed sources told me that he's been identified and the police are trying to reach his next of kin."

Eli chuckled. "Unnamed sources, eh? Should I take a guess? Are the initials F.T.?"

"I refuse to confirm or deny that." I didn't have to hide my grin since he couldn't see me. "You can wait a day or two like everyone else for the official announcement."

"Or not." I heard him trying to cover a yawn. "I have the day off. I've got my laundry to do and the next item on my busy schedule is a nap, but after that I can catch up on the news." He coughed. "If you catch my drift."

"Don't do anything that can get you in trouble," I scolded. "It isn't that important."

He yawned again. "It's not the company," he apologized. "I've been running on about five hours of sleep each night for the last week. But it was worth it. We landed a major contract as a result."

The way he talked about it seemed odd—but maybe he was using the "royal we." Either that, or he was a really loyal employee. I was going to tease him about it, but what he said next made me lose my train of thought.

"I dreamed about you last night. I was holding you in my arms and kissing your neck, planning what I wanted to kiss next." The longing in his deep voice made me quiver. "And then the alarm woke me. I miss you, Harmony."

"I miss you too, Eli," I answered in a whisper, almost slipping and saying the "L" word. I would have meant it, too.

Chapter 3

I tapped my mouse on the kitchen table as I studied the spreadsheet of requests from the writers' group. They were my priority, but it looked like most of the current requests were fairly easy. Three of the members had dropped out of the group, so there were fewer projects. In fact, based on the loss, I'd dropped my rate for them. I didn't think it was fair to ask them to pay me the monthly rate we'd negotiated in the beginning for less work.

I was trying to figure out where I'd get the money to pay for the cost of the wiring job at the Aldridge house. The quote came in way over the original estimate. If I didn't want to dip into my savings, I needed to rework my budget.

"Just use the money I gave you," my father, laughing, would have told me. "Consider the house an investment." But not only did I inherit his considerable estate, I also inherited his desire to depend on no one but himself.

With a plan in mind, I headed to my bedroom to

slip into something more comfortable before settling down on my loveseat to get to work. I paused at my bedroom door to flip on the overhead light. As my eyes adjusted to the bright light, I caught the faintest trace of a scent that didn't belong. Then, it vanished. I dismissed the sensation of something being wrong, telling myself it was just whatever Luke and Joe cooked for supper.

After changing clothes, I tugged the bedspread to smooth out the wrinkles and fluffed the pillows on my bed. Funny, I swore I'd done that when I made the bed in the morning.

Precisely at nine pm, I pushed the send button for the last of the emails responding to requests for research assistance. Regretfully, I glanced at the burner phone lying on my coffee table. Too late to make those calls to the numbers I'd found for Calib. And it didn't look like my schedule tomorrow had any empty slots with all the new projects I'd agreed to. That would give the cops one more day to find Booker's next-of-kin.

The next afternoon, I immersed myself in researching Colonial India. One of my authors wanted to write a romance story between a young English gentlewoman and the son of a wealthy local merchant. The more information I dredged up, the more plot twists I envisioned. I didn't notice Janine until, from across the table, she cleared her throat. Even then, it took me a minute to realize it was her, because the short haircut still threw me off.

"What's up?" I asked, leaning back and stretching.

"Do you have any plans for tonight?"

I did, but wasn't ready to reveal them. "Nothing much, just my normal stuff. You know, plot to take over the world."

She didn't groan at my well-worn old joke, and I wondered again why she was so happy.

"So can you come to the Flamingo tonight?"

On a Tuesday? This had to be big. "What's up?"

"Not going to tell you. You can wait like everyone else."

I glanced at her left hand. No engagement ring. Good, because I would've staged an intervention if she'd said yes to a guy she dated only once. Searching the internet for information on the Haida people of northern Canada, the only thing on my schedule for the night, would wait. Friends came first.

"What time?"

"Six. That will give everyone a chance to go home and freshen up." Her grin got bigger. "First round is on me, but after that it's everyone for themselves."

My eyes widened in surprise. Janine wasn't stingy, but she was notoriously careful about how she spent her money. Whatever her news was, it must be big.

In honor of the event, I left the library early to get ready. When I opened the door to my apartment, the odd feeling that someone had been there struck me. The memory of my apartment torn apart popped to the surface and I almost reached for my phone to call 911. That might have been the smart move, but instead I quietly walked through all the rooms. Nothing seemed out of place, and I decided my imagination was working overtime.

It didn't take long to read my mail, freshen up and get ready to go. As I went to grab my purse, my eyes fell on the burner phone lying on the coffee table.

"One call," I muttered. I sat, turned on my laptop, and pulled up the document with the numbers I'd found for Calib. Taking a deep breath, I silently prepared a speech, and dialed the first one.

"You have reached a number that has been disconnected or is out of service," the sparkly voice at the other end said. Drat. One down. I glanced at the clock, decided I had enough time, and dialed the next entry.

After three rings, I prepared myself for another recording, but was surprised by a male voice answering. "Yo."

"May I speak to Calib Booker, please?" I asked in my best phone operator voice.

"You got a wrong number, lady. Ain't no one here by that name. Whoever that Booker feller is, this isn't his number no more."

"Oh, sorry to bother you. Have a good evening." I grimaced. Two down and no more time. Janine and her news waited.

The parking lot of the Flamingo seemed unusually full for a weekday evening. Just how many people had Janine invited? I pulled Dolores in between two shiny new compact cars, hoping their owners would be careful when opening the doors and not scratch her paint. Most people in town seemed to be as protective of her as me, but I didn't want to take any chances.

A group of smokers hung around the back door. I recognized several of them and I waved in their general direction before heading towards the front entrance. My stomach growled as the aroma of a variety of freshly-cooked meals hit my nose. I nodded to the hostess in the restaurant portion of the building, and she smiled when she recognized me.

"The party's in the back," she said. "Have fun."

I snaked my way through the tables filled with families eating supper and headed toward the bar. Janine's birthday wasn't for another month and I tried to place what the occasion was, and if I should have brought a present.

Sarah was playing hostess, and she grabbed me by the arm as I stood in the doorway and scanned the dimly-lit bar. "What took you so long?" she asked as she guided me through the crowded room.

"Janine told me six," I protested. "And it's five 'till now."

"Well, we started early. Hey everyone, Harmony's here," she called loudly.

"Harmony!" a chorus of voices greeted me.

"Don't stand there, go get a drink." Sarah gave me a gentle shove.

With a faked grin, I went to get a beer, hoping Al still had that specialty brew from a local company on tap. Large crowds made me nervous, and this crowd was rowdier than I liked. Even Freddie, who I spotted with a glass of something, was getting into the swing of things.

With a beer in my hand I looked around, trying to locate Janine. A high-pitched squeal of laughter came from one corner, and as I turned in that direction, I almost collided with a man hurrying towards the front. Before I could get the words out of my mouth to apologize, he was gone.

"Well," I thought, taking a sip of my beer, "he must hate crowds too."

It was then that the scent of his aftershave hit my nose.

The shock froze me in place. By the time I recovered sufficiently enough to move, a quick glance assured me the man was gone and it was too late to follow him.

It couldn't have been Jake. Jake was still behind bars. I should have Freddie check on that. But if Jake had escaped, did I really want to let the police know he was in Oak Grove?

I wasn't absolutely positive that guy was Jake

anyway. His face had been turned away from me and he'd been wearing a hat and sunglasses. And it was hard to tell in the dark bar, but I thought his hair had been sandy brown in color, not dark brown like Jake's. No, it must have been a random stranger who happened to wear the same aftershave as my ex-boyfriend.

My train of thought was broken by someone loudly calling my name.

"Harmony! Get your butt over here!" Janine shouted.

Any possibility of sneaking out and begging for forgiveness later disappeared. With a forced smile, I headed towards the crowded booth. Freddie offered me his seat, but I turned him down, preferring to stand. If the opportunity arose, I could make a quick escape.

"So what's the big news?" I asked.

Janine giggled. "I'll make the announcement soon. Just waiting for everyone to get here."

I couldn't figure out who was missing, but this was her party.

During the next ten minutes or so, more of the employees and volunteers from the library drifted in. Merrilee arrived as well, bringing Lori with her. Lori looked as uncomfortable as I felt. I decided to help her out.

"How's it going?" I asked casually, sashaying up to the bar where she stood, looking out of place.

"Okay, I guess." Her eyes wandered around the room. "Merrilee didn't tell me this many people would be here."

"Janine didn't mention it to me either."

Her gaze settled on Freddie. "Is that Detective Thomason?" she asked in a whisper, surreptitiously pointing in his direction.

"Yeah, he and Sarah are pretty serious about each other." Another thing Merrilee forgot to tell her.

"Oh." Lori fidgeted with the glass she held, but didn't take a drink. "He makes me nervous."

"Why's that?" I suspected I knew the answer, but pretended innocence.

"He asked me a bunch of questions about some guy I never heard of before. Just because we share the same last name doesn't mean we ever met." She finally took a big swallow of whatever she was drinking.

"He gets very focused when he's working." I remembered all too well from the times he grilled me. Still, Lori seemed a bit too upset by a simple questioning, and I wondered what she was hiding. "If you haven't done anything wrong, you don't need to worry about it. So drink up and enjoy yourself."

The chance for further conversation ended when a shrill whistle broke through the overly-loud noise of the bar. I turned to see Janine standing on the seat of the booth, waving her arms. Freddie's hands were on her waist, making sure she didn't fall.

"Hey everybody," she called when the room quieted down somewhat. "Are you ready for the big announcement?"

The crowd cheered.

"It's about time!"

"Go for it!"

"Why else would we be here?"

I had to agree with the last person, whoever that was.

Janine grinned. "As you know, we've been without a head librarian since Andrea retired six months ago. In that time, the library board has done a tremendous job interviewing various applicants nationwide."

I'd considered applying for the job, but decided against it. There were still board members who looked at me suspiciously. Mostly the same ones who made it clear that I should resign after my arrest for drug trafficking. They figured even if I'd been cleared by a jury, the police wouldn't have arrested me if I hadn't done something wrong.

With a grin that stretched ear-to-ear, Janine continued. "I have the privilege of letting all of you, my friends, know they reached a decision today. It will be in the paper tomorrow. Your new chief librarian was the only internal candidate. Ladies and gentlemen, your new head librarian is me!"

I cheered along with everyone else as Freddie helped Janine down off the bench seat, but my heart sank. I fought back the jealousy and the tears. She deserved the position, but that had been my dream job for a long time. Just another thing Jake inadvertently took from me.

Chapter 6

Certain no one would notice, I took off after finishing a second beer—a non-alcoholic one. Between it being a school night and the middle of winter, the town's favorite make-out spot should be deserted. I could stargaze away from the city lights as long as I wanted. Or spend the time feeling sorry for myself.

With Delores's heater going full blast and the top down, I reclined my seat as far as possible and tugged my coat closed. The stars overhead sparkled brightly in a moonless, cloudless sky. I swiped at the tears dampening my cheeks.

Even with the warmth blowing from the heater vents, it didn't take long until I could see my breath. I pushed the button and watched as the convertible top eased into position and smoothly erased the stars. I was about to put Dolores into drive when my cell phone sang. I'd never changed the ringtone Eli set for himself and I almost smiled when I heard the opening bars of "Dream A

Little Dream of Me." I sniffed before I answered.

"Hey, Eli."

"I didn't wake you up, did I?" he asked.

"No." I sniffed again, this time because my nose was cold. "No, believe it or not I'm watching for shooting stars." Good lie, and I remembered something about a meteor shower. "What are you up to?"

"Missing you. Are you okay? You sound funny."

"I need to warm up, that's all. This was a spur of the moment decision, and I didn't bring a warm enough blanket."

"Harmony, Harmony," Eli scolded. "I wish I was there to take care of you. Or at least I could wrap my arms around you and warm you up."

"I like the sound of that," I said, my voice unconsciously dropping half an octave.

"Which one?" he asked with unspoken but not unheard longing.

"Do I have to pick one? I'll take both." I hesitated, not wanting to come off as too needy. "I miss you, Eli."

"I would be there in the morning, but I can't leave right now. Can you come here?"

The idea was tempting. Very tempting. It wouldn't take but a few minutes to throw some clothes in a suitcase. And Dolores had been tuned up just last week. The drive to Orlando would only take two days, and there wasn't anything to stop me.

"Harmony? You still there?"

"Yes, I'm here. I was thinking about it. Coming to Florida, that is."

My radio, tuned to a local station, suddenly blared a warning alarm, loud enough that Eli heard it.

"What's that?" he asked.

"Hold on, let me find out." I turned the volume control.

"A winter storm warning is in effect from midnight until ten pm Thursday," the announcer intoned. "Expected snow accumulation is in the range of twelve to twenty inches." I turned the volume back to its lower level.

"If I leave now, I might beat the storm." I pondered the possibility. How quickly could I get on the road?

"As much as I want you here, I don't want you to take any chances. Stay home where you're safe. You can come in a week or two," Eli said, but I heard the regret in his voice. It warmed me up better than the heater.

❋ ❋ ❋

Almost cheerful after talking to Eli, I headed home. My stomach growled as I unlocked the door to my apartment and pushed it open, reminding me the only thing I'd eaten at the Flamingo were peanuts. The package of frozen lasagna thawing in the fridge awaited me. Although leftover lasagna always tasted better when I rewarmed it in the oven, the microwave would have to do for once.

After flipping on the light, tossing my purse on the easy chair and hanging my coat on the coat tree, I headed towards the kitchen. As I filled a glass with water from the pitcher I kept in the refrigerator, I hesitated. Where did the package of lasagna go? I was sure I'd put it on the second shelf, right under the water.

"I must be losing my friggin' mind," I muttered and set the glass on the cupboard to free my hands. Either that, or I was still asleep and dreamed the whole thing. Not like I believed either one. Still, I moved aside everything from the front of the shelves and opened every drawer, and didn't find what I was looking for. I did find an out-of-date yogurt container, which I promptly tossed in the garbage, but no lasagna.

Puzzled, I opened up the freezer. Maybe it had been just my imagination. But no, there was an empty spot right where the package had been.

I considered the mystery as I warmed up a can of tomato soup, even checking the garbage to make sure I hadn't accidentally put the lasagna there. Sitting on top of the cereal box I'd emptied at breakfast, I spotted the balled up foil, all that remained of my lasagna.

While my soup cooled off, I rushed through the apartment, looking for something, anything, out of place or missing. I should have called 911 but experience told me they would find nothing. I certainly did. Even the ring was untouched and it was in plain view on my dresser.

Although I wasn't hungry anymore, I couldn't

waste the soup. After reheating it, I sat at my kitchen table and ate the soup straight from the pot. No sense in dirtying another dish. Whoever had been inconsiderate enough to eat my supper had been considerate enough to wash their own dishes. The contradiction puzzled and annoyed me.

It was too late to call Luke and Joe to ask if they'd seen anything suspicious, or if Piper had been acting up. Besides, the front door was locked when I got home—I distinctly remembered using my key to get in. No one had a spare key to my place except for the boys.

Sleep wasn't going to come easy, so I turned on my laptop and settled into my easy chair. Email first, and then I'd return to researching colonial India.

❋ ❋ ❋

Despite the impending winter storm, I headed to the library in the morning. I wanted to congratulate Janine again and more sincerely. Besides, I'd come across the diary of an officer of the British army who'd served in India during the years I was researching.

Around two in the afternoon, Janine caught me as I made another trip to the stacks.

"Go home," she said. "The snow and wind are starting to pick up. We're closing the library early. The police put out a bulletin asking everyone to stay off the streets if at all possible."

I hadn't looked outside for I didn't know how long, and was surprised when I saw nothing but a shifting whiteness through the large window in the reading room. "I guess the weatherman predicted this one right." I grimaced. "We should call off girls' night out too."

"I'll call Sarah if you call Merrilee. She can call Lori."

"Sounds like a plan. I'll see you on Friday if they get the streets cleaned off by then." I leaned in and gave Janine a hug.

"What was that for?" she asked, startled. I'm usually not the touchy-feely type.

"Just because." I grinned at her. "I'm glad we're friends."

Janine reached out and touched my forehead. "You don't have a fever. You must be working too hard," she said solemnly. "Take the rest of the afternoon off."

"I think I will, doctor."

After clearing off Dolores's windows, and while waiting for her to finish warming up, I called Luke to open the garage for me. It was good to have friends I could count on.

❈ ❈ ❈

The first thing I noticed when walking into my apartment was the afghan I kept on the back of the recliner. It was on the floor and hadn't been like that when I left. "So who's been sitting in my chair?" I asked. "Eli?" I called hopefully to no response.

Then I noticed the dirty dishes in my kitchen sink. "So who's been eating my porridge?" I whispered to myself. Surely a thief wouldn't have stopped to make himself a sandwich.

I tip-toed down the hallway, holding my breath. The bathroom was empty, but my bedroom door was partially closed. I carefully pushed it open and peeked inside. A familiar head nestled on my pillow. "So that's who's been sleeping in my bed."

Perched on my loveseat, with my hands clasped in my lap, I waited. Around four, my alarm went off. My guest must have set it. The springs in my bed squeaked, and I heard low swearing and the thump of feet hitting the floor. From my position, I knew I'd remain unseen until my visitor came into the front room. The door to the bathroom closed, and re-opened in a few minutes.

I listened to his movements while he returned to the bedroom, probably putting on his shoes. Finally, he shuffled back down the hallway, rubbing his hand through his short hair as he headed towards the kitchen.

"Hello, Jake," I said to his back.

To his credit, he didn't jump. Clearly, prison hadn't destroyed his rock-steady nerves. He turned to me with a brilliant smile.

"Angel! You're home early!" He moved towards me, opening his arms for a hug, but I held one hand up in the universal motion for "stop." He did.

"How did you get in here, Jake? I know you don't have the key. The lock was changed a few months ago after some of your 'friends' broke in. Seems they thought I had something they wanted." I frowned, and loaded my voice with sarcasm. "Oh, that's right, you're a world famous jewel thief, aren't you? I guess my little ol' lock isn't a problem for you."

I studied him. Prison had changed a few things about him. He'd lost weight, his hair was in a military-style buzz cut, its color a light brown, almost a blond. Had he dyed it? There were new lines in his face and I wondered what internal scars he'd acquired. The twinkle in his eyes that I used to love was nowhere to be seen.

He inched closer to me during my rant, and in one quick movement he closed the rest of the gap between us and wrapped his arms around me. "I'm so sorry. I never meant for you to be involved."

For a moment, my body sank into his familiar warmth. But in the long wait for him to wake up, I'd prepared myself for this. "What are you doing here?" I asked as I pried myself out of his grasp. "You have another six months to serve, according to my calculations. What did you do, escape?"

He laughed, that hearty, low laugh that used to make me quiver. "No, I'm out legally. Between the couple of months I put in while waiting for trial and the early release program for good behavior, I've done my time."

"Then why have you been hiding out at the Aldridge house?" The sleeping bag I found there made sense now. After all, he'd been the one who had shown me how to get in through the kitchen window. "And why did you sneak in here instead of just knocking on my door?" Something didn't fit, and I wouldn't be satisfied until I got the round peg into the square hole.

He sighed. "Can we at least sit while we talk about it? Have a beer or something?" Like he didn't already know I had a six-pack in the fridge.

I glanced out the kitchen window on my way to the refrigerator. The snow was falling harder than before, and the wind blew hard enough to make the lacy curtains tremble. Although it was still late afternoon, heavy clouds blocked the sun and the street lights did little to break the gloom. I closed my eyes and leaned my forehead against the refrigerator door. How was I going to be able to toss Jake out into the blizzard?

With a bag of pretzels and a couple of napkins tucked under one arm, and an opened beer in each hand, I returned to the front room. Jake was casually reclining against one arm of the loveseat. I set his beer down on the coffee table in front of him, and took a seat in my easy chair, putting the pretzels in between us. One of his eyebrows raised as if he wanted to ask a question, but he must have chickened out or decided to bide his time.

"By the way, I like your new car," Jake said as he

picked up his bottle. "Did you finally get tired of George?"

It amazed me that he remembered the name of my old car. "No, George exploded. It may have been mechanical failure, but the police aren't sure. A couple of teenagers attempted to steal him." I took a drink of my beer before continuing. "I bought Dolores as an investment."

He nodded and grinned. "Dolores, huh? Yeah, I can see that." Jake was one of the few people who didn't find the fact that I named everything funny. His attempt to change the topic of conversation almost worked, but I was on to him. I stared at him, hoping he would start talking without me having to nag. It didn't work. I guess prison had hardened him.

"How long have you been out?" I asked. "And why were you hiding?"

"A couple of weeks."

I did the math in my head, wondering why he was being so vague, and why he hadn't answered the second question. "How did you manage to stay hidden when the cops were swarming the house?" I asked quietly. "And why are you in Oak Grove anyway? Why didn't you go back to Atlanta or wherever it was you used to live? Or was that story a lie like everything else you told me?"

He carefully set his beer bottle on the coffee table and stood. "I guess I'd better get going," he said.

"Have you looked outside? You're not going anywhere, Jake."

I saw his fists clench. "I can't do this right now."

"Just look me in the eyes and tell me you had nothing to do with the murder. Make me believe that and I'll wait until you're ready to tell me the rest."

He walked over, knelt in front of my chair, and stared into my eyes. "I did not kill that man."

I watched as his eyes shifted. "But?"

He sighed. "I knew him."

Chapter 7

Three beers weren't enough to get Jake drunk. I nursed my two beers to make sure there were four for him and I wasn't positive that would be enough.

Jake still wasn't talking. Not about the things I wanted to know, anyway. In between long, uncomfortable silences when we both stared out the window at the still-falling snow, we did discuss a few things. Like a couple of the more interesting research projects I'd done, how much it was going to cost to bring the wiring up to spec in the Aldridge house, and Janine's promotion.

I studied him with each lull in conversation. The material of his pants was snagged and the elbows of his shirt looked ready to tear at the slightest stress. His hair was definitely a lighter brown than I remembered, and had hints of silver. Had he been dyeing it when we were dating or had he started going gray in prison? What worried me more was how dull his eyes were, as if he was recovering from a week-long drunk.

Supper was simple because I hadn't planned for company. I always kept everything I needed for omelets on hand, and I remembered he liked them. It only took a few minutes to whip them up while he made toast.

"Best food I've eaten for a while," he said with a smile when he finished off his last bite.

I could only imagine. At least the stuff they served in the local lockup, although nothing fancy, was edible. Prison grub, on the other hand, barely qualified as food based on reports I'd read. And what had he been doing for food since he got out?

He answered my question without me actually asking it. Either the beer or the food had loosened him up. "I've eaten so much food from the local convenience stores that the clerks started giving me discounts and letting me do odd jobs for what they couldn't sell." He looked at me sheepishly. "I hope you didn't go hungry last night. I figured you were going to eat at the Pink Flamingo, so I ate the lasagna you had in the fridge. Even your leftovers are better than what the quickie marts sell as fresh."

"Are you stalking me?"

"No." He ducked his head. "More like going places you always go, although I didn't expect you at the bar last night. I wanted to make sure you were all right."

"I'm fine." Now I was anyway. For a while last fall, it had been iffy.

"Yeah, I see that." Jake grinned. "In fact, you're looking pretty darn good."

"Thank you." I wasn't immune to Jake's charm, based on the blush rising in my cheeks

"So did you miss me?"

How could I break the news to Jake? I stood, gathered up our dishes and took them to the kitchen sink. "You want a glass of wine?"

He picked up our empty beer bottles and put them in the recycling bin under my sink. "I missed you, Angel," he said, coming to stand close behind me, his breath warm on my cheek.

I turned, keeping my face blank, although my stomach was doing flips. "The night we got busted I saw a side of you I'd never seen. You scared me. Then I saw those pictures of all the other women you were with and a piece of me died. I'll never get over it. Did you ever really love me?"

He reached up and softly rested one hand on my cheek. "I still do."

Shit, I'd set myself up for that. One look in his eyes convinced me he meant it, too.

I turned my back to him and started running water in the sink to wash the dishes. "A lot of things have changed," I said as I stared out the little window over the sink. The glow of the streetlights illuminated the heavy snow. "We aren't the same people we used to be."

"I know why *I've* changed," he said, pressing his body against mine and turning off the faucet. "What changed you?"

I stiffened at his touch and laughed harshly.

"Besides being drugged, kidnapped, having a gun pointed at me and threatened with death? How about thinking that you could have fixed it all with just a few words and you didn't?"

He pulled away. I held myself motionless and continued staring out the window while I listened to his footsteps move away. The sound of the front door opening broke me out of my trance.

"I guess I'm stuck here," he said as I rounded the corner from the kitchen. He closed the door against the blast of frigid air, and wiped off snowflakes from his clothes. "You sure there's no more beer?"

A six-pack of beer normally lasted me two weeks. We'd finished it off in one night. "I'm sure."

"You know what I haven't had forever?" he asked with a crooked grin. "Hot chocolate. Got any?"

Hot chocolate I could handle. I always kept some stashed in my cupboard. I even had miniature marshmallows to put on top.

To fill the silence between us, I turned on the TV before settling into my easy chair with my cup. Jake was already sprawled out on the loveseat, clearly hoping I'd sit beside him, but I wanted to maintain a physical distance. The first sip I took was too hot for my liking. I blew on the surface to cool it down and watched the marshmallows crowd up against the edge of the cup. From the corner of my eye, I noticed Jake doing the same. He looked as nervous as I felt.

I didn't remember him ever being nervous. His self-assurance was one of the things that attracted me to him. There were hundreds of things I wanted to ask him, to say to him, but I decided to wait.

I found an old sitcom to fill the time. Surprisingly, I enjoyed the subtle humor and sexual innuendo. When one of those obnoxiously loud commercials came on I muted the sound. That's when he broke.

"I have a confession to make, Harmony."

What happened to calling me Angel? Still, I didn't say a word.

"I was scared. Prison is not a good place to be." Jake put his elbows on his knees and stared at the floor.

No shit, Sherlock.

"They tell you when to sleep, when to wake up, when to take a piss. No matter how hard you try to follow their rules, there's always some asshole of a guard that wants to make your life more miserable than it already is. You jump when they say jump, but it isn't high enough. If you aren't awake ten minutes before the whistle goes off, you're sleeping in late. This one particular guard made it a mission to try to get me in trouble. Guy by the name of Wesley. No clue what I did to upset him in the first place, but it was bad enough that I overheard other guards telling him to lighten up.

"You know me, I was used to coming and going on my own time and answering to no one. In prison, someone was always watching me. Hell, the other inmates told me they'd never seen anyone in the general population be under such intense scrutiny.”

I turned off the TV and went to sit beside him, putting one hand on his shoulder.

“When those pictures of you showed up in my cell, I had no idea how they got there.” I knew which pictures he was talking about. They’d been taken when I’d been kidnapped last fall. Jake took a shaky breath. “The attached instructions said to put the exact location of the necklace on the back side of the paper and leave it on my cot when I went to lunch.” He looked up at me. “If the authorities were able to connect me to the necklace, I would spend years in prison. So I convinced myself the pictures were bogus. Someone snapped a picture of you and altered it. Besides, I had my cousin looking out for you.”

“Is this about forgiveness, Jake?” I asked quietly. “Because I can’t forgive you. I’m not the only person who was hurt by your cowardice. Two good men might have died trying to protect me. Both of them carry the scars to prove it.” I held out my wrists to him. “I have a few scars myself.” Small ones, but they were there. For the most part, I tried to pretend there were no emotional scars.

He lightly ran his fingers over the lines on one wrist and groaned.

“And you aren’t the only one who lost their privacy,” I continued. “I was being followed by both the FBI and Stephen Sallis’ goons. Somebody bugged the apartment and put a tracker on my car. Hell, one of the town cops was on his payroll.”

Another one worked for the FBI, but I decided not to mention that. "Wouldn't surprise me if the prison guard who gave you such a bad time didn't answer to him as well."

His head jerked up. "Stephen Sallis? I've heard the name. What does he have to do with anything?"

"His wife wanted the necklace. The one you stole."

Jake turned and took my hands into his. Looking me in the eye, he said "Stay away from him. He's bad business."

I snorted. "You think I don't know that? He managed to get out on bail, but the other four men are still under lock and key until their trials." Sighing, I added, "And since they're facing charges on the federal level, it might be a long time before they get in front of a judge and jury."

"Is that why you're taking shooting lessons?"

"You have been stalking me." I pulled my hands away from his. "Why are you in Oak Grove anyway? I don't believe it's because you wanted to make sure I was all right. You could have done that with a phone call."

"Why else would I come back to a town like Oak Grove?" he asked, desire coloring his voice. He rested one hand on my upper thigh.

I believed him for all of two seconds, then brushed his hand away. "Are you trying to play me, Hennessey? Because it's not going to happen." It made me wonder how much of the story he'd told me was true.

He gave me a wry grin. "Damn it, I'm out of

practice. Of course, you never fell for my lines. That's one thing that attracted me to you."

Maybe or maybe not, but I'd fallen for him hook, line, and sinker. Even though that was oh-so-long-ago, my heart remembered. It also remembered how he'd broken it.

"Strike two. You wanna try for a third one?" I crossed my arms across my chest.

His shoulders slumped. "You want the truth? The condo I told you I had in Atlanta? It doesn't exist."

I wasn't surprised. Disappointed, maybe.

"I did have a place there. A little two-room barely-furnished excuse for an apartment. Its biggest attraction was a landlord who didn't pay any attention to my schedule. Hell, most of the time he was either drunk or high on whatever drug was available. He wouldn't be able to tell the cops anything. All he cared about was getting the rent money to pay for his next fix. But it gave me a legal address."

"Why didn't you go back there?"

He grunted. "After my conviction, a friend moved what little stuff I kept there into storage. I figured at least it might be there for me when I got out if I wanted it. If Marty had figured out I was locked up, he would have sold my stuff in a heartbeat. And then when I showed up he'd claim it got stolen. Once I figure out where I'm going, I'll make a trip up and retrieve it. Although I need to make a trip to Florida first to get my car. My cousin is keeping it for me."

"Eli?" I asked. He'd never mentioned it to me.

Jake nodded. "I told him to drive it once in a while. I hope it's still in one piece. I'm not so worried about his driving as all the old ladies down there who can't see over the steering wheel."

I grinned at the image. We had our share of those in Oak Grove too. But the conversation triggered another thought. "Does Eli know you're out?"

"Not yet," he said, shaking his head. "I wanted to get a plan pulled together before I called him. Mostly so he has something to tell his parents. They worry about me more than my own parents ever did."

Jake had always avoided talking about his parents. "Have you called them?"

"My father is dead. And I don't plan on contacting my mother. She's not a person I want in my life."

I couldn't imagine feeling that way about my mother, but decided it wasn't the time to push. "I think you should give Eli a call." I glanced at the clock. It was almost midnight. "Shit, is it that late? You can call him tomorrow."

"I guess I should go." Jake stood and stretched. "Thanks for the supper and the company. Is it okay if I come back by tomorrow?"

"It still hasn't gotten through to you, has it? You're stuck here tonight." It wouldn't be the first night Jake had stayed at my apartment, but I didn't plan on sharing my bed with him this time. He raised an eyebrow and grinned. I rushed to finish. "The easy chair is really quite comfortable."

"Your bed is big enough for two. Wouldn't be the first time we shared it," he said, his voice husky.

I stared at the floor. If I looked him in the eye, I might find it hard to resist. "I'm sorry, Jake. Not happening."

"Okay then." He hesitated, like he wanted to argue. Then his shoulders slumped. "I'll take the chair. Although I wish you'd kept your old couch."

"I didn't have a choice. Someone shredded the cushions and the back of the sofa looking for the necklace. That's why I have a new mattress too."

Suddenly his arms were wrapped around me and he pulled me into his chest, my head resting on his shoulder. "I am so sorry," he murmured. "I never meant for any of this to happen. You should have been safe here." He shifted his weight back and forth from one leg to the other, rocking me. It almost felt like we were dancing. I used to like dancing with him.

But the thought popped into my mind that his presence might put me in danger—again.

Chapter 8

It threw me for a loop when I woke to the smell of freshly brewed coffee. Even in the days when Jake and I were together, I'd always been the first one up. I pulled on my robe and put my hair into a ponytail and went to see what he was up to.

Greeted by a scene of domestic tranquility, I wondered if Jake had been replaced by a house brownie in the middle of the night. Last night's dishes, including the cups we'd used for hot chocolate were washed and drying in the rack. Two mugs sat on the table, along with the sugar, and a spoon neatly placed on a napkin beside each. Jake was nowhere to be found.

From the amount of light filtering in through the curtains, the snowstorm had ended. As I went to pull them open, I heard someone moving snow from the steps. Luke and Joe must have started early this morning, but usually I did my own steps.

I pulled open the front door, prepared to yell at one of them—and saw Jake, broom in hand, his pants covered in snow. The Florida-raised man looked up at me with a worried expression on his face.

"I don't think I'm doing this right."

"Your first problem," I told him as I brushed his clothes off and tried not to laugh, "Is that you can't use a broom when there's this much snow. You have to use a shovel."

"Okay." He sounded puzzled. "So we dig holes in the snow?"

I held back a laugh. "A snow shovel. They're made with a flat edge. You fill the blade up with snow and toss it into a pile somewhere else."

"Where do I find one of those?" Judging him to be as cleaned up as he was going to get, I let him into the house and closed the door.

"They're in the garage. After I get dressed and we come up with different shoes for you, we'll go get them."

He looked down at his wet loafers. "My feet are cold."

It took three pairs of athletic socks to make sure Jake's feet wouldn't slip around in a pair of Luke's old fishing shoes. By now, Luke and Joe had already started clearing the sidewalks. I put Jake to work helping them while I tackled the stairs.

After a few minutes, Joe headed inside. I couldn't help but notice, because he walked right under me, and I considered dumping a load of snow on top of his balding head. But considering he's won every snowball fight I've ever had with him, I kindly let him get away without a single flake dropped on him. Okay, I chickened out. And he knew it too, because he glanced up and winked.

When he came back out, Joe stomped up the stairs behind me, out of sight from Luke and Jake. "Is this on the up and up?" he asked.

"He says it is. And it's hard to believe that if it wasn't, he'd be out in public shoveling snow."

Joe grunted. "Just to be on the safe side, I left a message for Detective Thomason."

I wished he hadn't done that, but I couldn't blame him. It was my first instinct as well. I prayed that Freddie wouldn't send in several squad cars, sirens screaming. The best option was to give up on the stairs and help Joe on his stretch of sidewalk while keeping an eye on Jake. There didn't seem to be any way to warn him ahead of time.

My first clue that something was about to happen was the snowplow driving down the street. Oak Grove does a fairly good job of clearing the streets, but naturally, they take care of the main streets first. The fact that Luke and Joe's house sits away from any main traffic route is one of the things that attracted me. So I shouldn't have been surprised when shortly afterward, I spotted a red Mustang headed our way.

I stuck my shovel into a snow pile and went over to greet Freddie. The grim look on his face told me this was an official visit.

"Take a deep breath," I told him. "Jake hasn't done anything wrong."

"I'll be the judge of that," he growled.

When I turned, I saw Jake watching us. When he started to move, I wondered if he planned to run.

Instead, Jake carefully placed the shovel on the sidewalk and held his open hands out to his sides. "Hello, Detective," he said. "How have you been?"

"Move away from the shovel," Freddie ordered.

I held my breath.

"Of course. Do you want me to step closer to you or backwards?"

Freddie's eyes widened at Jake's easy acquiescence. "Towards me is fine."

Jake took three steps and stopped. "Good?"

"You got paperwork to show you're out legally?"

"Yes. Not on me, but I have it. It's stored in a locker over at the Salvation Army."

"I've got a call in to check your status, so you'd better not be lying."

"I understand." Jake's shoulders twitched. "Is it okay if I put my arms down now? They're getting tired. Or would you like to search me first?"

I exhaled loudly and noticed the neighbors across the street watching the spectacle. "Can we move this inside, Freddie? We're drawing a crowd."

He nodded. On an impulse, I walked over and picked up the shovel Jake had dropped, and wrapped my free arm around his waist. Even through the several layers of sweaters I'd made him wear, I felt him shaking.

"What are you doing?" he asked in a whisper.

"Proving a point. I don't like bullies," I whispered back.

Luke, Joe, and Freddie were all fuming, but there wasn't anything they could do. When our procession reached the bottom of my stairs, I hesitated as I considered my options. If we went to my place it would be crowded, which might be uncomfortable for Jake. On the other hand, it was familiar ground to him. And it was my territory and they would be my guests, which would put all four of them under an obligation to behave themselves.

My decision made, I leaned the shovel against the fence and asked Jake loudly, "You don't suppose that coffee you made earlier is still hot, do you?"

His eyes searched my face. "I hope so. I'm freezing."

I grabbed his hand. "Only one way to find out."

After climbing a few steps, I plastered a bigger smile on my face as I swiveled to face the others. "Are y'all coming?"

Under other circumstances, it would have been funny to watch the scramble for seating. Joe and Luke headed for the loveseat as I predicted. Freddie—I was debating whether or not to demote him to Detective Thomason—grabbed a chair from the kitchen table. I considered having Jake sit in the easy chair, but decided that was like putting a match to an already flammable situation. Instead, I put him to work helping me in the kitchen.

"Do you want to grab the creamer out of the fridge? You know where I keep it." I dumped the now-cold coffee out of the pot and rinsed out the filter. Just to equalize things, I added, "Freddie, will you get the cups out of the dish strainer? I barely have enough to go around."

Freddie lingered in the kitchen while Jake took the cream and sugar into the front room. "What do you think you're doing?" he said between clenched teeth.

I grabbed his arm. "Would you excuse us for a minute please?" I asked no one in particular as I pulled him towards my bedroom. I shut the door behind us.

"Let's get something straight. This is my place, my rules. Jake is my guest. You have no probable cause to treat him as anything else. You may not like it, but either you treat him with respect or you *will* leave. And you *will* need a warrant to get back in. Do I make myself clear?" Heat rose in my cheeks as I let go of the anger I'd been restraining. I had to stop myself from shaking my finger in front of his face.

Freddie backed up a step under the onslaught of my words. "He's a convicted felon!"

"And he's served his time." I softened slightly. "Look, I get you want to protect me. But he and I have some unfinished business, and it has nothing to do with the law." At least, I prayed it didn't. There was still the puzzle of the dead man to solve.

"Hennessey says he's done, but I want to verify there wasn't a paperwork error." Freddie's phone buzzed and he tapped a few buttons before looking back at me. "Text message from the station. Evidently he's telling the truth."

"Now, if you're ready to play nice, let's go have coffee like civilized people."

No one was talking when we returned to the front room, so I turned the TV on to a weather channel to get an update on the storm. With any luck, it had passed by and we wouldn't be getting any more snow. But no, the weatherman was making his pronouncement of doom.

"Another wave of snow is on the way," he said all too cheerfully. "Sometime late this afternoon, we should see the clouds rolling back in." I turned the TV off.

Luke carefully balanced his cup on the arm of the loveseat. "I bet the kids love it. No school again tomorrow."

"Is that old sled still in the garage?" I asked. "Maybe we should take Jake to the park."

Before Luke had a chance to respond, Freddie's phone beeped. He squinted at the screen, and without saying a word walked out the front door. The rest of us exchanged glances.

"That's weird," Joe said.

"He'll be back." I pointed my chin towards the entrance. "He didn't take his coat."

I was right. In less than two minutes, Freddie came back inside, dusting off a scattering of snowflakes that had settled on his shoulders. I watched his eyes roam around the room, stop for a moment on Jake, then settle on me.

"I have to take off. Thank you for the coffee, Harmony. I'll call you later."

I couldn't read his face. "Drive safe," I told him as I handed him his coat. He nodded, then leaned forward and kissed me on the cheek.

"Call me if you need me," he whispered in my ear before leaving.

Joe was silently chuckling when I turned around, and coughed when he realized I'd caught him. "We should try to finish up the sidewalks before it snows again." As one, he and Luke stood. "You gonna come and help us, Jake?"

"Give me a minute to get back into the pile of sweaters Harmony made me wear," Jake said from the kitchen. The smile on his lips wasn't reflected in his eyes.

As Luke and Joe tromped down the steps, Jake moved to a spot near the window to watch them. It struck me as strange, but I just picked up the cream and sugar to carry back into the kitchen. I made a second trip to gather the dirty cups, and Jake was still peering out of the window.

As I piled the cups in the sink and turned on the water, I heard him come into the kitchen behind me. Suddenly, the dish cloth was yanked out of my hands and tossed in to the sink as he pressed me against the edge of the counter.

"You call him Freddie now? And you let him kiss you?"

I considered placing an elbow into Jake's side to

make him back off, but decided I didn't want to physically hurt him. Instead, I pushed against him and he backed up enough that I could turn around. It was time to come clean, and the next few minutes would do more mental damage than I liked.

"Did you think I'd wait for you?"

He blinked rapidly. "Yes. At least I hoped so. What's that got to do with Thomason?"

"Really? After the police showed me the pictures of the other women you'd been with?"

"Answer the question, Harmony. What's going on between you and the cop?" Jake's voice was strained.

"We dated. It didn't work out. Now he's seeing Sarah, so we're friends. Or at least we've called a truce."

The lines of tension in his face eased.

"Is that why you were able to stand up to him?" Jake asked. "Do you know how bad you scared me? Knowing I couldn't protect you? And when we heard you yelling at him in the bedroom, I thought he'd drag you back out in cuffs." He laughed, shakily.

I wondered why all the men in my life thought they needed to protect me. But I had been pushing the limits of my friendship with Freddie. "Did you notice Freddie's limp? He got that when one of Saliss' goons ran him off the road because of his connection to me, so I owe him. On the other hand, I identified a crooked cop on the force and took the guy down, so Freddie owes me."

"You did what?"

I shrugged my shoulders. "It's a long story. Let's just say my self-defense lessons paid off."

Jake smiled, a real smile. "I knew you had it in you. I wish I'd been there to see it."

"You should have seen me when I managed a Bootlegger's 180 in Dolores."

"Are you going to let me drive her?"

I'd distracted him, just as I'd planned. "Nobody's driving her anywhere in this weather, and that includes me. Now we'd better get outside and finish shoveling before the boys come looking for us."

I lied. Mid-afternoon, despite the ominous clouds, I pulled Dolores out of the garage to take Jake to the shelter to get a change of clothes out of his locker. Turns out that he'd been spending the colder nights at the Salvation Army, but all the beds were spoken for, so he was going to spend another night with me. After clearing the sidewalks, he needed a shower—badly—and wanted to change into clean clothes afterward. I drove, of course.

We stopped at a package store on the way home for more beer. Luckily, my favorite place was open. It was my favorite for several reasons. First, it was close to home. Second, the owner wasn't afraid to stock unusual varieties of beers and wines. Third, the owner was my cousin, Jane, and I could always trust her recommendations for the perfect wine.

Jake headed over to the beer coolers while Jane and I chatted. We may have been cousins, but we didn't look too much alike. She took after her mother, while I took after my dad. In my opinion, she got the better end of the deal. About the only thing we shared was brown hair and eyes.

While Jane went to the back to get me the bottle of Columbia Gorge Viognier I'd special ordered, Jake brought his selection to the counter. Guinness. I wasn't surprised. To be on the safe side, I sent him back for a second six-pack.

"I'll pay you back, once I get my money," he said quietly, before Jane returned. She'd been stopped by some other customers looking for help.

"No problem. Remind me to tell you about all the extra business I've been getting." Of course, if I told him Eli was sending it my way, I'd have to explain why.

The beer and wine tucked behind our seats, I glanced in the rear-view mirror before pulling into the street. A shiver ran down my spine when a black sedan fell in behind me. "Fasten your seat belt, Jake. We have a tail."

He swiveled around. "Shit." He turned back around, clicking his belt closed and grabbing the dash with one hand. "Hang a right."

"I got this," I said, and swung to the left instead, mentally cataloging which streets should be fairly clean.

"They're still with us."

"Yep. Can you get my cell phone out of my purse?"

"What good is that going to do?" He reached behind my seat and grabbed the phone.

I didn't answer right away because I was busy

fighting Dolores as she slid on a patch of ice. To my satisfaction, the black sedan spun one-hundred-and-eighty degrees behind me. I made a hard right and then another right, hoping to lose the other vehicle.

"I've got Freddie's direct line in my contacts," I said. "Call him and tell him I'm on my way to the police station. I hope he's still on duty."

"You can outrun that guy," A swift glance at Jake showed me the spark was back in his eyes.

"Yeah, but wouldn't it be fun to have him follow me right into the waiting arms of the cops?"

"You have a warped sense of humor, Harmony. I love it." He punched the buttons on my phone and I listened to his side of the conversation.

"Detective Thomason. This is Jake Hennessey… I'm with Harmony, but she's busy right now… We're on our way to the station… No…Listen. We're being followed… Late-model, black, Ford… Two-three minutes… Yeah, we'll stay on the line."

He put the phone on his thigh and twisted around again. "He's still back there."

"Yes. Hopefully he doesn't know where we're going." I took a chance and headed down a narrow side street that led to the back side of the station. If I stopped Dolores just right, the sedan would be stuck with nowhere to go.

I had one shot to get this right. As I reached the end of the lane, I stepped hard on my brakes, and barely turned my steering wheel. My tires squealed. Freddie dashed out the front door of the building, his service revolver nestled in his hand.

Chapter 9

Freddie was followed by two officers, guns drawn and pointed at the black car that screeched to a stop halfway down the block. Another man exited the station from the back door, trapping the other driver. As Freddie advanced, I swung my door open.

"Stay in the car," Freddie said, his voice urgent. "And leave it running, just in case."

"Okay." I gripped the steering wheel and kept my eyes on him as he approached the other vehicle. The driver's window rolled down. After a brief, murmured conversation, papers were handed through the opening. Jake reached over and put his hand on my knee. I'd been unconsciously tapping my foot on the gas pedal and revving the engine.

Freddie studied the papers, handed them back, and returned his gun to its holster. Straightening, he called, "It's clear." As all the other guns were put away, he leaned over and said something to the occupant of the car. Freddie shook his head before walking towards me.

"Do you mind coming inside for a few minutes, Harmony? You too, Hennessey." He sighed. "You're both a part of this."

Jake and I sat in Freddie's office, waiting for him. After looking around to make sure no one was watching, I swiped a piece of scrap paper and a pen off Freddie's desk. I wrote three letters on the paper, then slipped it to Jake. I didn't want to take a chance on our conversation being recorded.

He looked at it, at me, at it again, then at me. "FBI?" he mouthed.

I nodded just as Freddie entered. As Freddie pulled out his chair to sit, Jake stuffed the piece of paper into his pants pocket. At least I was able to give him a warning.

"The guy who was following you is meeting with the Chief," Freddie said. "After he gets done there, I think he'll have something to say to you."

"He was number three, right?" I asked.

"Number three?" Freddie asked, puzzled.

"Last fall. The day when Eli and I were assaulted by Steven Saliss' goons. When Agent Felton owned up to being a Fed and those other agents came up from Pittsburgh. I couldn't keep track of everyone's names, so I assigned them each a number. He was number three."

Freddie tried to hide his smile. Jake looked stern but I spotted the hint of a grin. They both knew of my fixation with names. "How did you get involved with the FBI?" Jake asked.

"Another long story. To keep it short, they were following you so they started following me. They bugged my apartment, and put a tracker on Dolores."

"That's pure speculation," Freddie interjected.

"Yes, but it's the only thing that makes sense since it wasn't the local police. Once a month, I still get my place professionally 'swept'. But I thought that whole business was over. So why is number three here?"

Already pale after spending several years in prison, Jake somehow became even paler.

"Agent Garza," Freddie said, "or number three as you call him, is explaining that to the Chief. Common courtesy calls for the FBI to inform us when they operate in our jurisdiction, and it didn't happen. There's no law that says they have to, but the Chief is real unhappy that they chose not to. Especially as it could have put the lives of our people in danger. Your life too, Harmony, and the Chief is doubly upset about that because you're a civilian."

I noticed he didn't mention Jake, but I wasn't going to bring *that* up. "I don't get it. You told me the museum got their necklace back, so why would the FBI still be interested in me?"

"It's not you they're tailing," Jake said. "It's me."

Freddie nodded. "That's the same conclusion I reached."

Jake abruptly stood, his chair's legs screeching as

they scraped the tile floor. "I won't be responsible for making your life hell, Angel. Thank you for trying to help me out. Detective, I assume I'm not being held for anything and I'm free to go?"

"Are you sure you don't want to stick around and listen to what Agent Garza has to say?" Freddie asked.

Jake shook his head. "Why? You think he'll waltz in here and offer me a job tracking down who really stole that necklace? That only happens in badly written movies. Once the Feds make up their collective minds that you're one of the bad guys, there's not a damn thing you can do to change it. Even if this asshole offered me a job, it would be so they could set me up and arrange things so I'd spend the rest of my life in prison."

For a second, Jake had *me* believing he was innocent.

"Don't you belong in prison?" a voice rumbled from the doorway. "For killing Calib Booker? Didn't he used to be your fence?"

"Agent Garza, I presume?" Jake asked, as three heads swiveled in that direction.

The assumption was an easy one. The man standing in the doorway wore the classic black suit, black wingtip shoes, and a scowl on his face.

"What proof do you have that I had something to do with anyone getting killed?" Jake continued smoothly. "Or that I ever used a so-called fence?"

"But you don't deny knowing him," the agent said, advancing one small step.

"No. We discussed a couple of real-estate deals at

various times. None of them worked out. He was way too greedy. But just because I didn't like the guy doesn't mean I killed him."

"But you didn't seem to be surprised to hear that he is dead. Which I find interesting, because his death isn't public knowledge."

I caught my breath. The FBI man had a point.

"Have you ever been in this town before, Agent?" Jake asked. "Pick five random people off the street—maybe not today but on a normal day—and ask them what they've heard about the murder. Two will know he was found at the house Harmony is renovating, two his name, and the other one would pretend they didn't have the foggiest idea what you were talking about."

Jake was right. The rumor mill in Oak Grove never took a break, not even during a major snowstorm.

"Has it ever been determined when he was killed?" I asked. "Or where?"

"The coroner's report places the time of death from fifteen to twenty-four hours before the body was found," Freddie said. "Because it's unknown how long the body was outside, the coroner is unwilling to get more specific than that. It appears he was shot where they found the body."

I'd research how they figured that out later.

Freddie had a question of his own. "What I want to know, Agent Garza," he said, using that polite but firm tone of voice he used when questioning a suspect, "is what interest you have in this case? Murders are not normally in the FBI's line of duty."

"I don't have to explain that to you."

"No, you don't. But I bet you explained it to the Chief. And I'm sure he'll share it with me if he feels it's appropriate." As Freddie talked, the agent crossed his arms defensively. I wondered what he was hiding. "So why are you here instead of sneaking out the back door?"

The tight line that was Agent Garza's lips got impossibly tighter, and I worried Freddie had gone too far. "I need a moment alone with Miss Duprie."

"I don't think so," I said. I reached for my cell phone to call Dan, my lawyer. "But if you have something to say to me, I don't mind if Freddie and Jake hear it."

Garza's right eyebrow lifted when I said "Freddie" instead of "Detective Thomason." "I prefer not to waste my time."

I smiled my best artificial smile. "Why don't you satisfy my curiosity and tell me anyway? You drove all the way up from Pittsburgh in this weather, you might as well save yourself another trip."

"Okay then." He moved until he was mere inches away from me. "I intended to offer you a deal," he said, staring down at me. "You help us get the evidence we need against Hennessey and I'll make sure that you don't get charged."

I don't intimidate easily. "You sound like you've been talking to Agent Felton," I said with a smirk. I stood, and moved closer to him in a deliberate invasion of his personal space. We were almost touching. "And he was all talk. You don't have anything on me and you know it, because I haven't broken any laws. And you don't have anything on Jake either, or you wouldn't need me. Which tells me he hasn't done anything illegal." At least, that's what I wanted to believe, but what it told me was that Jake was good—really good. I put a finger to my cheek and cocked my head. "But as I'm sure your files say, my job is doing research. So if you want to hire me to do computer searches for information, I'll be glad to add you to my list of potential clients."

Agent Garza's face reddened. "You don't know who you're messing with, Miss Duprie."

"Why, Agent Garza, that sounds like a threat. Freddie, doesn't that sound like a threat to you?" I said, my voice dripping sweet syrup. Then I sighed and took half a step backwards. "Look, I'm just a small-town ex-librarian and that's the way I like it. Hell, I only leave town once or twice a year. And the FBI knows that because they had a tracer on my car and a bug in my apartment for god-knows-how-long. So I would appreciate it if you would just back off and let me go back to being me, instead of trying to make me into a gun moll or drug lord or whatever it is you're trying to make me out to be."

I sensed Jake shifting uneasily. Agent Garza reached into his pants pocket retrieving a small leather case, and pulled out a card. Handing it to me, he said, "Call me if you change your mind, Miss Duprie. I wouldn't wait too long." Then he turned and stormed out of the office.

I sank back into my chair. "Wasn't that fun?"

Jake put his hand on my shoulder. "Is there somewhere in town—a church or something—that opens up beds for the homeless in weather like this, Detective?" he asked. "The Salvation Army is full, and until I get a job, I can't pay for a room."

Freddie took a thoughtful breath. "Off the top of my head, I don't—"

I interrupted. "You're staying at my place again, unless the chair is too uncomfortable," I said firmly.

"Actually, I was going to suggest he stay with me," Freddie said to my amazement.

"Keeping an eye on the suspect?" Jake asked dourly.

"I've got a spare bed, and I consider it doing Harmony a favor." The two men exchanged glares. I decided my best course of action was to keep my mouth shut.

Jake's shoulder slumped. "I'll take you up on that offer. I don't want to drag Harmony into this mess any deeper than she is."

I was already in deeper than either man realized, but that would remain my secret.

The least I could do was invite Freddie for supper, which meant inviting Sarah as well. And since the predicted additional snowfall had missed Oak Grove, the streets were clear enough for people to get out of their driveways. With that in mind, I decided I needed to make extra food in case anyone else showed up. This meant I needed to make my almost world-famous baked spaghetti. It froze well if there was extra.

So after he'd showered and changed, I put Jake to work making a tossed salad while I cooked the spaghetti and prepared the other ingredients for the main dish. It didn't take long for me to figure out he had no experience cooking. I had to show him how to shred the lettuce and remove the veins from the celery. It didn't matter if the result wasn't quite up to my normal nit-picky standards, because he certainly tried hard.

With half an hour until Freddie and Sarah were due to arrive, everything was ready except for the garlic bread. All it needed was to be popped into the oven when they showed up on my landing. Jake was busy doing something on my laptop, so I decided I had time to do a quick check of the apartment.

I'd bought a small counter-surveillance device. It wasn't as accurate as the equipment the security company out of Pittsburgh used, but it claimed to catch most bugs. As I walked around the front room, I felt Jake's eyes on me.

"Portable scanner," I told him, holding up the small black box. "Figured it was worth taking the extra precaution with Agent Garza in town. I want to check the rest of the apartment but at least this room is clean. And by the way, I have something for you."

He frowned and shook his head. "You've done

more than enough for me," he protested. "I can't take anything else from you."

"It's no big deal." I opened the junk drawer in the kitchen, pulled out the burner phone and tossed it to him. "It still has several hours' worth of time on it. It can't be traced to me which means it can't be traced to you."

"You're kidding me," he said in amazement. "Who the heck are you? And who are you working for? Internal affairs for the FBI or something?"

The thought made me laugh. "Yeah, right. I've spent my whole life undercover in Oak Grove just in case a rotten agent showed up here."

"Why are you helping me, anyway?" Jake put the laptop on the coffee table.

I bit my lip in concentration as I waved the scanner around the kitchen. "Maybe," I said, with my back towards him. "It's because I'm hoping if I help you out, you won't go back to your previous 'job'. Or because I feel responsible for you going to prison. If you hadn't been here to see me so much, the cops would never have been able to bust you. Or," I put the scanner down and opened the refrigerator door to get the butter out, "it's because I used to love you and although I don't anymore, I don't hate you either."

"Are you sure you don't love me? And that you're trying to convince yourself you don't?"

I decided now was the time to tell him. Freddie or Sarah might let it slip at supper. Besides, it would be a relief to get it out in the open. "I'm in a relationship with someone else, Jake."

While we'd been talking, he'd come into the kitchen and was standing in front of me. "Anyone I know?" he asked evenly, but I detected the strain in his voice.

"As a matter of fact, yes." I drew in a deep breath. "It's Eli."

Chapter 10

Jake slammed his hand on the kitchen counter so hard the cups in the mug tree rattled. "Eli? My cousin, Eli?"

"Yes, your cousin Eli." It hurt to hear the pain in Jake's voice, but there simply wasn't an easy way to tell him the truth.

He raised a fist. For a second, I thought he was going to hit me, and I prepared to take a defensive move. Instead, he lowered his hand and backed away. He muttered something about "that little weasel," pounded on the counter again and dropped more than a few swear words.

"Is that ring on your dresser from him?"

I'd forgotten about my recent purchase. "No, I bought it from a pawn shop. It needed a good home."

A shadow of a smile almost reached his face. "Here in Oak Grove or somewhere else? Cleveland, maybe?"

My jaw dropped. Literally. I stared at him for a

long moment, while a zillion questions jumbled together in my brain. The knock on the front door jolted me from my semi-catatonic state.

Jake reached out and gently ran his fingers down the side of my face. "Your company is here," he said quietly. "But we're not done yet."

Amazingly enough, no one extra showed up. So the four of us sat around my table and acted like we were old friends and nothing was wrong. Except I caught Freddie scrutinizing Jake when he thought Jake wasn't watching. And Jake took every opportunity possible to touch me, and each time he did he let his fingers linger a moment too long. Sarah was the only one who didn't feel the tension. Either that or she was a better actress than I'd realized.

"Did you hear about the snow sculpture contest in the park?" she asked.

"No," I said. How did I miss that? "Who's sponsoring it?"

"Oh, it's unofficial." She put more grated cheese on top of her spaghetti and passed the container to Freddie. "Started with some little kids building old-fashioned snowmen, and then a bunch of high schoolers got involved. Pretty soon parents got into the spirit of things as well. Now there are dragons and castles and all sorts of creations scattered on the shore of the lake. Makes me hope the cold weather sticks around so they last longer."

"You and I should go see them tomorrow," Jake said smoothly, touching my forearm.

I would have loved to go, but not with Jake. "I really need to go to the library tomorrow," I said. "If I get too far behind, I'll never catch up. I have a deadline coming up in a day or two." I hadn't even checked my email to see if I had any new requests.

Sarah sighed. "It's not like you have to punch a time card. Sometimes you take yourself too seriously."

We'd had this discussion before, and I had no desire to rehash it now.

But Sarah was on a roll. "You loosened up for a while, now you're slipping back into your old habits." She winked at Jake. "You were good for her, except for that whole drug and attacking the police stuff."

Was she flirting with Jake in front of Freddie? She'd hardly touched her wine, so she couldn't be drunk. Unless she'd been drinking before she and Freddie got to my place.

I glanced at Freddie. His expression was more puzzlement than anything else. He caught me looking, and barely shook his head. He didn't know what she was up to either.

Jake, on the other hand, winked back at her. "I'll try to change that."

"Yeah, the whole long-distance relationship thing she's got with Eli isn't working out if you ask me."

"Sarah!" I hissed.

Jake leaned towards her, ignoring me. "What makes you say that?"

"Do you know they haven't had sex yet?" She

giggled. "At least the last time we talked about it. But it might have changed when he was here a couple of weeks ago."

My face burned as she reached for her wine. Freddie distracted her by putting his hand on her shoulder. "Did you take one of your pills today?" he asked.

Sarah had occasional bouts with a panic disorder but the prescription her doctor gave her usually helped. She laid a finger across her lips and looked thoughtful. "Yes. I had a really bad day today. In fact, I may have taken two. One this morning, and one before we came here."

That explained it. "Let me get you something else to drink, Sarah," I said, rising. "How about some ice water?" A trip to the refrigerator would give me time to regain my composure.

"Why, am I acting loopy?"

Freddie's mouth twitched. "Just a little. But it's probably better you don't drink any alcohol."

Sarah frowned. I could sense her objection coming, so I jumped in. "Water sounds good. I'll have some too. Anyone else?"

We made it through the rest of supper without further discussion of my love life. But the snow starting falling again and Sarah started yawning like crazy, so we called an early end to the evening. Jake eyed me speculatively the entire time, so I shouldn't have been surprised when he stopped in the doorway after letting Freddie and Sarah leave before him. "I'll be right there," he called after them. "Forgot something."

I glanced around, trying to spot what he'd left behind. His duffel bag was on the floor beside him. "Did you leave something in the kitchen?"

"No." He closed the gap between us and wrapped his arms around me. "I didn't want to forget this."

His lips were suddenly pressed against mine. As he leaned me backward, I wrapped my arms around his neck to keep my balance. Big mistake, because I'm sure he read it as a sign of encouragement.

I tried not to respond, but my mouth remembered all too well how nicely we'd meshed, and I think I kissed him back.

He chuckled, his lips still gently touching mine. "So you haven't had sex with Eli yet." It was more of a statement than a question. He allowed me to straighten, and I hastily dropped my arms and gave him a small push. He chuckled again and released me.

"Good night, Angel," he said with a smirk as he picked up his duffel bag. "Sweet dreams."

I closed the door behind him, locked it, then leaned against it. Shit. I was in so much trouble.

A trip to the library usually relaxed me, but there was too much on my mind. I'd left my place early, texting Freddie first so he wouldn't drop Jake off when I wasn't there. With only a few hours of sleep, I wouldn't get anything done if I'd stayed home.

I'd considered calling Eli after everyone was gone, but ended up texting him instead. The kiss Jake and I had shared left me feeling guilty enough that talking to Eli would have been a bad idea. The message was simple enough, "Thinking about you." His response, received an hour later, was just as direct, "Wish you were here."

Before I settled in for a long day at my favorite table, I scooted behind the front desk to say hi to Janine in her new office. She smiled and put down the file she was leafing through. "Just what I needed," she said. "A reason to take a break."

"How long have you been here?" I asked, noting her empty coffee cup.

She glanced at the clock. "Four hours. I came in at six. There's so much I need to learn and so much to get caught up on at the same time. And then there's still a constant stream of well-wishers who come by and want to spend hours chatting. The only way I have time to get anything done is to come in before the library opens."

"It'll get better," I assured her. "Once you get the hang of things."

"I certainly hope so. I'm afraid this job may turn out to be more than I can handle."

"There's not much I can do, but if you need help, let me know."

"Can I convince you to come back to work? It'll be better with me as your boss."

"That's sweet of you, but don't forget the politics behind me leaving. You can't jeopardize your new job by fighting the Board." After my arrest for drug trafficking, the board had "requested" my resignation. When I was found not guilty, they didn't change their minds. As much as I appreciated the offer, I wasn't going to put her in a bad position. And I certainly wasn't going to let on it was her job I wanted.

"Excuse me, Miss Janson," said a small voice from the office door. I turned to see one of the newest volunteers from the local high school. I swore they got younger every year. "But someone at the front desk wants to talk to you."

"Case in point," Janine said with a sigh. "I'll be right there, Lacey."

Social niceties fulfilled, I went to work and hid behind my normal stack of research materials. With my nose stuck in a book about the social habits of penguins, I blocked out the world. The pictures were cute and the information was fascinating. I hadn't realized that penguins fight for nesting spots by having stare downs.

I jumped when someone nearby cleared their throat. "Miss Duprie," said Agent Garza from across the table.

"To what do I owe the pleasure of your company, Agent?" I asked, pouring every bit of sarcasm I could summon into my voice. "Weren't you headed back to Pittsburgh?" I didn't bother to ask how he'd found me. Everyone knew where I worked. Hell, it seemed most of the town knew where I lived and my daily schedule.

He pulled out a chair and sat, leaning forward with his elbows resting on the table. "We need to talk."

"Funny, I have no need to talk to you. Didn't I make myself clear yesterday?"

"Are you blind? Do you really believe Hennessey is innocent?"

"Despite popular opinion, there's no proof he isn't." I stared at him and didn't blink as I flat-out lied. I knew where the evidence was, but it was well-hidden and would remain that way. "And I remember hearing something about being innocent until proven guilty."

"A fairy tale, Miss Duprie," he snorted. "Surely you're not that naive."

"Or I refuse to become as cynical as you are."

He leaned back, and closed his eyes. "I didn't use to be that way. But this job has a way of sucking hope out of you." His eyes snapped back open. "And I will deny I ever said that."

So the man was human after all.

"Are you married, Agent Garza?" I asked. "Have children?"

Another one of his typical snorts. "In this job? Not a chance. Not that it's any of your business."

"You're right. But being with children might be good for you. I used to run story hour for the library, in fact I still fill in when they need me. It's amazing what hanging out with kids will do for a person."

"That's your opinion." He shifted in his chair. "But back to business. Jake Hennessey is a dangerous man. He hasn't killed anyone yet, but it's only a matter of time. It would be a shame if you were his first murder."

That took things way over the line. Time to put an end to the conversation. "Tell me, Agent, exactly what crimes does the FBI figure Jake has committed? I've heard a variety of stories."

"A whole string of things. Mostly jewelry theft. A bank robbery or two. But he's smart, and we can't make any charges stick. We need someone who can get him to talk. That's where you come in."

"What do you want, for me to wear a wire and interrogate him?"

He shook his head. "Too risky. No, the plan would be for you to get him out to a restaurant where we've installed recording equipment, and get him to admit to what he's done."

I stared at him, stunned. "Not a chance. You're asking me to betray my friendship with Jake and trap him into admitting something I don't believe he's done in the first place."

"There's a nice reward offered for information on a few of the thefts. I could make sure you were eligible to receive some of it."

"Now you're trying to bribe me?" I pushed my chair back and stood. "I'm walking away for a few minutes. I'd appreciate it if you were gone by the time I get back."

"You'll wish you'd cooperated when you get charged as an accessory."

I took a deep breath. "And there you go with the threats again. Good-bye, Agent Garza." I picked up several books I was done with and headed for the second floor. I half-expected him to follow me, but when I reached the landing and turned, I saw him stomping towards the front door. "Good riddance," I muttered, but when I reached for the railing, my hand was trembling.

❃ ❃ ❃

I was on the floor, under the table, when I saw a pair of men's black wingtip shoes stop by my chair. The feet in them paused and rotated, as if surveying the library. "Hey, Jake," I said.

He bent over and I grinned into his upside-down face. "What are you doing under there?"

"Looking for my earring," I answered as I crawled out. I wondered if he would remember I didn't wear earrings on a daily basis because I was sensitive to the base metal used in the posts.

"Do you need help?" He extended his hand and helped me stand.

I swatted at some imagined dirt on my knees. "Thanks, but no. It's probably at home on the counter of the bathroom. I bet I forgot to put it in this morning. I was in a hurry."

As I had hoped, he picked up on my storyline. "Wouldn't be the first time," he said.

I grabbed a stack of books and handed them to him. "Come on, you can help me put these away. I'm done with them."

Without a word of protest, he followed me as I made the trip up the stairs to the second floor. I grabbed the top book from his arms and wandered all the way down to the end of the stacks. It may have appeared like I was looking for the shelf the book belonged on, but in reality I was cataloging the location of each patron.

The row at the very end offered the most privacy, and that's where I led Jake. With one last peek to ensure the next aisle was still empty, I turned to him.

"You think I'm crazy?" I asked, noting the slight smirk on his face. "Let me set you straight. I had a visit from Agent Garza. He's still trying to use me to take you down. He even tried to bribe me."

"Why are you telling me this? Didn't you accept the money? You need it."

I couldn't help myself. I laughed loudly. The irony of the statement was overwhelming. Thankfully we were where no one could see us. I didn't want Janine to yell at me for being noisy. "Are you telling me you never researched me as a potential target?"

"Target for what?"

"Theft. Robbery. Whatever it is you specialize in."

Jake hesitated, then put his stack of books down on a shelf. "Let's go for a walk."

His tone of voice almost sounded threatening. "I can't just leave these books here, I have to put them away first," I told him, knowing it would give me time to decide whether to go with him. Or, time to make a getaway.

As I worked, I kept an eye on him. He stood at the top of the stairs and seemed to be scanning the main floor of the library. I wondered if he was watching for anyone in particular.

With all the books returned to their proper places, we went downstairs and I grabbed my coat from the back of my chair. Jake hadn't ever taken his off, but he zipped it up as he headed towards the front door. I let him go first—if I wanted to get away from him, this was my last chance. But this was Jake, and deep down, I didn't believe he would hurt me.

So I followed him outside, down the fifteen steps, and down the street. He hunched his shoulders and leaned forward as if fighting a cold wind, although it wasn't much more than a strong breeze.

I expected him to head towards the nearby coffee shop, but he stopped where the trunk of a big oak tree broke the force of the wind. He looked around one more time, making sure no one was nearby. "What makes you say I'm a thief?"

"The spreadsheet. And the postcards. And the damned necklace you tried to give me. The one you hid in my closet. The one I almost got killed for."

"I understand about this much of what you're talking about," he said, pinching his thumb and first finger together.

"The postcards. The postmarks didn't match the

location of the pictures. So I developed a spreadsheet to figure out where you really were when you mailed them. And I figured out a pattern of robberies that matched your travels."

He stiffened. "Who else knows about this?" he asked, his voice urgent.

"Eli. And Scotty and Lando, his coworkers. I can't imagine they would ever tell anyone. But if I can figure it out, so can the Feds."

His eyes searched my face. "And why do you think they were after a necklace?"

"Because one of Sallis' goons told me so when they kidnapped me."

"And how did they come to the conclusion you had it?" He slumped against the tree.

"Crooked cop, I guess. They had a picture of us the night you gave it to me." I pulled my coat closed as a particularly cold gust of wind hit me.

He scrunched his eyebrows. "I'm confused. What necklace are we talking about?"

"You know, the ruby and diamond necklace." I put my hands on my hips.

He took a deep breath. "All this time I thought you were talking about something else. You're talking about the ruby necklace? The one you wouldn't take?"

I nodded.

"That necklace was a fake."

Chapter 11

Jake waited while a car drove down the street. I imagined its occupants considered us crazy, standing outside in the bitter cold when there were perfectly good stores nearby. "I was ashamed to tell you. I wanted to give you something extra nice, but I couldn't afford the real thing. But the replica was such a high quality it still took a chunk out of my wallet."

"It looked real." I said.

He swiveled to face me. "Like I said, good replica. The stones were artificially created, and the chain was heavy electroplate. When I gave it to you, I didn't even know the real one had been stolen."

"Then why did Saliss think I had the real thing?"

He sighed. "Good question."

"And why does the Museum of Fine Jewelry say they got the real thing back if I sent them a fake?"

"You did that?" Jake actually grinned. "I wondered. Where did you get another copy?"

"Eli and I found it where you'd left it in my closet. No one else knows."

The smile vanished. "I didn't put the necklace in your closet."

"What do you mean, you didn't put it in my closet?"

"I still have it. Well, I think I do. Hopefully my friend put it in storage along with the rest of my stuff."

"Why didn't you tell someone that before? Like when people were trying to kill me?" Bitterness washed over me, and suddenly I didn't like Jake anymore.

"Because I honestly thought they were talking about a different necklace. One that had nothing to do with you," Jake said.

"That's damned convenient. And look how quickly you came up with it. It would take me much longer to come up with that good of a lie."

"It's not a lie. I'll admit to doing things you wouldn't approve of, but I'd never mix you up in them."

"Too late. You already have."

In the silence that followed, I watched a few flakes of snow, knocked from the branches of the tree, shimmer on their way to the ground.

"I know," he said. "And I regret it."

"Then do something about it." I kicked at a clump of snow that had been shoved into the gutter by the snowplow. It was more solid than

I expected and I swore as my toes got crunched.

"You think I don't want to?" Jake put his hands on my shoulders. I knocked them off.

"I figured if you wanted to, it would be done by now."

It was as if someone stuck a pin in a balloon. In front of my eyes, he deflated. "I'm not that good," he said.

It was too cold to continue our discussion outside. We returned to the library and I did my normal end-of-the-day routine of returning all the books I'd used to their proper places. Then we went to my place to scan the apartment again before we got into any serious topics—okay, our argument.

I seethed while I made a careful tour of my apartment, waving my magic wand around, waiting for a suspicious beep. After a cursory check of the entire place I returned to the front room.

Jake was sitting in the recliner, with an empty beer bottle in front of him, and a full one in his hand. "I see you got started without me," I said.

He jerked his head towards the kitchen. "There's one on the cupboard for you."

That was real thoughtful of him. Barely controlling my anger, I stalked into the kitchen to get it. With my prize clutched firmly in my hand, I sat on the loveseat to keep an eye on his reactions. It was too early to start drinking, but with everything that had happened, I felt justified in making an exception to my rule.

"So what did you plan to steal from me?" I asked, my voice as brittle as the icicles hanging from the edge of the roof.

He spread his arms open. "Really? When I look around, I don't see anything worth my effort." He shook his head. "You were never a 'person of interest', Angel, you were a happy coincidence. I came to town because there's an old couple here with a large coin collection, and they seemed to be an easy target. But then I met you, and those plans went away. I wasn't going to mess up my chances to come back here and be with you."

I knew exactly who he was talking about. The Jansens had collected coins for years. I'd spent a wonderful afternoon with them a year or so ago, interviewing them about their hobby for one of my authors.

"Which brings up a question," he said. "How big are the payments on that sweet car of yours? What do you call it? Dolores? How do you afford them?"

"That's none of your business," I snapped. If he didn't know I had a large sum of money sitting in the bank, as well in a variety of investments, I wasn't going to tell him.

"Okay, okay," he said, holding up his hands as if to ward off my anger. "I was just curious. I wasn't planning to steal her."

"So tell me, Jake, why is it you can't do something to fix this mess you got me into?"

He put his beer bottle down, leaned forward, and stared at the floor.

"Because I'm not good enough."

"All my life, I've always been 'pretty good.' Never great, never the best. And I've tried. But no matter how hard I try, there's always someone better than me. I pretend not to care but I can't fool myself.

"When it comes to being a thief, I'm good. Not great, not the best. And whoever stole that necklace—shit, they're damned good."

I almost felt sorry for him. Almost. "Any idea who it is?"

He picked up his beer bottle and took a swig. His adam's apple bobbed up and down as he swallowed. "I've heard stories about a guy capable of it. But he's been out of the business for years."

"Is there a way to reach him?"

"What do you think we're going to do? Pick up a phone and call him? That's not how this business works."

I opened my laptop and waited while it loaded. "What's his name?"

"What are you doing?" Jake got out of the chair and sat beside me on the loveseat, leaning over to peek at my screen.

"Doing what I do best," I answered as I logged in. "Sometimes it doesn't matter if you're the best, just that you tried your hardest."

Orson Wallington was a unique enough name that I had no trouble finding the right guy. Especially as he had made a career as a security expert after retiring from the business of being a world-class thief. At least, that's what his web page advertised.

"The guy's a freakin' legend," Jake said as he scrolled through the website. "I can't believe he sold out and went legit."

"He's how old now?" I asked, trying to see his biography. In his picture he appeared to be a distinguished old businessman, with neatly groomed gray hair and beard and a tailored pinstriped suit.

"Doesn't say," Jake answered, "but he's got to be in his sixties or seventies now."

"Well, I don't imagine he ever paid into Social Security so this might be how he's funding his retirement."

"As good as he was, I figure he'd have some money stashed away."

"And maybe this is a new way of stealing people's money? Giving them advice on how to avoid being robbed when he's really checking them out? Casing the joint?"

"Casing the joint? No one uses that expression any more. You've been reading too many bad novels." But the expression on Jake's face was thoughtful.

Crap. I hoped I hadn't given him an idea.

"Wouldn't work long-term," he said. "After one or two jobs, your reputation would tank and the police become suspicious." Jake continued to browse through the information. "That makes sense, he's living in California and is a consultant for various movie companies. I'd say he's as smart as his reputation makes him out to be."

So much for dropping by and interviewing him. But a phone call was still feasible.

"You still have the burner phone I gave you?" I asked.

"Not on me. It's stashed." Jake grinned. "It turns me on when you talk like that."

"Like what?"

"Burner phones, casing the joint, plotting alternative methods of income. You missed your calling, Angel, you would have made a great sidekick when I was in the business."

I wasn't going to be anyone's sidekick. But that wasn't as important as the other thing Jake had said.

"So you're out of the business?"

He put the laptop down and laid one arm across my shoulders, pulling me closer. "I don't have much choice, do I? Not when the Feds are watching every step I make. No, I need to go legit. Make a deal with the bank, get the house back, and restore and sell it." He fiddled with the band wrapped around my bun. "Why are you still over there all the time?"

I pulled myself upright. "Because I own it now, Jake."

He blinked several times. "Well, aren't you the one for surprises."

"I hated to see it sitting there empty. So once the

bank got all the paperwork done to get the title, I convinced them to let me take it off their hands. I'm waiting for the electricians to finish up before I tackle the next project. Luke and Joe are going to help me put up new drywall on the first floor. I'm going to rework the rooms like you'd planned. I've added a few things, but we're basically sticking to your concept."

"That's a big risk. Your research gig must be doing well if you can afford rent, a mortgage, and the payments on that fancy car." I could practically see the gears in his head turning and his body stiffened. "Or did you get money somewhere else? Have you sold me out?"

I put my hand on his knee and turned to face him. "Jake, look at me. Right in the eyes, Jake. I did not sell you out. I wouldn't do that. I have money, Jake. I always have. I just don't spend it." I shrugged. "Until recently that is. But while Keith didn't approve of it when I bought Dolores, he sees the house as a good investment strategy.

"Who's Keith?"

"My financial consultant."

"You have a financial adviser? How much money are you talking about?" he asked with wonder in his voice.

"More than enough. Only a few people are in on the secret and I like it that way."

For a moment, the predatory gleam my father taught me about flickered in Jake's eyes. Then he shook himself like a wet dog and it disappeared.

"If I had known…" he said. "But I'm glad I

didn't. It's better that you know I wasn't after your money when I fell in love with you."

I sighed. "It was fun while it lasted, but it's over now. I'm helping you as a friend. You understand that, right?"

"That's not what the kiss last night told me." He lightly ran one finger over my lips.

It was tempting. All it would take was the smallest move on my part and things would end up in the bedroom. Or maybe on the loveseat. Or that one time on the table.

My body remembered all too well how good we'd been together.

But the Hennessey I wanted in my bed wasn't Jake. I gave him a small push and retrieved the laptop from the coffee table to use as a shield. It was still open to the website of the so-called master thief.

"He's even released a book," I said. Now *that* was something I could get excited about. "And hey, he's doing a promotional tour. He'll be in Pittsburgh next week."

I should have known right away it was too convenient.

Beside me, Jake chuckled. "You're not getting off

that easy," he said. "But I'll let it drop for now." He leaned over my shoulder to see the screen. "Got plans for Tuesday? I'd kinda like to meet him."

Which brought up another line of thought. "Just what are your plans, Jake?"

He leaned back against the arm of the loveseat. "I guess I can't go back to what I was doing."

"I should think not," I huffed.

He had the gall to grin. "I still think you would make a good sidekick."

I punched him in the shoulder. "Be serious."

"Yes, Mother," he said.

I punched him again, and he rubbed the spot.

"That one will leave a bruise. Do you want to kiss it and make it better?"

He pretended to cower in fear when I raised my fist again. "Sorry. Truth is, I haven't given it much thought. First thing I need to do is get to the little bit of money I stashed without the Feds tracking me. I've about used up the cash I'd hidden here. Then I need to head to Florida and get my car. But I guess my priority should be to prove I didn't murder Booker."

"That reminds me. I wonder if they ever located his next-of-kin."

"From what he told me, his wife left him years ago, and took their daughter with her. 'Course, I had the feeling he didn't try too hard to get them back."

"Do you remember his daughter's name?" I asked, trying to contain my excitement.

Jake shook his head. "He never mentioned it. Why?"

"Merrilee has a new coworker by the name of Booker. The lady claims she's no relative but it's a heck of a coincidence."

"You have a picture of her? I could tell you if they look like they're related."

I didn't make a habit of taking pictures of my friends unless it was a special occasion. Hell, I've never once snapped a "selfie." "No." Another dead end. But I still had a few more phone calls I could make. I just needed to buy another phone.

Jake stayed for supper, but Freddie came to pick him up soon after we'd finished. I insisted Freddie stay and eat a piece of the raspberry shortcake I'd whipped up. I hadn't heard any updates on the investigation and wanted to pump him for information.

"Have they found the kid who shot out the window?" I asked casually as I put a swirl of whipped cream on top of his shortcake.

Freddie shook his head as he took the plate from me. "I doubt we ever will. Most of our attention has been diverted elsewhere." He shot a glance toward Jake who was watching TV in the front room. "There's a lot of pressure to bring our guest in for questioning."

"Agent Garza still in town?"

With his mouth full of cake, Freddie nodded vigorously.

"Has anyone located Booker's next-of-kin?"

He swallowed. "His daughter got in contact with

us finally. She doesn't want anything to do with him even now. So I'm guessing his body will stay in the morgue until the county pays for cremation."

The whole situation kept getting worse and worse. I couldn't imagine ending up in a morgue with no one who cared enough to bury me. Which reminded me, it was time to make a trip to my parents' gravesite.

"Is the daughter a suspect?" I asked. I'd heard stories of victims killing their abusers years later.

"No, she's out in Nevada. Her mother's there with her, so we can't pin it on the ex-wife either. Although there are rumors Booker remarried, we haven't been able to verify that information. If he did, it wasn't in Ohio."

I scrunched up my mouth. "So no other possibilities?"

Freddie half-laughed. "You're beginning to sound like me when I'm questioning a suspect. There's a whole list of people with motive. What we don't have is any evidence to point at anyone in particular."

I let him finish his cake without asking more questions, but my mind was racing. Was there anyone on his list that wasn't on mine? And how would I find out? "So what happens next?"

"I get yelled at on a regular basis until something else comes along to distract the mayor and it goes into the books as unsolved." He put one hand on my shoulder. "Try not to get involved more than you already are, Harmony."

If I wanted to help Jake, I didn't have a choice.

The apartment seemed empty after they left. Jake had the ability to make everything brighter with his eye-catching smile, and in the last few days, I'd seen that smile more often. But I had to wonder how much of it was fake.

For the moment, it didn't matter. I had plans now that I was alone. With any luck, Eli wouldn't be in a meeting. First, though, even without my burner phone, I wanted to call a couple more numbers on my list.

The first number went straight to voice mail for a man with a heavy Indian accent. It didn't fit the expected profile so I hung up. Next call was answered in a very business-like way "Twenty-Seventh Street Pawn."

"Sorry, wrong number," I said. I assumed it was one of the pawn shops that Booker had owned, but surely the police had already spoken to the employees there.

There was one more number on the list, and it had an Ohio area code. As I prepared to dial it, I hesitated, wondering if the FBI was tapping my phone. If they were, one more call wouldn't make a difference.

After the third ring, I figured I'd get voice mail. So I was surprised when a lady picked up.

"Hello?" a muffled voice said.

"Hello, is Calib Booker available?" I knew the answer, but planned to bluff my way through the call.

There was a long silence. "Who is this?"

"This is Martha Stone," I said, channeling Aunt Martha once again. "I'm researching the history of pawn shops, and wondered if Mr. Booker would be available for an interview." The lie rolled easily off my lips.

"He's not here."

"Any idea how I can reach him?"

Another long pause. "No."

"Can I ask who this is?"

The silence in my ear let me know the call had ended. At least I'd made a start.

Chapter 12

There were ways to track down people by their phone numbers, and I knew just the men for the job. My next call went to one of them, although that wasn't the main reason I wanted to talk to him.

Eli picked up immediately.

"Hey, beautiful," he said. Even over the phone he could make me blush.

"Hey, yourself. You have the night off?"

"No, but no meetings tonight, so I'm catching up on paperwork. What are you up to?"

"Missing you. And trying to figure out how I can prove Jake's innocence."

"Jake? What's he got to do with anything?"

"Hasn't he called you yet? He's out of prison, and here in Oak Grove."

I sensed a shift in Eli's mood. "What's he done now?"

"Nothing as far as I can tell. But there's an FBI agent in town who would love to tie him to the dead guy they found at the house."

Eli mumbled a few choice words. "The police detain him?"

"No, because there's no evidence. He's bunking with Freddie for a few days since I don't have a spare bed."

"How hard did you beg to make that happen?"

"Freddie volunteered. I suspect he wanted to keep Jake away from me as much as possible, and keep an eye on him at the same time."

With a chuckle, Eli said "Remind me to thank Freddie next time I see him. But you should let the police do their job and stay out of it."

"Freddie says they aren't getting anywhere in their investigation. And the FBI guy alternates between threatening and trying to bribe me to help them."

"It's not Felton, is it?"

"No, this guy's name is Garza. If anything, he's worse than Felton."

"That bad, eh?"

"Yes, that bad. So can you ask Lando and Scotty to do some research for me?"

Lando and Scotty were a couple of computer geeks who worked with Eli. On top of their programming skills, they had considerable hacking abilities. They saw it as a game and claimed they only used those powers in 'white hat' capacities. I didn't quite understand the distinction.

I gave him what limited information I had.

"That's not a whole lot to go on," he said. "But we'll see what we can do."

"Thanks. I don't know what else to do."

"You could just let him take care of himself. Especially after the situation he got you into. He sure didn't help you out any."

"But he was responsible for getting us together."

"He was, wasn't he? I guess we owe him something." I had a vision of Eli shaking his head.

"Besides, he claims the necklace he gave me was a fake and that he didn't leave it in my closet."

"And you believe him?"

"When he told me, yes, but now I wonder. Something doesn't add up." I should have told Eli then about our planned visit to Pittsburgh, but I didn't.

"Can I talk you into coming here and letting Jake sort out things for himself?"

"Not until I'm sure Jake and Freddie won't kill each other," I said regretfully. "But keep asking and one day I'll surprise both of us and say yes."

"Tell you what. I'll call The Towers and book a room for Jake. That way he's still in town but not complicating things for Freddie. Although I fully intend to wring his neck for not contacting me himself."

Why didn't I think of that?

"And the next time you see him, you can tell that son of a b…gun that he'd better call me," Eli added.

It tickled me the way Eli tried so hard not to swear around me. "Got it."

"And Harmony…?" he started, and stopped.

"What, Eli?"

He took a deep breath. "Never mind, just be

careful, will you? It's driving me nuts that I can't be there."

"I know. Don't worry, nothing bad is going to happen. Besides, Jake's here to help out."

"That's what I'm afraid of," he muttered

Was he jealous?

With him in Florida, I didn't need to hide my smile. "What was that?" I asked, pretending I hadn't heard.

"Nothing. Just thinking out loud."

We talked for quite a while longer, until I could no longer cover my yawns. "As much as I hate to say good night, I have to get to bed."

An answering yawn came from the other end. "No fair," Eli said. "Now I'm doing it too. And I have more paperwork to finish before I head home."

"Can't it wait until next week?"

"I wish," he said regretfully. "I'd do it tomorrow, but I promised Dad I'd drop by and help him with yard work. What I really want is to tuck you in."

"One of these times," I sighed.

Neither of us said anything for a long moment, then I couldn't help myself, and yawned again.

He chuckled. "Go to bed, beautiful, and sleep well."

As I tucked myself into bed, I wondered if he really thought I was beautiful. Or was that just a line?

✳ ✳ ✳

Jake was pacing in front of the hotel entrance when I pulled up Tuesday morning, and I was even a few minutes early.

"Let's get out of here," he said, closing Dolores's door with a little too much force for my liking.

"What's going on?" I pulled out of the driveway and made a mental note to keep track of the black sedan that followed in a few seconds.

Jake opened and closed his fists. "I was talking to Anna this morning, and she let it slip that Garza pressured management into letting him into my room while I was out yesterday."

"Anna?"

"One of the housekeepers. Sweet little old lady."

"You should have called me. I would have brought the scanner with me." I glanced in the rearview mirror, and wasn't surprised to see the black car still behind me. However, we hadn't gone far, so it might have been a coincidence that it was traveling in the same direction.

"You can pick it up before you bring me back tonight."

"Yeah." Without warning, I changed lanes. I'd already made sure none of Oak Grove's unmarked cars were nearby. Unless they'd acquired a new one in the last month or two, I was golden. When the black car switched with us, I got a look at the driver and confirmed my suspicions. Agent Garza was along for the ride.

I decided not to say anything to Jake. He was agitated enough. The next couple of street changes, I signaled ahead of time. I didn't want the FBI man to know I was on to him. In fact, I was going to waste as much of his time as I could.

My "no eating food in Dolores" rule was about to get broken again. I pulled into a convenience store's crowded parking lot, taking the last available spot, grinning as I watched the black car roll past. "Do you want coffee?" I asked.

"Sure," he said, reaching to unbuckle his seat belt.

I put my hand on his to stop him. "I'll get it. Why don't you wait here?" As he started to protest, I added, "I saw some shady characters around the corner. I don't want to leave Dolores unguarded."

He grinned. "Shady characters? Where do you get these expressions, Angel?"

Bad books, probably, but I just shrugged my shoulders. "Two sugars, one cream, right?"

As busy as the store was, it took longer than I'd hoped to pay for the coffee. The line wasn't terrible, but the man in front was arguing with the clerk over the cost of a pack of cigarettes. Once that sale was completed, everyone else paid and left quickly, including myself.

I surveyed the parking lot and the street beyond

as I left the store, a coffee cup in each hand. Jake sprang out of the car to assist me. "Nobody bothered her," he said, indicating Dolores with his free hand. "She gets plenty of second looks, but I expected that."

"Most of the locals are accustomed to her," I told him. "At least that's my theory."

He opened my door and then held my coffee for me as I slid into the driver's seat. After handing me my cup, he hurried around to the passenger side, and balanced his cup on the dash while he settled in. It gave me time to locate the black sedan parked across the street.

This made my choice of direction easy when we left. Garza's car was parked facing east, so I headed west. He'd have to risk a U-turn if he wanted to follow. That would give me the opportunity to lose him.

But the plan didn't work out. Two blocks away, I got stuck waiting for a funeral procession to go by. That gave the agent time to catch up, although he was several cars behind me. As I waited for the tail end of the motorcade to pass, I tried to come up with another method of losing him.

Jake must have noticed my attention was focused behind me, instead of in front of us. He twisted around in his seat. "What's going on?"

"Don't look now, but Agent Garza has decided to spend some time with us."

"For how long?"

"Ever since we left the hotel. If it hadn't been for the funeral, we'd be in the clear."

Jake reached for his seat belt. "Let me drive."

The last car with the funeral home's placard drove by. "Not happening," I said as I pushed the gas pedal. "I'm familiar with how Dolores handles, and you aren't. Besides, I'm hoping he doesn't realize I know what's going on yet."

"So what's the plan?"

"Next stop is the post office. After that the library. I'm trying to fool him into thinking we're just running normal errands and lull him into complacency. Then when the moment is right, I'll leave town heading north towards Erie and away from Pittsburgh on the county roads. I can pick up the interstate from an on-ramp in about twenty miles. That will still give us time to make it to the book signing."

"Have I told you lately that I love how your mind works?" He adjusted the back of his seat and settled in for the show.

It should have worked. In fact, it almost did, but Agent Garza was more determined to stick with us than I'd anticipated. By the time we'd reached the interstate, he was still behind us, although he'd lost ground on the curvy country road. I had one more chance.

The intersection was a basic cloverleaf, with one ramp heading north and another going south. If I played my cards right, he'd make a wrong guess about which way I'd gone. As I made my turn, I said "Keep an eye out while I watch traffic."

Jake leaned forward to get a better view in his side view mirror. I was at the top of the ramp and preparing to merge into the light flow of traffic when he exclaimed "Yes! You did it! You're a genius! He's headed the other way."

"You taught me well, sensei." Maybe too well. Nothing I'd done had been illegal, but I was sure the FBI wouldn't look kindly at it.

I had one more trick up my sleeve. I left the interstate several exits before Pittsburgh, and took surface roads the rest of the way. If Garza had alerted his colleagues to our trip, they might be waiting for me.

We arrived at the bookstore downtown with no further sightings of our FBI "friends." There were a surprising number of parking spots along the street, but I followed the signs to a small pay-by-the-hour private lot. That meant we had to walk a couple of blocks, but it also hid our destination.

Inside, a small group of people sat on folding chairs, most of them holding books. Jake and I took seats in the last row. "Do you see him anywhere?" I whispered.

"Not yet." He took my hand. His was sweaty. "Can you believe I'm nervous? This guy is a legend!"

In a few minutes a female employee of the store walked to the front.

"Mr. Wallington will give a short talk, answer a few questions, and then be available to sign books," she said. She glanced around the less-than-overwhelming audience. "Please don't ask him how to perform any illegal activity."

There was a tittering from the audience, but it hushed when she escorted an elderly gentleman in from a side door. "There he is," Jake hissed.

"Ladies and gentleman," the lady said, "Mr. Orson Wallington."

Amid polite applause, the man took a seat behind a table and picked up a microphone. "Hello, everyone," he said, and looked surprised when his voice blared from a set of speakers. The woman hurried to adjust the volume. "Let's try this again," and nodded in satisfaction. He scanned the room, and I suspected his eyes rested on Jake longer than they did anyone else.

To my disappointment, his little speech didn't tell me anything new. It was mostly tips on how to make your home less vulnerable to theft. Things that were common knowledge, like putting wood on the inside of glass sliding doors to block them from opening. Jake seemed even less interested than me.

But when Mr. Wallington started talking about his current career as a movie consultant, Jake leaned forward and paid close attention. Was he debating doing the same thing? At least it would be better that going back to a life of crime.

After his speech, the author sat behind a table and signed books. I bought one and stood at the end of the small line while Jake hung back.

"Anything in particular you want me to say?"

Mr. Wallington asked as I laid the book in front of him, without glancing up.

"No, your signature is fine," I answered. "But I wondered if I could ask you a few questions now that the crowd's gone."

He looked up. "Not here," he said to my surprise. "Why don't you and your friend over there join me for supper?"

A second man showed up at the little Thai restaurant a few blocks away that Orson, as he asked me to call him, suggested. Orson introduced him as Steve, his manager. The stiff way in which Steve held himself made me suspect he'd had a previous career, one with the FBI or a similar agency.

To play it safe, I introduced myself as Martha Stone, historical researcher, and Jake as Jacob, my assistant. Orson's mouth twitched when I did that, but he didn't comment.

I kept my questions to generic queries about working with the various Hollywood producers mentioned on the website. It wasn't until Steve excused himself for a few minutes that things got interesting. Orson leaned forward across the table.

"I know who you are, Jacob Hennessey," he said, staring at Jake and whispering. "But does the lady?"

"Actually, I do," I answered for Jake, placing one hand on his suddenly-tense shoulder. "At least I have a pretty good idea."

"Then you aren't really Martha Stone."

"Does it matter who she is?" Jake asked. "She's trying to help me out. Somebody set me up and made it appear I pulled off a major jewelry theft and used her as a decoy. To clear her name, I have to prove I wasn't involved. If you were still in the business, I'd suspect you, but since you've retired, I thought you could tell us who might be responsible."

Orson nodded his head and brought his hands together so just his fingertips touched. "We need to talk more but not here where we can be overheard. Miss Stone, perhaps you would meet me in my hotel?"

Was he hitting on me? "Not without Jake," I said.

Orson smiled broadly. "You can't blame a man for trying." He took a pen from his pocket and scribbled something on his napkin, tore the corner off and handed it to me. "Ten tonight," he whispered just before Steve returned.

I dropped the paper into my lap without looking at it. As Steve settled back into his seat, I asked "So where's the next stop on your book tour?"

With several hours to kill before the meeting with Orson at his hotel, there was plenty of time to buy the new burner phones. I bought two, so I could alternate between them. We told the salesman that one was for me and one for Jake, using false names of course. I convinced the sales clerk to activate "mine" on the spot, claiming—truthfully enough—

that I was from out-of-town and didn't have a phone to call the carrier from and I needed the phone right away. The twenty I slipped him as a tip may have helped more than the sob story.

Even that didn't use up all the extra time. I longed to make a trip to the main library downtown, but worried I might run into someone I knew there. So instead we drove through some of the historic neighborhoods. Most of the old homes were lit by only a porch light or two, but it gave us the opportunity to make sure we weren't being followed. It's not paranoia if there's a legitimate reason for it.

After we'd killed enough time, I checked the scrap of paper that Orson had given me to make sure I remembered his hotel and room number correctly. The hotel, part of a well-known chain, was located downtown. It didn't take me long to find a parking spot as most nearby businesses were closed.

Jake and I sauntered through the lobby as if we belonged there, and took the elevator to the fourth floor. Although we were a few minutes early, Orson must have been waiting for us. He pulled the door open at the first knock.

"Nice to see you again." With a sideways glance at Jake he added. "I hoped you'd change your mind and come alone."

"I thought I made myself clear about that," I answered.

He grinned. "You did. Please come in. Would you like something to drink?"

Since I would be driving later, I turned him

down, but Jake took him up on his offer of a beer. While they busied themselves with discussing the meager options available, I took time to study the room and our host.

The room wasn't anything special, just a basic high-end hotel room with a single king bed covered by a heavy-duty flowered quilt. The nautical theme of the pictures of the wall seemed out of place for a hotel in Pittsburgh. Perhaps the decorator had caught a glimpse of one of the city's three rivers and used it for inspiration.

Orson didn't look anything like I expected a jewelry thief to look, except for his nose, which appeared to have been broken once or twice. My expectations may have been skewed by bad movies, but I always figured a jewel thief would be more like an acrobat versus a pudgy old accountant. Didn't they need to be able to squeeze into tiny spaces? Whether he fit the expected mold or not, Orson was the only lead Jake and I had.

"So what is it you do for a living, Martha?" he asked as we took seats. He and Jake took the cushioned chairs while I chose the desk chair.

"Research," I told him. "I dig up information on topics of interest for people willing to pay for my time. That's how I found you. Although, frankly, you've made it easy."

He sighed. "It's the price I pay for making sure the right people know I exist and are willing to pay for my services. In that respect, Martha, or whatever your name really is, you and I are more alike than it might appear on the surface."

I hadn't thought about it that way. The more publicity I got, the more customers I attracted.

"So where's Steve?"

"In his own room, down the hall. The publishing company may have made me agree to have him along, but I insisted I needed some privacy." He grinned. "They assume his presence will safeguard them from lawsuits if there are any high-profile thefts in the cities on the tour." He shifted in his chair and looked me straight in the eye. "Truth is, I can't pull off the big-time heists anymore. This body got old on me. That's why I retired."

I had the distinct impression he was hoping for a compliment, so I obliged him. "Your biography said you are seventy-three. You don't appear to be a day over sixty."

That earned a chuckle. "That biography is mostly made-up bullshit that the PR firm put together. Had to come up with something to satisfy the IRS since I never bothered to get a social security number. Every one I've ever used was fake. Fake numbers to go with fake names."

Jake butted in. "Rumors say your real name isn't Orson Wallington either."

Orson shook his head. "This business was so much easier before the government started tracking us on computers. Used to be I could hop a bus into a town using whatever name I felt suited the area, pull a job and leave with no one the wiser. It's not like that these days. Now, you need an ID to even check into a motel."

"So your name isn't Orson Wallington?" I asked.

"Orson has some class to it, don't you think? Better than Harry or Joe. Besides, Martha," and he rather pointedly emphasized the "Martha." "Names aren't important here, are they?"

With answers like that, he should have been a politician, not a thief. Although some people would say they were the same thing. I decided to get down to business.

"The real question is, can you help us or not?"

"What is it you want?"

"Information. Who besides you has the skills to steal The Marquesa's Necklace from the traveling exhibit of the Museum, and then stash it in my apartment? Especially while I was under surveillance by my town's police department?" Because how else had the real necklace gotten there? "And of course, the real question is why?"

Orson picked up his beer and swirled the liquid around in the bottle before taking a swallow. "The why is easy, my dear," he said. "Consider the company you're keeping. I imagine your friend has made a few enemies along the way."

It couldn't be that simple. There had to be more, but clearly Orson wasn't ready to talk. "But who has skills to carry it out?"

"Information has a price." He leaned back. A bad sign. "What's in it for me?"

I didn't know what to tell him.

Chapter 13

But Jake did. "How about if I promise not to bust this cute little scheme you've got going?" he spat out. "The real Orson Wallington is a mechanical wiz and loves computers. Plus, he's all of five feet tall, according to the stories. You're nothing but a con artist using his name to make yourself look good."

Holy crap. Why hadn't Jake said something earlier?

The fake smile that had been pasted on Orson's face since we'd walked in the door disappeared.

"What's more," Jake continued, "If Steve was here to make sure you didn't get into any trouble, there's no way he'd let the real Orson Wallington out of his sight. Hell, I'm just a bit player compared to the big guys, and I've spotted two ways for me to get out of this building and back in with no trace. The real Orson would have twice that many ways figured out."

I'd have to remember to ask Jake how to get past

the hotel security cameras later. Strictly for research, of course.

"My guess is that Steve is an actor, and I've got you figured out." Jake slammed his beer down on the dresser so hard that I was afraid the bottle would shatter. "You're a groupie. But you don't follow rock stars. Or serial killers. You worship jewelry thieves. You track their careers. That's why you can pretend to be Orson Wallington and get away with it. Hell, you probably have a map hanging on the wall of your bedroom tracking every theft the real Orson Wallington is accused of. Am I right?" He stood and grabbed my hand. "Come on, we're out of here. This guy is a waste of our time."

"Wait a minute," Orson said as I stood, his voice a harsh whisper. "Don't go. This gig is the best deal I've ever had. Don't blow it for me. Please."

"What's in it for us?" Jake asked.

"Information. I have some that might help. Really."

I saw it in Jake's body language the minute he made his decision. But this was his area of expertise, so I let him handle it.

"I can't trust you, so why should I believe anything you say?"

"Because I've been a fan of yours, too. Figured you would be near the top of the game soon," Orson answered, a little too eagerly. "Saw you as Orson's competition before long."

The thought of Jake having a groupie—a male one at that—was enough to make me giggle, but I turned it to a cough when Jake glared at me.

"I'll make you a deal. Tell me what you know, and if it's worth my time I'll promise to keep quiet. But if you ever let anyone know we were here, the deal is off. Agreed?"

Orson hesitated. "Does that include her, too?" he asked.

Jake growled, and I swallowed another giggle. "The lady will speak for herself."

I lowered my voice and tried, unsuccessfully, to sound threatening. "If the information checks out—and I *will* try to verify it—I promise not to reveal where it came from. And I won't tell anyone about who you really are—or aren't."

The old man nodded, and, after finishing what remained of his beer, told us what he knew.

Which turned out to be long on rumor and short on hard information. The story was gathered from several internet forums that Steve monitored. Supposedly, Jake had been approached by some anonymous guy who was trying to recruit talented burglars to work for him. By turning down the offer, Jake had pissed him off. The forums didn't have anything to say about me, which was good in one way and bad in another. The limited information didn't put us any closer to figuring out who the real culprit was, but at least let us know that somewhere out there, someone had it in for Jake.

Before we left, I managed to get information about the forums from Orson. He was so computer-phobic that Steve would print out copies of interesting posts for him to read. He had a couple stashed, and unwillingly, gave them to me.

"The people who run these forums are crazy," he said, his hand trembling as he handed them over. "They're very particular about who gets access. If they find out I told you about them, I don't know what they'll do. But it won't be good."

"Don't worry, I can cover my tracks," I assured him, stuffing them into my purse. "No one will find out."

Jake had one hand on the doorknob and the other on the small of my back to walk me out of the room, when he stopped. "One thing's been bothering me," he said. "Does the real Orson Wallington know you're doing this?"

The smile returned to Orson's face. "Yes. As a matter of fact, he dropped by to visit me one night. Nice guy. Said he'd be keeping track of me. As long as we don't visit the same city at the same time, I provide him with an alibi. Like you said, he's good with computers and he watches my website for my schedule. Every now and then, he feeds me a bit of information to keep my speeches fresh and makes it sound as if I'm an expert. Works out for both of us."

Jake was still shaking his head as we started the drive home. He'd insisted on using my flashlight, laid on the ground, and looked under the car first in case we'd picked up any attachments while we were in the hotel. As far as he could see, it was clean.

"That was a waste of time," he said when we hit the interstate.

I felt the same way, but decided to put a positive spin on the night. "Well, at least we got some data." I checked my rear view mirror one more time, but it was hard to tell if we were being followed or not with all the traffic, even though it was a little after midnight. "And if I can get on those forums, who knows what I'll find out."

He shook his head. "I've heard about them, even checked one out once. Everything on those forums is pure speculation unless the information is planted by the cops." A series of street lights we passed under revealed his gloomy expression. "And that information is somebody's best guess. If it was real evidence, they wouldn't be revealing it."

I'd check them out anyway, out of curiosity, wondering if they would say who the mysterious person with a grudge against Jake was. As I checked my mirrors and switched lanes, I heard Jake chuckling.

"What?" I asked.

"I get a kick out of the fact that Orson is out there somewhere, still doing what he does better than anyone else."

"You think that's a good thing?"

"Gives me hope I'll be able to get back into the game one day."

I was tempted to pull over, stop the car, and order him to get out. I probably should have. "God damn it, Jake," I said instead. "You don't think I'm helping you so you can go back to a life of crime, do you?"

He giggled. Jake didn't giggle. Ever. "I love when you talk like an ol', private eye movie, Angel," he answered, slurring his words. He reached to turn off the heater and flipped to air conditioning, despite it being below freezing outside. "I'm hot." He fanned himself with one hand.

I took my eyes off the road long enough to glance at him, and spotted sweat beads on his forehead. "Are you okay?"

"Sure," he muttered, adjusting the back of his seat so it reclined. "Jus' tired all of a sudden."

I took one hand off the steering wheel long enough to touch his cheek.

Shit, he was burning up.

My choices were limited. Watch for a hospital sign and take him to an emergency room. Or get him home as quickly as possible and try to treat him myself. The decision was made for me by the flashing blue lights in my rear view mirror. Luckily, the road had a nice, wide shoulder and I pulled over. I hadn't been speeding, so why was I being stopped?

I rolled down my window, turned off the engine, put both hands on the steering wheel, and waited.

"Was goin' on?" Jake muttered and closed his eyes.

"I've got it covered," I answered, although in truth, I didn't. It took a few minutes before the officer climbed out of his patrol car and approached. He'd probably been running my plate, but still, the wait made me nervous.

"License, registration, and insurance please," he said with no expression in his voice.

"Of course," I reached over Jake, popped open my glove box, pulled out the registration and handed it to him. "My license and insurance are in my purse behind my seat." Freddie had taught me it was a good idea to tell an officer exactly what you are doing.

"Any weapons in the car?" he asked as I twisted in my seat.

"No." I extracted my wallet from my purse. "Why did you stop us anyway?"

He didn't answer until he got done examining the documents I handed to him. "You were swerving back there. Have you been drinking?"

"Only one beer with supper, and that was hours ago."

"What's up with your friend?" the officer asked, leaning down and peering into the passenger's seat, where Jake slumped against the window, his breathing rapid and shallow.

"He's sick." I allowed the worry to seep into my voice. "Running a bad fever. It came on quickly." I reached over and touched Jake's cheek again. Still hot. "I was checking his temperature just before you stopped me."

"Do you want me to call an ambulance?"

"No, I don't think it's that bad." At least, I hoped not.

The officer hesitated, and handed me back all my paperwork. "Tell you what, ma'am," he said. When had I gotten old enough to be called ma'am instead of miss? "I'm going to let you off with a warning. In the future, pull over when you're distracted."

While he went back to his car, I returned all my documents to their proper places and restarted my internal debate about what to do with Jake. A snore from his side of the car made my decision for me. I'd take him back to his hotel, get some ibuprofen into him, and hope for the best. I didn't think there was any way I'd ever get him up the stairs to my place.

The officer was back at my window in a few minutes. "If you'll sign here," he said, handing me a piece of paper and a pen. I scrawled my name on the dotted line, and handed it back. He tore off the bottom copy for me, and when Jake snored loudly again, shook his head. "I hope your friend gets better soon." He straightened up. "Drive safe." He patted Dolores's roof and walked back to his vehicle.

It didn't even upset me when he followed me for a few miles until we got to another off-ramp and he exited. In fact, it made me feel more secure. Like help was just a few feet away in case Jake stopped breathing or something. I'd eliminated food poisoning from my list of suspected ailments, but the quick onset of symptoms baffled and bothered me. When Jake started twitching, I wasn't sure if he was dreaming or shivering. I turned the heat back on. I was cold, so he must have been as well.

Luckily, the exit for Oak Grove wasn't too much farther. As I pulled into a parking spot at the hotel, I realized I had no idea where Jake kept the key card to his room. I didn't want to search each and every one of his pockets looking for it. That could lead to complications I wasn't prepared to deal with.

Just getting his seat belt undone was risky enough. When I opened the passenger side door and reached over him to undo the belt, he woke up. "Hey, Angel," he said weakly. "Where are we?"

"Back in Oak Grove. Think you can make it to your room?"

"Don't want to move right now. Except to do this." One arm unexpectedly shot up, pulling my head down to his. With no sign of weakness, he planted his lips on mine. Shocked, I let it happen, although I tried really, really hard not to kiss him back.

"I've been wanting to do that all night," he said, letting me go and leaning back in the seat. "Hell, I've wanted to do it since the last time we kissed."

"You rat! Get out of the car!" I pulled myself out of the passenger compartment and straightened up. Only his condition saved him from a swat or two, like a parent would give a misbehaving child. As we'd kissed, his lips were hot, and not from passion. He still had a roaring fever.

He laughed, undid his seat belt, and swung his legs out of the car. I noticed his hand shaking as he reached for the car door to support himself, and rushed in to help.

"Couldn't stay away, could you?" he grinned. But he didn't refuse my arm when I offered it to help him stand.

The elevator to the upper floors was only a short distance through the main lobby, but it took too long to get there. Jake needed to stop and rest every few steps, and during the ride to the fifth floor he slumped against the wall. When he tried to stick the key card into its slot, he missed. Several times. Finally, I grabbed it from him and unlocked the door myself.

Once in the room, I shoved him down on the bed. "So eager?" Jake asked, but I just "harrumphed."

I pulled his shoes and socks off. "If you want anything else off, you'll have to do it yourself."

His answering smile was weak, then turned into a frown. He slowly rolled off the bed, then rushed to the bathroom and closed the door. It wasn't enough to block the sound of his distress as he emptied the contents of his stomach. I needed to rethink the food poisoning angle.

Jake was in there long enough that I contemplated opening the door to check on him. About the time I decided to do it, he emerged, paler than ever. I helped him back to the bed, and, still fully clothed, he crawled on top of the covers.

"Go home," he whispered.

"In a few minutes." I held my wrist to his forehead. The fever was as bad as ever. "I'm going to see if the front desk has any ibuprofen and then I'll be right back."

He shook his head. "Couldn't keep it down. Go home, don't want you getting this bug."

I don't get sick very often, and had no idea how to take care of someone else who was sick, but I couldn't leave Jake alone. "Go to sleep," I said. "I'll stay a few minutes, and be back in the morning to check on you."

His eyes were closing by the time I got done talking. I pulled the spare blanket off the shelf of the closet and covered him with it, then sat in one of the easy chairs. If I got my laptop out of Dolores, I could research what to do for him. I watched him for a few minutes, wondering if turning on the TV would wake him.

I woke to the sound of pounding on the door. The lights were still on, but the light leaking in through the crack of the curtains made me suspect it was early morning. I yawned and stretched. Why was housekeeping wanting in?

Jake shifted on the bed, but didn't wake up. The blanket I'd put over him was in a pile on the floor. Only half-awake, I couldn't decide whether to cover him back up or answer the door first.

The pounding on the door got louder, and a voice called "Open the door, Hennessey. We'd prefer not to break it down."

Chapter 14

What the hell was Freddie yelling about? And what was he doing here? I undid the security lock and yanked the door open. "Will you keep it down? People are sleeping," I scolded him, gesturing at the other doors in the hallway with their 'Do Not Disturb' signs. Then I noticed the uniformed officer hanging a few feet behind him. "What's going on?"

Freddie's stern face got grimmer. "Where's Hennessey?" he asked and "What are *you* doing here?" How had he not seen Dolores in the parking lot?

"I'm here," Jake said. "Let him in, Angel."

I turned to see Jake sitting on the edge of the bed. I walked over and put my hand on his forehead. His temperature was down, but still not normal.

"What's up, Detective?" Jake asked, taking my hand away from his forehead and kissing it before letting go. Even in his weakened state, he wouldn't stop playing games.

"We're here to take you to the station for questioning," Freddie answered.

Jake stiffened, took a deep breath, and blew it out. "Am I under arrest?"

"Not yet."

Whether due to the fever or the tension, the spark that had returned to Jake's eyes over the last few days was gone when he glanced at me. "Do you mind if I change first?" he asked. "I slept in my clothes."

Freddie nodded, and Jake stood and headed for his closet. Halfway there, he stopped abruptly, switched directions, went to the bathroom and closed the door behind him. The officer with Freddie started to say something, but stopped when the sound of Jake getting sick carried into the main room.

"That does it, I've got to get him to a doctor," I said.

"How long has he been like that?" Freddie asked.

"Since last night. He was fine during the day."

"You were with him all day?"

"Pretty much. I picked him up mid-morning to go to a book signing in Pittsburgh with me. I wanted company."

"You didn't go to Erie?"

"Erie? No. What gave you that idea?" Erie was north of Oak Grove. The original direction Jake and I had gone the day before. In spite of the situation, I smiled. "A certain FBI agent tell you that?"

"This is serious," Freddie said. "Not a game."

He didn't answer my question. "You might tell Agent Garza that he either needs to get a different car or improve his hiding skills."

"Do you have any proof of where you were?" Freddie was still in his official mode.

About that time Jake came out of the bathroom, shirtless. "Sorry," he mumbled, and opened the closet door.

"Hold off for a minute, Hennessey," Freddie said. "Harmony, do you have proof you were in Pittsburgh?"

I took my purse off the dresser. "Sure." I opened my wallet. "Here's a receipt for the book I bought. And one for supper." I handed them to him. I hadn't bothered with receipts for parking.

Freddie glanced at them. "Anyone who can verify Jake was with you?"

"The waiter at the restaurant might remember him." I frowned. "I doubt the clerk at the bookstore would, as busy as they were."

"Anyone else?"

I blushed. "The Highway Patrolman who stopped me on the way home might."

One of Freddie's eyebrows rose. "HP stopped you?"

"He just gave me a warning," I rushed to explain. "He saw me swerving when I was checking Jake's temperature and not paying attention to the road."

"Did he give you a ticket?"

"No, just a written warning." I dug into my purse and found my copy.

Freddie studied the slip of paper and turned to the officer. "You know an HP guy by the name of Ferguson?"

The officer nodded. "If it's the same guy, I met him at training a couple of months back. Good guy. I owe him a beer or two."

Jake had returned to his seat on the bed. "What did I do?"

Freddie hesitated before answering. "You're suspected in a theft that occurred last night in Erie. A witness identified someone matching your description."

His lips a tight line, Jake shrugged. "Not me."

"I need to verify your alibi, but you can stay here for now. Do yourself a favor, and don't go anywhere."

"Agreed." Jake lay on the bed. "Don't think I'm up to any trips, anyway."

"Can I talk to you outside, Harmony?" Freddie asked.

The officer excused himself when we exited the room. Freddie and I stood in the hallway. I left the door to Jake's room opened a crack so I could get back in without disturbing him. "What are you doing here?" Freddie asked again in a low voice.

"Taking care of a sick friend." I felt like stamping my feet in frustration. "I may not be very good at it, but I didn't want to leave him alone."

"What you're doing is putting yourself in a bad spot."

"Why? Because you're hell-bent on proving Jake is a bad guy?"

"Not me, Harmony. But if Agent Garza can tie Hennessey to something, there's a possibility he'll try to charge you as an accessory. And there won't be anything I can do to help you at that point."

"So help me *now*. Figure out who killed Mr. Booker."

"You don't think I'm trying? Everyone on the force wants to get credit for that. Whoever solves the case will be up for a promotion." Freddie didn't get excited easily, but he waved his hands in the air as he spoke.

I sighed. "So what am I supposed to do? Throw him to the wolves? I'm a sucker for the underdog, and right now Jake is a textbook case."

We both fell silent. "By the way," I said eventually, "What are you doing here? It's not in your normal job duties."

Freddie grimaced. "The Chief asked me to do it as a personal favor. He figured Hennessey might be less likely to fight me off than anyone else on the force. 'Course, you did notice he didn't send me alone."

Yeah, I noticed.

Jake was asleep again by the time I slipped back into his room. I decided to make a quick trip home to change clothes and get my portable scanner to check his room for any "gifts" Agent Garza might have left behind. On the way, I'd stop by the drugstore, pick up a thermometer and get some advice from Sean, the pharmacist. I put Jake's room key card in my wallet but left him a note so he'd know where I'd gone if he woke up.

When I returned to Jake's room, he wasn't in bed, and I didn't see him anywhere. I panicked for two seconds, then heard the shower running and relaxed. After setting the bags from the drugstore on his dresser, I started to check his room with my portable scanner.

I was running the device along the door frame leading to the bathroom when I realized the water wasn't running anymore. It didn't register until the door opened and there was Jake. And except for the towel he was using to rub his hair dry, he was stark naked.

I couldn't help myself. I stared. A wide grin spread across his face.

"Like what you see, Angel?" he asked.

Truth was, I didn't. He'd lost both weight and muscle tone in prison. The scar on his shoulder seemed more prominent. The new tattoo on his chest didn't compare in style or skill to the ones he'd had done previously. And although some of the color had returned to his cheeks, he still looked sickly. But I lied.

"Looking good, Jake," I said. "As always."

His smile got bigger. "I can't believe you slept in the chair last night. You're welcome in my bed anytime."

My brain overloaded trying to formulate a response that wouldn't get me into more trouble. I was saved from having to respond when his expression turned to one of dismay. He dashed back into the bathroom, slamming the door shut behind him. I moved to another part of the room so I didn't have to listen to the sounds he was making.

When he came back out, he headed straight for the bed. "I thought I'd finished with that," he moaned as he collapsed upon the mattress, pulling the cover over himself.

I put one finger from my right hand on my lips, stretched out my left hand and opened up my fist, exposing the small device I'd found attached to the underside of the desk. "If it's the flu," I said a tad too loudly, "It'll take at least a couple of days to recover."

Jake got my unspoken message. "I hoped it was a twenty-four hour bug or food poisoning or something, I thought the pad woo sen I ate last night tasted funny."

"Mine was fine. Maybe your taste buds were off." I walked into the bathroom and set the device on top of the toilet tank. If Jake got sick again, it would serve Agent Garza or his buddies right to listen to it. Or, they could suffer through Jake singing in the shower. He was almost as bad at singing as me.

From the bed, Jake's eyes questioned me as I picked up the scanner and started my hunt again. I paused long enough to write a note which I handed to him. "Could be more than one." He nodded his understanding.

"So what did you pick up from the drugstore?"

"I thought we'd try ginger ale," I told him. "See if it settles your stomach. It works for morning sickness, I'm told." He groaned and I grinned. "I bought a thermometer too." My device gave another suspicious beep as I ran it over the window frame.

Pushing aside the heavy drapes, I tried to find the cause of the alert, but didn't spot anything. I ran the scanner over the spot again, waiting for the alarm. Nothing happened, so I moved on to another part of the room, even though I had the all-too familiar prickle at the back of my neck.

I wrote another note for Jake, "I don't trust it," and gave it to him along with a glass of ginger ale. "Sip it slowly," I said. "If it stays down we'll move on to something more challenging like crackers."

"You're enjoying torturing me, aren't you?" he asked.

"Not at all." I wandered back to the window and this time ran my hand along the frame. If I had a pair of white gloves I could check and see how clean it was at the same time. My fingers met with an obstacle in a strange place. I nodded, more to myself than anything, but also to let Jake know. He'd been tracking my movements.

It took a few seconds to pry the second bug from

the metal. I held it up for Jake to see, then walked to the bathroom and set it down next to its partner.

"Is there any more?" Jake asked. He held out his now-empty glass, but I understood what he was really asking.

I shrugged. "Let's not overdo it. We'll take it a little at a time."

Which is exactly what I did. Every ten minutes or so, I'd interrupt whatever I was doing—mostly watching TV while Jake slept—and scan some part of the room. I didn't know if it was possible to turn the devices off and on remotely, but didn't want to take any chances. By the middle of the afternoon, I hadn't found any more.

Jake successfully ate some chicken noodle soup from the restaurant next door, and I counted that as a victory. I'd forced so many glasses of sports drinks on him he made a face each time I poured him another. I figured it was good practice if I ever had a child of my own. I wondered if Eli wanted kids. We'd never talked about it. Our relationship wasn't anywhere near that level.

"Have you talked to Detective Thomason again?" Jake asked at one point, when the same commercial I'd seen four times in the past two hours popped up on the TV. He set his glass on the nightstand. I figured he was trying to distract me to hide the fact that he hadn't taken more than two small sips from it.

"No, I didn't expect to."

Jake threw the covers off and sat up. While I'd been out getting the soup, he'd put on boxers and a t-shirt so I didn't have to avoid looking at him anymore. "I hoped he'd tell you when my alibi checked out," he said.

Me too, but Freddie wasn't too happy with me at the moment. "I'm sure when he gets a definite answer, he'll tell us," I said, yawning. It had been a long night and an even longer day, and I couldn't help myself.

"Why don't you go home?" Jake said instantly. "I'm feeling a lot better." He wiggled his eyebrows suggestively. "Unless you want to take a nap with me."

The suggestion to go home sounded awfully good. Playing nurse was a lot harder than I'd anticipated. Either that, or it was the stress and lack of sleep, but I was worn out.

"Thanks, but I'd rather sleep in my own bed. I'll bring you supper later."

"No," he said firmly. "I'll order in something. Go take care of yourself. I'll call you if I need anything. I promise." I was so tired I didn't think to ask if he had money.

Tired enough that I didn't see the man standing by my car until he spoke.

"You're playing a dangerous game, Miss Duprie."
I spun around, instinctively swinging my purse.

It's not that big of a purse, but with the scanner shoved inside, it could do some damage with a solid hit. Agent Garza managed to move just before it would have connected with his arm.

"What would that be?" I asked, not bothering to hide my irritation.

"Providing an alibi for a suspect."

"And I suppose the Highway Patrol is in on it too? You're the one playing games, accusing Jake of being involved in a crime in a city miles from where he was." It was a rash assumption, but Garza's tactics crossed over an invisible line in my mind.

He took a step closer and was tall enough that I was forced to look up at him. Damn, I didn't like it, but backing down wasn't an option. I stood my ground.

"You'd better take a closer look at your informant," I continued. "Figure out why he's lying to you, and what's in it for him."

That shut him up for all of two seconds. Conflicting expressions flashed across his face. First surprise, then anger, then a tightly controlled blankness. "There's still time for you to change your mind," he said, "But there won't be much longer." He wheeled around on one heel and marched off.

First thing I checked back at my apartment was the small piece of clear tape I'd stuck across the door frame. Just another trick I'd learned from a James Bond book, and a new habit I'd developed. Unless someone watched me attach it, they'd never know it was there. At least, that was my theory. The tape was undisturbed, and nothing seemed out of place inside when I opened the door.

Once inside, I hesitated. I'd lost two days of research time, and I hadn't checked my email either. I didn't want to destroy my carefully-honed reputation for being responsive to inquiries as well as being quick to answer back with information. My bed called for me, but instead I sat down on the loveseat, turned on my laptop, and opened my email.

When I snapped awake with nonsense typed into the reply box, I gave up. I dragged myself to my bedroom, crawled under my covers, and counted the stars on my ceiling.

Disoriented, and with a killer headache, it took a minute to figure out where I was. The familiar glow of the numbers on my alarm clock caught my eye, and I panicked for a different reason. It was Wednesday, six in the evening, and I'd forgotten about girls' night at the Flamingo. If I didn't let them know I was alright, I'd have Freddie pounding on my door in no time flat. Either that, or pounding on Jake's door at the hotel again.

My priorities shifted from getting something to ease the pain in my head to making a phone call. I swung my legs over the edge of the bed, sat up, and regretted it as a wave of dizziness struck me. Damn. Had I picked up Jake's bug? I gripped the edge of the mattress and waited for the feeling to pass. When it did, I slowly stood, hoping it wouldn't return.

I made it to the front room with no further lightheadedness, although the ache hadn't diminished. I picked up the phone and hesitated, trying to decide who to call. Which of the ladies would be most likely to answer?

I settled on Sarah. If Freddie wasn't with them, she'd be watching for a call from him. She answered after two rings.

"Where are you, Harmony?"

"Home. I have a headache, and won't be coming tonight. Don't worry, it's nothing serious, and I'm sure it'll go away after I take some aspirin."

She hesitated. The background noises at the Flamingo seemed subdued. "Maybe we should come over there," she said.

Instantly on edge, I asked "Why?"

The question was followed by an even longer silence. "We'll tell you when we get there," she answered. "We'll have Al put our orders in to-go boxes. Do you want us to bring you something?"

I catalogued what leftovers were in the refrigerator. "No, I'm good. Can't you give me a clue?"

Silence followed, and for a moment I thought we'd been disconnected. But she must have put the phone on mute, because about the time I was going to hang up and call her again, she was back.

"Lori has been arrested for the murder of Calib Booker."

Chapter 15

The smell of burgers and fries filled my apartment, but the girls were barely nibbling their food. I'd settled for getting some aspirin in my system, not trusting my stomach to handle anything solid. The queasiness might have been Jake's bug, but I suspected not. It reminded me of how I'd felt before every big test in school.

"What made the cops suspect Lori?" I asked Sarah, taking a sip of my water, not taking any chances of upsetting my stomach. And if anyone would know, it was Sarah. Freddie was at the station, working.

"She was his wife," Sarah told us, "working on being his ex-wife."

"That might make her a suspect, but it's not enough to arrest her," I pointed out.

"No, but they found a text message from her on his phone threatening to kill him if he didn't leave her alone."

Crap.

"She claims she didn't do it," Sarah said. No surprise there. "But Freddie isn't telling me anything more than that. The department is trying to keep a lid on leaks so it doesn't compromise the investigation."

"I wonder if she'll be able to claim battered-wife syndrome," I said thoughtfully. "Does she need a lawyer? I'll contact Dan in the morning and see if he can help."

My friends stared at me. "What do you know that we don't?" Merrilee asked.

I avoided their eyes. "I've done some research of my own," I said. "Calib Booker didn't have the best track record. Let's just say any number of people had reasons to hold a grudge against him. Including at least one ex-wife he allegedly abused."

"Have you told Freddie this?"

"No, I guess I should. I figured if I dug up the information, so could he." Everything I'd found was publicly assessable, after all. Well, most of it.

Sarah was already calling him. "I'll leave him a message if he doesn't pick up."

I was torn. As long as Lori was a suspect, Jake would be off the radar. But my gut told me Lori hadn't killed her husband, and I couldn't let an innocent person take the rap for his death.

While Sarah was leaving a message, I grabbed my cell phone and went into the kitchen to call Dan. I doubted he'd be able to do anything for her right away, but it helped to know he'd be at her side for the initial hearings. The local public defenders were nice enough people, but terribly overwhelmed by their caseloads.

I wasn't surprised to get his voicemail since his office was closed for the day, and I hadn't called the "emergency" personal number. The message I left explained the situation and told him to talk to me about the bill. Keith, my financial adviser, would have a fit.

My conscience at least partially appeased, I returned to my friends. After all, I'd been the one who'd told Freddie about Lori in the first place.

Another night when nobody wanted to talk. Sarah kept staring at her phone, as if she could force it to ring. Having been at the other end of the situation, I knew what was going on at the police station. She wouldn't be hearing from Freddie any time soon. If she was going to date a cop, she needed to understand there would be nights like that. Rare in Oak Grove, but always a possibility.

"Is she going to be all right?" Merrilee asked eventually.

"They won't shine a bright light in her eyes for hours, if that's what you're asking," I said, trying to crack a joke. It fell flat. I sighed. "Hopefully she requested a lawyer. If so, they'll put her in a cell for the night and won't question her until the morning when a public defender shows up." Or, if he got the message in time, Dan. "The cots aren't very comfortable, but at least she'll get a pillow and a blanket and can try to get some sleep." Although the night I spent in jail, sleep had been the last thing on my mind.

"And don't worry, our local guys will make sure no other prisoners bother her, if there are any. It's not like those shows on TV." In fact, when they brought DoraLee in during one of her "episodes," they'd moved me to an empty office until her son arrived with her meds and took her home.

No one wanted to leave, and I didn't blame them. I didn't want to be alone either. But finally Merrilee made her goodbyes and took off, needing to be at work the earliest. That "broke the dam" as my mother use to say, and soon Sarah and Janine left as well.

Stress would keep me from sleeping, so I plugged in my laptop. The deep, dark corners of the internet would keep my mind occupied. I thought about the information Orson had given me, and those chat rooms that might hold clues to the person responsible for last fall's events. With Jake no longer a suspect in a murder, it didn't seem as much of a priority as it had a few hours earlier.

I'd been asked to find out what impact the era of US nuclear research had on the families of the scientists involved. The overwhelming loneliness of the young wives of the workers at Los Alamos nearly brought me to tears as I read their stories. If it wasn't for the unimportant jobs many of them held—a few hours a day while the children were in school—it would have been much harder for them. I couldn't imagine living my life behind a barb-wire fence, even if it was supposedly for my protection.

So I cursed when the ringing of my cell phone interrupted my reading. It was past midnight and I wondered who'd call me this late. It had to be bad news.

I scrambled to get to my cell phone from the kitchen table before it stopped ringing. Not easy to do with the laptop's power cord creating an impromptu obstacle course. Still, I got to it in time to hear Freddie say "She's probably asleep. Can it wait until the morning?"

"I'm here, Freddie. What's up?"

"Harmony. Sorry to disturb you. Are you home or still babysitting Hennessey?"

"I'm home."

"Sarah said you might have information about the Booker case."

"I don't know if it will help," I said. "You must have information I don't since you arrested Lori."

"I can't tell you anything at this stage of the investigation." I heard him conferring with someone in the background. "The Chief says I can tell you we doubt she was capable of pulling this off on her own, but she's not talking. Unless we can come up with something else, the DA's going to file charges."

Damn it, was he blackmailing me? I hesitated. "I've asked my lawyer to represent her. I told him I would pay his fees."

"We're not enemies in this," Freddie said softly. "I just want the truth. Can you help me?"

Double damn it. I owed him.

The coffee got done a minute or two before Freddie knocked. We were both going to need it. He looked almost nervous when I answered the door.

"Are you alone?" he asked.

Not a good way to start. "What did you think, that I invited Jake to spend the night?" I spoke more harshly than necessary.

"You're spending a lot of time with him. I wasn't sure if the two of you were picking up where you left off."

That explained Freddie's attitude. I should have known the rumor mill of Oak Grove would kick into high gear.

"As far as I'm concerned, we're just friends." I grinned wryly. "I'm not sure if I've convinced Jake of that. Circumstances keep trying to push us together."

"Have you considered he might be manipulating those circumstances?" Freddie asked.

Shit. No, I hadn't. Was it possible that Jake was playing me? But I didn't think it was possible to fake a fever. And he had sent me home when I'd offered to stay. I decided I was just tired.

"Don't worry, I've got my eyes open."

I'd created a folder for the web pages where I'd found information about Booker, so returning to them was easy. Freddie browsed through them at his own pace, occasionally asking me to help him find the right post in a forum otherwise lost in miscellaneous clutter. I figured most of them would be worthless for his purposes, but left those decisions up to him.

Despite my afternoon nap and the coffee, I nodded off as he scrolled through the many pages I'd bookmarked.

"Why didn't you share this with me before?" he asked, waking me up from a dream about leaky pipes.

"How much is admissible in court?"

"Almost none of it. Unless we can track down the people who posted in these forums and get statements."

"And there ya' go. That's why I didn't tell you. Besides, I figured anything I found, so would someone on the force. I know a few of the guys are computer whizzes." I yawned. "Some of those postings are years old, and the names are just made-up handles. Even with warrants, I doubt the records exist to connect them to real people."

"Why were you doing the research anyway?" Freddie asked abruptly. I saw him slipping deeper into cop mode.

"Truthfully? At first I wanted to find out who this guy was who had the balls to end up dead on my property. I wanted to find his family so he could be put to rest properly. Then, when Jake showed up and everyone wanted to blame him, I felt guilty and wanted to clear his name. Now?" I pushed back a loose lock of hair from my eyes. "Now I want to make sure that the right person goes to jail for the crime. Maybe Lori did it and maybe she didn't, and maybe she had a good reason for it. Have you checked her medical records yet?"

The look in Freddie's eyes told me he hadn't, but he was plotting how best to make it happen.

"I'm going to share this information with Dan too," I added.

"I can't stop you, but I hope word doesn't get out to too many people. It could hinder our investigation."

"I'll make sure Dan is aware of the need for confidentiality." I yawned again, covering my mouth with my hand. Like I needed to remind a lawyer of that.

"Be done in a couple of minutes. Only a few more links to check out." Freddie followed my lead and tried to hide a yawn.

I leaned against the corner of the loveseat and closed my eyes. It would only be for a second, enough to wash away the dryness, and I'd be right there if he needed anything.

I woke to a hand gently shaking my shoulder. "Wake up, little Susie," Freddie said.

"Do you need help finding something?" I asked, stretching. "What time is it anyway?"

"No, I need to leave. It's four. I fell asleep too." He grinned. "I thought about letting you stay right where you were, but I didn't want you to wake up with a sore neck. We must be getting old. Can't even stay up all night anymore."

"Speak for yourself. I never pulled an all-nighter,

even back in college." Of course, the library science majors I hung around with weren't exactly known as the partying types. We were happier with our noses buried in books then hanging out in a bar, trolling for dates. "Did you get everything you need?"

"If I think of anything else, I'll call you." He paused while he pulled on his coat. "If that's all right?"

"Sure. You know where to find me." Most of the time, anyway.

When Freddie was gone, I closed the lid on my laptop without shutting it down and went to bed. As I crawled under the covers, I thanked my lucky stars that my research about Orson was stored in a different folder, buried under several layers of harmless links.

Chapter 16

Shit. I couldn't believe I'd set my alarm before tumbling into bed. I rolled over to turn it off, but when I pressed the snooze button the noise didn't stop. It took me a minute to realize it was my phone ringing from the front room, and not my alarm.

Naturally, by the time I located the phone buried in the cushions of the love seat, I'd missed the call. But a quick glance at the recent calls made my irritation disappear. With a smile, and without checking voicemail, I hit send.

"Good morning, gorgeous," Eli answered. "I hope I didn't wake you."

"You did, but I half expected you to be at my door this morning, so it's okay." Good thing he couldn't see me, because I had bags around my eyes, my hair was a tangled mess, and I looked like I hadn't showered for two days. Not gorgeous at all.

"What happened?" he asked anxiously. "I only called because I'm missing you."

The man knew how to make me feel good. "A

couple of things. One, I got stopped by HP for swerving on the road."

"Damn, I never thought about monitoring their system."

I should have kept my big mouth shut. Too late now.

"And Jake's sick. Probably the flu. Or maybe a twenty-four hour bug. I spent most of yesterday taking care of him."

"Is he okay?"

"He seemed to be getting better when I left him. I'll call him later to see how he's doing and if he needs anything."

"I wired him some money, you know. You don't need to spend any of yours on him."

No, I didn't know. Jake hadn't told me. That answered a couple of questions I'd had.

"I just picked up a few basic first-aid supplies. I never replaced the thermometer I broke last year."

"Sounds like you've been busy. Anything else happening?"

"The police arrested someone for the murder."

That got his attention. "Oh?" he asked casually.

So I told him the whole story. Well, most of it. I left out the part about the trip to the pawn shop in Cleveland. And the meeting with Orson Wallington.

"Even Freddie seemed unsure that she's the perpetrator. Or that she didn't have help, anyway." I wished Eli was sitting next to me on the loveseat and we were cuddling as we discussed the case.

"You've done everything you can," he said. I

wondered if he was staring out his window at sunny Florida skies while I watched snow clouds roll over Oak Grove. "Now let the police and the lawyer do their jobs." He'd told me that before, and I hadn't listened then, either.

"Yeah, I'm so far behind it's crazy. Hey, did Lando and Scotty ever dig up any info on the phone number for me?"

"I haven't had a chance to ask them."

"It probably doesn't matter, but if they find anything, give me a buzz. So what have you been up to?"

He groaned. "Work, work, work. I need a day off. But it's not going to happen any time soon."

"Would you like me to call your boss and yell at him for you? Tell him you work too hard?"

"Sounds like a great idea, but it wouldn't do any good."

"Or I should come down there and rescue you. I can see it now, me busting down the door of your office with a pistol in each hand, ready to blast the chains holding you to your desk chair. Oh yeah, I'll be dressed all in black, wearing a mask so I can't be identified." My mouth twitched. "Better yet, I'll leave you chained to your chair, lock the door behind me, and have my way with you."

"That might work," he said, with a hitch in his voice, "if you remember to close the blinds over the window to the hallway first."

I heard what sounded like a knock on his door, and a voice in the background say "Got a sec?"

"Be with you in a minute," Eli's muffled voice

answered. Then, to me, "I have to go now. This guy is as hard to catch up with as I am. Have a good day, Harmony."

"You too." I blew a kiss into the phone before hanging up.

I never learned to whistle, so I hummed happily through my morning routine, my headache gone, my stomach behaving itself and no longer tired despite the lack of sleep. Even the large headlines of the morning paper blaring the news of Lori's arrest couldn't destroy my cheerful mood. I had an inkling that she'd be free sooner than other people expected.

I set my laptop alarm to go off at ten. Before I called Jake, I'd get in a couple of hours of work.

Of course, it didn't turn out that way. Dan called me around nine to tell me he'd be meeting with Lori in a few minutes. Freddie called a little bit later to tell me the chief wanted to thank me for my assistance in the case. I tried to get an update, but he wouldn't tell me anything new. And just before ten, there was a knock on my door.

"I should've gone to the library," I muttered under my breath as I went to answer it. Of course, I remembered to look through the peek hole before I opened the door. "Isn't one FBI guy hassling me enough?" I asked a stunned Agent Felton.

Other than replacing the blue uniform with a dark suit, he hadn't changed since last fall when he'd pretended to be a rookie on the Oak Grove police force. His blond hair was cut a shade shorter, and I thought he had some new wrinkles around his eyes. He seemed to be holding himself stiffly, as if he expected me to yell at him.

"Can I come in?" he asked, pulling his coat together as a blast of cold wind whipped around the corner of the house.

No longer in a good mood, I asked "Do you have a warrant? Or should I call my lawyer?"

"No need for either one." Felton looked sheepish. "I'm here to inform you that Agent Garza has been assigned elsewhere." Another gust of wind blew a clump of snow off the roof and into his face. "Can I please come in?" he pleaded.

I even made him fresh coffee.

But I made him sit at the kitchen table. I still had dirty dishes to clean from the previous night, and I could work and keep an eye on him while he warmed up and got ready to talk. Until then, I gave him the silent treatment.

He was on his second cup, and I was considering cleaning the refrigerator when he said "You don't fit the profile."

Thank heavens for that! "What profile?" I asked.

"Any of them. No matter how I manipulate what little data we have, you're an anomaly. Which should be suspicious on its own, but maybe I'm just jaded. Everyone has something to hide, but I can't figure you out."

If he only knew what I knew he might think differently.

"So what are you hiding, Agent Felton?" I asked, grabbing my coffee cup and sitting at the table opposite of him.

He grinned. "Nope. You can't catch me that easily. Good try though."

"I thought you guys were trained not to smile."

"That's a myth. We are human, at least most of the time."

"I believe you just told a joke, Agent." I smiled at him in return. "But you didn't come to exchange pleasantries. Why are you really here?" If he asked me to try to trap Jake into recording a confession, Agent Felton would be out the door so fast it would make his head spin.

"First, we want to apologize for Agent Garza's behavior. He has been assigned elsewhere."

Which of the several things Garza had done was the FBI apologizing for? Felton didn't look like he was going to tell me, so I didn't ask. "I suppose you're taking over the case?"

"Only on the local level. Which is basically non-existent at this point. In fact, Erie police napped a suspect in the jewelry theft the other night. Your friend is off the hook for that one. You won't be seeing me unless new evidence is introduced."

"Hate to tell you, but that doesn't break my heart."

"Now that's a normal reaction." Agent Felton pushed his chair away from the table, stretched, and stood. His face returned to his normal, expressionless void. "Thank you for the coffee, and for your time. I believe an old dog can learn new tricks, but a zebra doesn't change its stripes, Miss Duprie. Tell your friend to keep his nose clean and he might do all right for himself."

The string of clichés made me cringe. "I'm not sure what you mean, but I'll pass the word along. But tell me something, Agent Felton, why are you doing this? Why not a phone call instead of showing up here in person?"

He frowned. "The Special Agent in Charge asked—no, ordered me to do it. His reasons weren't shared with me. Which makes me suspect pressure from up the chain of command. Who do you know, Miss Duprie?"

I shook my head. "No one important." Most definitely, no one with that kind of pull.

I waited by the open door to watch Agent Felton leave. Two steps down, he paused to button his coat. "Tell me one thing," he said. "How the heck did you outsmart Agent Garza the other day when he was tailing you?"

"What?" I put one hand to my chest, widened my eyes, and fluttered my eyelashes. "Was he following me? Whatever for?"

"Right." Felton grinned, gave me one of those manly chin-lifts, and continued on down the stairs.

I closed and locked the door behind him. With a purely instinctive move, I grabbed the scanner out of the closet, turned it on, and "swept" the entire apartment. Then, to be on the safe side, I ran our cups through the rarely-used dishwasher, changed the tablecloth, and crawled under the table to make sure no "presents" were left behind. Even though I found none, it would be several days and several more scans before I was satisfied with the results.

With my plans for the day totally shot, I needed to revamp my priorities. I needed to get caught up on so much work it was crazy. At least my stomach and head had settled down, so nothing should hold me back. Which reminded me, I'd forgotten to call Jake.

It would have been easy enough to pick up the phone, but guilt overwhelmed me. What if he had gotten sicker, and was unable to eat or get out of bed? Or his fever returned, and he couldn't call the front desk for help? As I turned the key to start Dolores, I scolded myself for being so silly. Jake was fine, I assured myself, but it wouldn't hurt to drop by and see if he needed anything.

At the hotel, I waved to the clerk at the front desk, and walked swiftly to Jake's room. I knocked lightly on his door and pressed my ear against it to try to hear any noises from inside. I almost fell when the door was abruptly pulled open. Instead, I tumbled into Jake's chest.

"Throwing yourself at me? You must have missed me," he said as he put his arms around me.

I blushed as I pushed myself away. Although he was shirtless, at least he was wearing pants, and looked freshly showered.

"Obviously, you're feeling better." I pushed a non-existent lock of loose hair away from my face.

"Yeah, whatever I had, I've kicked it." He smiled broadly. "Are you coming in or are you going to stand in the doorway? I'd like to thank you properly."

The leer on his face made me afraid of what he had in mind.

Chapter 17

When I didn't move right away, Jake grabbed my arm and pulled me into his room, shutting the door behind me. "There was a draft coming in from the hall. You don't want me to have a relapse, do you?"

"Of course not." I struggled to regain my emotional equilibrium, his gentle teasing reminding me of why I'd fallen for him.

"Or did you come by to torture me some more?" He waggled his eyebrows at me, the innuendo plain.

"Now I know you're feeling better." I moved over to the dresser, re-arranged the bottles of medicine, and tossed some trash into the wastebasket.

"Why so nervous?" He stood behind me and buried his face in my neck.

"Jake, no." I swiveled so we were face to face. "Friends, Jake, just friends."

"You keep telling yourself that, and maybe you'll believe it," he said, reaching up to stroke my cheek.

I tried pushing him away again, but he stood his ground. "I'm stronger than you," he grinned.

Yeah, but I'd learned a few moves recently that he might not be expecting. Still, I didn't want to hurt him. There was a better way to get him off balance.

I ran my fingers down his chest and purred. "Such nice muscles too." Clearly, he hadn't been expected *that*, and his body tensed. I moved my hands further down, and he leaned his body into my light touch.

"Whoa," he gasped. "What are you up to?"

I grinned at him, grabbed his left arm, and tugged. He fell forward and I stepped to the side. He caught himself on the dresser with his right arm, but by then I was several steps away, laughing at him.

"Too easy," I snorted, crossing my arms over my chest and glaring at him. "Men."

When he turned around, the look on his face almost scared me. But then he shook his head, and laughed. "Let's see you try it again."

"Nope, it's one show to a customer. Now, do you want to know why I'm here?"

Jake got the abbreviated version. My personal life wasn't any of his business, so I didn't share the phone call with Eli. Or the one with Dan. Or the visit with Agent Felton. I figured he might be on his best behavior if he still thought the FBI was trying to nail him. I did tell him he was off the hook, temporarily at least, for the murder. Then I told him about Lori.

"What are your plans for the rest of the day?" he asked.

"Work. I have to get some work done. Why?"

He frowned. "I hoped you'd keep me company. I don't feel up to going out yet, but I don't want to sleep all day either. Can you stay here and do your thing? Talk to me about what you're researching or something?"

My laptop was in the car, the WiFi in the hotel worked great, and I couldn't come up with a justifiable reason to tell him no, other than I liked having access to the physical books in the library. But I didn't want to spend more time alone with him than necessary.

"Why don't you come to the library with me?" I asked, my smile bright. "You can kick back and read a book, or grab a few magazines, and keep me company there. Or take a nap, there's some comfortable chairs in the periodical section. We can grab lunch first."

It was clear from the look in his eye he wanted to refuse, he'd been hoping for a more intimate afternoon. But he nodded, reluctantly, and said "Lunch is on me, as long as we go someplace cheap. And not greasy or spicy."

He didn't want to admit it, but I think Jake actually had fun. We ate lunch at George's Diner, a place where the home-made soup was a treat. The day's special was an old-fashioned chicken noodle soup, just the thing for a person recovering from a stomach bug. At the library, I sent him on several "missions" for me, trying to locate books I needed. The first time, he took so long I was about ready to send a search-and-rescue squad to look for him. He caught on quick, however, and soon started returning with his prizes in a few minutes

He snuck off and took a nap mid-afternoon. I spotted him in a chair near the magazine racks, a newspaper in his lap and his eyes closed. Eleanor, the little old lady who volunteered in that area, put her finger to her lips and winked at me. Smiling at her, I returned to my table.

I got a lot accomplished that afternoon. No, I didn't get all caught up, but by the time Jake wandered back to the table and asked if I was ready to go, I was.

Even after his nap, Jake seemed worn out, and he didn't argue when I suggested we pick up something to take back to his room for supper. "I hope I didn't make you overdo it," I said, as we set the bags of food down on the little table in his room.

"I guess I wasn't as recovered as I thought," he said, with a half-hearted smile. "And if it's okay, I'll wait to eat this." He indicated the bags with a wave. "I'm going to lie down for a few minutes."

What he bought would warm up nicely in the microwave in his room. "See you in the morning," I said, as he lay down and closed his eyes.

The package of spaghetti I'd pulled from the freezer and reheated sat half-eaten on my coffee table. I'd responded to all my waiting emails, accepting only a few of the more interesting research jobs. Some of the requests I'd received were so trivial I could only assume pure laziness on the part of the requester. How hard was it to find the name of the president of the Thirty-Second Bank of Omaha?

And those papers in my purse—the ones from Orson—had been nagging me all day. Jake might not be a murder suspect anymore, but I still wanted to see what those dark-net fan forums had to say about him.

Without a user name and password, I could only see bits and pieces of topics. So after going through several proxy sites and setting up a new, bogus email account, I put in my request, I figured it would be a day or two before I got a response.

Either I got lucky or the administrator of the group was marvelously efficient, but I got a response within half an hour. The email wanted to know where I found out about the group, and why I wanted in. My answers were half-true. A friend told me about the forum, and I was a fan of Orson Wallington. In less than five minutes, I had access.

I decided it might be wise to maintain the fiction I was interested in Wallington, so I spent the first fifteen minutes reading about his supposed exploits.

And then the next fifteen, because I found it fascinating.

True, much of what his fans claimed he'd done were huge exaggerations. No way a man could jump out a sixth floor window onto a concrete street, get up, and run away. Or squeeze through the bars of a safe-deposit vault in a bank with no one seeing him, and the security cameras failing to record the event. There was a heated discussion about whether he should get credit for that theft, because the theory of many members was that it took inside help.

Eventually though, I turned the focus of my reading to posts about Jake. A few of the crimes he supposedly committed were so outlandish I laughed. The group gave him credit for stealing a coin collection in Washington State on a day he'd spent with me, thousands of miles away in Oak Grove. One person claimed he'd stolen an antique music box from a museum in New Mexico for the thrill, only to break back in the next day and return it.

The more I read, the more I decided Jake was right. Some of the information had to be planted by officials with law-enforcement agencies. Once I'd fully accepted that idea, it didn't take too much effort to wonder if the whole site was a trap set up by the authorities.

I disconnected from the site and turned off my wireless access to the internet. I cleared my browsing history, deleted all cookies, and shut down the computer. If law enforcement tried to track me, I'd made it impossible.

My paranoia is what saved me. As I sat in my darkened apartment, without even the glow of the laptop screen to provide light, I heard them. Stealthy footsteps sneaking up my exterior stairs. And from below, Piper, Luke and Joe's dog, barked wildly.

I held my breath and fumbled for my phone. My mind first went to Jake. But no, he didn't need to sneak into my apartment any more. All he had to do was knock.

The sound of my doorknob being tested came next. Thank God I'd remembered to lock it when I came home. I slipped into my bedroom and dialed 911. As I whispered to the operator, I made a silent pledge to go gun shopping in the morning.

Barb, the operator on duty, told me the police were on the way, but weren't using their sirens. They hoped to catch the intruder unaware. As I listened to her with one ear, I kept track of the noises at my front door with the other.

The lock seemed to be holding. Whoever was trying to get in wasn't as good as Jake. Funny, I found that reassuring in a warped kind of way.

In the darkness, I fumbled to find the doorknob to the stairway that led down to Luke and Joe's part of the house. If I needed an escape route, I had one—as long as they hadn't piled any more "treasures" into the space, after cleaning it out last fall. Luke liked to hoard things, and Joe liked things uncluttered, so there was a constant flow of boxes in and out of the house.

"The officers are almost there," Barb said quietly in my ear. "Are you still okay?"

"Yes," I whispered. "He hasn't gotten in yet." Then came the squeak of the hinges as the door was pushed open. Tine to oil them again. Or maybe I should leave them alone. The squeakier the better. "Cancel that. He's in."

"Can you get to a closet or is there someplace where you can hide?"

Not too many places to hide in my apartment. I twisted the door knob to the stairway. Damn, it didn't turn. I tried again, with no luck. How had it gotten locked? Desperately, I tried one more time, but my failsafe escape route had failed. Time for plan B.

I tried to figure out what weapon I could easily reach. Everything in the kitchen was off the list, the intruder was between me and them. The closest thing to a weapon I kept in the bedroom was a fake samurai sword hanging on the wall next to my Grateful Dead tapestry. The plastic blade would crack the first time it hit anything hard. There had to be something I could use to protect myself.

I stiffened when something large crashed to the floor, followed by muffled swearing. Barb must have heard it as well.

"Are you okay?" she asked.

I nodded my head but realized she couldn't see me. "Yes," I breathed as I used the noise from my front room to cover any sound I might make slipping into my bathroom.

"Hang on. The officers are pulling up in front of the house."

They'd better hurry, or they were going to miss out on all the fun. I grabbed the can of hairspray I kept for those rare occasions when I wanted to do something with my hair besides put it in a bun.

A flashlight's beam illuminated the hallway a few seconds later. I'd made it to the bathroom's relative safety just in time.

As the man inched down the hall, I held my breath and prayed he didn't wear glasses. The shaft of light flashed into the bathroom itself. I raised my arm and prepared to push the button. The noise of loud footsteps outside caused the intruder to raise his head. It gave me the perfect shot. With the quickness of a rattlesnake going after a field mouse, I aimed and pressed the trigger.

His cry of anguish was heard even over the yells of the police as they smashed through the front door.

Chapter 18

With the adrenalin rush a memory, I sat in my easy chair, trying to fight off the shakes. Even the afghan I wrapped myself in wasn't enough to keep me warm as I watched the paramedics work on my victim. They'd borrowed a stack of towels and I watched as they poured yet another bottle of eye cleanser over his face. With his hands cuffed behind his back, there wasn't a way to prevent the solution from splashing. The carpet would still be damp in the morning, and I resigned myself to a major clean-up job after I woke up.

If I ever got to sleep in the first place. The cops hadn't even started questioning me yet, so it was going to be a long night. The thought made me even more tired, and I yawned. One of the paramedics noticed.

"We're almost done. We'll have this guy out of here in a minute or two."

I wondered if I could convince the police to come back later to ask their questions.

The paramedic nodded at the two officers, and they each grabbed the suspect by an arm. As they helped him to his feet, they swung him around so he faced me. "I don't suppose you've ever seen this guy before, have you?"

"As a matter of fact," I said slowly, drawing out the moment and recognizing the consequences. "I have. He goes by the name of Steve."

The officers made it surprisingly easy for me, getting only the basic information before they left. Just the standard who, what, where, when and why. I regretted it now, because two very angry men held me hostage in my apartment bombarding me with questions and scolding me for taking unnecessary risks. And if history had anything to say about it, a third one would be pounding on my door at any moment.

Freddie showed up on my doorstep first thing, acting in his official capacity. Why wasn't I surprised that he'd been assigned to the investigation? He barely touched the coffee I gave him before grilling me on my knowledge of Steve. Who wasn't Steve at all, no surprise, but a small-time con man with a rap sheet a mile long. The ID in his car listed his name as Alexander Thermopolis, but Freddie suspected it was another alias.

Next, Jake showed up. The story of the break-in made the local morning news, and he bribed one of the housekeepers to give him a ride. He didn't even get a cup of coffee into his hands before he started yelling at me about not hiding in a closet or something when I knew the police were on their way.

All I wanted to do was to grab the towels, take them down to the basement, and throw them in the washer. Then I could turn my attention to getting rid of the rest of the evidence of a police visit. My apartment had become overdue for a deep cleaning. I needed everyone out of the way for that.

But I predicted that my misery wasn't complete. I expected another set of footsteps on my stairs soon. Jake started talking about moving in to protect me and I wondered when the next flight from Orlando arrived in Pittsburgh.

"Look," I told Jake rather heatedly. "Last fall, when Eli hired a professional bodyguard to watch me, I made him stay out in his van most of the time. I like my privacy, and if you think I'm going to make an exception for you, you're wrong!"

"I'm not so sure it isn't a good idea," Freddie said to my amazement. "Until we figure out what this guy wanted, it might not hurt for Jake to hang out here. It'll make you less of a target. We don't have the resources to do anything but step up patrols in the neighborhood."

"You're ignoring the fact that I did a mighty fine job of protecting myself last night," I pointed out.

"You got lucky this time," Jake said. "Next time, you might not be."

"Last night wasn't the first time I saved myself."

"Are you talking about yesterday? I let you do that, Angel."

"Do what?" Freddie asked.

"It doesn't matter. That's not what I was talking about anyway. You tell him Freddie, you saw it last fall when I tackled Clearmont." Clearmont was the bad cop who'd threatened me.

Freddie grimaced. "So you got lucky twice. The third time might not be the charm." He glanced at Jake. "I'll tell you the story later."

Their minds were made up and I wasn't going to get anywhere. Time to switch the topic.

"Has Steve said why he chose my apartment, of all places, to break into?" It was easier to keep thinking of him as Steve.

"He's not talking. Demanded a lawyer as soon as they got him down to the station. He's clearly done this before." Freddie gripped his coffee cup tightly, as if to squeeze information out of it. "We found something unusual in his pocket. A gold wedding ring. But it wasn't his size and looked like a woman's ring. One of the guys said the design was Celtic. Are you missing a ring, Harmony?"

My eyes met Jake's. "Let me take a look." I rushed to my bedroom. Steve hadn't made it this far, so how could he have snagged my ring? But there it was, still in the tray on my dresser. "No, it's here," I called, and carried it out for the men to see.

"Hmm." Freddie walked to the front window to examine it in the sunlight. "I didn't see the other ring, so I don't know if they're the same or not." He fiddled with his cell phone. "I'll ask for a picture."

He headed outside to place his call in privacy, and I seized the opportunity to go to the kitchen and gather up cleaning supplies.

Jake followed me, took the cleanser and sponge out of my hands, and set them on the counter. "That can wait."

I picked them back up. "I like to keep the place clean. Besides, it'll help reduce my stress."

He cocked his head. "Cleaning reduces stress? I'll give it a try." With a crooked smile, he took the sponge away from me. "What do you want me to tackle?"

"Scrub the front door, inside and out. It's covered with fingerprint powder residue." I dug under my kitchen sink and found the spray cleaner which I handed to him. "I'll start on the walls in the hallway."

We barely got started before Freddie came back. He grinned when he saw what we were doing. "Picture should be here shortly," he said, tapping the screen of his phone. "Where did you get your ring?"

"Pawn shop in Cleveland," I answered promptly. "It was an impulse trip and an impulse buy." I didn't have anything to hide. Well, not much. "I'd heard a rumor they might have some books I'm interested in, but it didn't pan out."

"How long ago?"

I shrugged my shoulders. "A while back."

"Before or after Calib Booker showed up dead?"

I wouldn't be able to lie my way out of this one. "After."

"Pure coincidence, I suppose?"

I scrubbed a stubborn spot harder. "Absolutely. Can you stand somewhere else? You're blocking my light."

I stopped cleaning long enough to study the picture on Freddie's phone. It was hard to be sure on the small screen, but the ring looked identical to mine. "Well, that's weird," I said. "It must have been a popular design."

"Who knew you had this ring?" Freddie asked.

Who had I told about it? I could think of only one person, and I didn't want to throw him under the bus. He must have sensed my dilemma.

"I did," Jake volunteered. "Spotted it in her bedroom a few days ago. Complimented her on her choice of jewelry." That wasn't exactly the way I remembered it happening, but I kept my mouth shut. I figured if I tried to explain what he was doing in my bedroom it would only make matters worse. "I'd like to see the other ring in person," Jake shocked me by continuing. "And compare them side by side. Can you arrange that, Detective?"

"Why?" Freddie asked, logically.

"Heritage jewelry used to be a hobby of mine. For example, I suspect this ring…" Jake picked it up from my palm "Is a knock-off of a ring from the late 1800's. The story is that an English lord fell in love with and married an Irish governess, despite his family's opposition. The design on the wedding band he gave her was a combination of symbols from their two different backgrounds. I don't know how much truth there is to the story, but the ring design was popular for a number of years.

"Because of the lack of fine details in the design, I can tell this one wasn't expensive brand-new. The more costly rings had fine lines in the knots and the rope pattern. Even worn down, some of those markings should remain. It's hard to tell looking at a picture."

Shit, did Jake make that up as he went along or did he really know all that? He sounded like one of those experts on the shows where people bring in their old stuff to have it appraised. I couldn't tell. Freddie nodded seriously and said "I should be able to arrange it."

Jake handed me the ring back, and I slipped it on the ring finger of my right hand. It fit perfectly, and I rubbed the pattern with the tip of my finger, wondering who'd worn it before.

❀ ❀ ❀

My cleaning delayed, I was putting away the sponges before we went to the police station, and wondering if I should leave Eli a note. It worried me that he hadn't shown up yet and hadn't called. I was itching to get my hands on my laptop and see if he'd emailed me or something. I needed to make sure it was still working anyway. Steve had tripped over the power cord—that was the crash I'd heard—and yanked the cord right out.

Freddie and Jake waited impatiently for me, grinning at each other as I put everything in the proper place. I had to re-arrange the cleaner that Jake had tossed into the first empty spot he'd seen rather than putting it back where it belonged. It irritated me they found it funny, so I dragged the process out longer than necessary.

Finally ready to leave, I grabbed my coat off its hook, threw it over my shoulders, and glared at them. "Well, are you two clowns coming or not?" I snapped.

I yanked open the door in time to spot a figure starting up my stairs. My heart fluttered for a second, but then my brain kicked in. It wasn't Eli, or anyone I wanted to talk to. I debated the wisdom of clomping down the stairs and brushing by him as if he wasn't there. Probably not a good idea. I turned to the men. "We have company," I said. And not the welcome kind.

Chapter 19

I gave Agent Felton the most uncomfortable chair in the apartment, a chair I pulled from the kitchen table. Unlike my normal hospitable self, I didn't offer him coffee, so he sat with his hands tucked in his pockets, trying to look relaxed.

Jake and I sat in the loveseat, and Freddie had the easy chair. We all looked at each other, as if trying to decide who would start. Freddie took the lead.

"Have you informed the Chief you're in town yet?" he asked. "He's tired of the FBI interfering with local cases."

"This, unfortunately, is much more than a local case," Felton answered, his mouth a taut line. "As I'm guessing Miss Duprie can tell you."

I shifted uneasily as the attention turned to me.

"Harmony?" Freddie asked, tentatively.

"I have a few ideas." I picked at a piece of lint on the loveseat. "But I haven't had time to do the research yet, so they are pure speculation."

"I'd like to hear them anyway," said the FBI man.

He asked for it. I fiddled with the ring, suddenly ill-fitting on my finger.

"The FBI has had their eyes on Orson Wallington and his book tour for some time now," I said "And they've noticed a string of thefts that follow it. But they're unable to make a connection. Orson always has an alibi. He's in public, doing a book signing or giving a speech to a local literary group. Or maybe even a neighborhood watch, telling them what to look out for. But no one has ever suspected his manager—Steve or Alexander or whatever his name is. Someone made a rookie mistake and assumed wherever Orson was, Steve was with him." At Freddie's sharp intake of breath, I raised my eyes and studied Felton's face. It was expressionless.

"Go on," he said.

"What little research I've had time for indicates the sales of Orson's book aren't doing that well. So where is he getting the money for hotels, foods and transportation? I can't believe the publishing company would sink all that money into a lost cause. I want to check out the publishing company and see how reputable they are."

"What do you mean?" Felton asked, a spark of interest in his eyes.

"Have they published other books and what kind and how many? How long have they been in business? It's easy to set yourself up as a publisher these days. Even easier to publish a book electronically and make it print-on-demand. I haven't opened the copy of the book I bought yet, so I don't know if it's done right or if it's full of mistakes."

Felton looked thoughtful. "We'll check into that."

"Are all those supposed jobs Wallington had with movie companies for real?" I asked. "Or are they bogus too?"

One corner of his mouth twitched. "Those jobs were real, but not as important as he makes them out to be. He's lucky the studios aren't calling him out on it."

"How hard is it to tell when someone's been poisoned?" I asked abruptly.

"What?" Felton, startled out of his act of nonchalance, leaned forward.

"It's been bothering me. How Jake got so sick so fast. Sure, it could have been a bug, I'm no doctor, but it just seems weird to me."

"It depends upon the poison used. We could run lab work but it's been several days already and might be too late for anything to show up." His attention focused on Jake. "Would you be willing to have a blood test done, Hennessey?"

"What good would it do?" Jake ran one hand across the top of his head.

"We could hit these guys with a new charge," Felton said, excitement creeping into his voice. "Something with a bigger kick than breaking and entering that will give us a bargaining chip and get them to confess to a whole litany of past crimes without us having to spend hours on investigation."

"You're talking attempted murder," Freddie said.

"Exactly," Felton agreed.

Wow. That escalated quickly.

"Murder?" I squeaked. "And I thought all we were talking about was a nice little triple-scam."

"Triple?"

"Yes." I ticked them off on my fingers. "One, Alexander-Steve is pretending to protect the public from the master thief. Two, Orson is ripping the public off with shady advice and stories he gleaned from the internet. And three, the real Orson Wallington is still out there stealing God-knows-what from God-knows-who."

"Slow down, Harmony, what do you mean the real Orson Wallington?" Freddie asked.

"The guy doing the book tour? He's a fake." I glanced at Felton. "I figured the FBI knew that."

"If it's in the case file, I didn't see it. Of course, I only had time for a quick review." The agent exhaled loudly. "How did you find out, Miss Duprie?"

I thought rapidly. I wanted to keep Jake out of this. "His height. He was too tall. The research I did before we went to the signing claimed Wallington was a short man. The guy who showed up at the book signing was about average. Weight and the color of your hair you can change, you can make yourself look taller, but it's hard to make yourself shorter except by hunching over."

"All true, but not something I'd expect a librarian to know," Felton said accusingly.

Freddie rushed to my rescue. "You have no idea what Harmony knows or doesn't know, so stop looking for a connection that doesn't exist. She is an invaluable if unofficial resource for the Oak Grove Police."

Invaluable resource? I liked the sound of that. I'd ask Freddie what he meant later.

Agent Felton wanted to see the *other* ring. To make him happy, Jake and I rode to the police station with Freddie. Jake volunteered to sit in the back, and I got a kick out of watching him try to squeeze into the small space that pretended to be a back seat. I had mercy on his knees, though, and pulled the passenger-side seat as far forward as it would go. Agent Felton followed in his own car.

When we got to the station, we weren't allowed into the evidence room until the sergeant in charge figured out a way to mark my ring. He didn't want to take a chance on the two being mixed up. He finally settled on a strip of clear tape wrapped around mine while the other ring had the official evidence tag string tied to it.

Jake hung in the background while Felton, Freddie and the sergeant examined the two rings. The sergeant gave up first, and grinned at me. "The only ring I care about is the one on my wife's finger, and it's been there thirty years."

Felton gave up next. "It's not my area of expertise."

Freddie motioned Jake to join him. Jake didn't bother looking at my ring, but honed directly in on the one found in Steve's clothing.

He held it up to the light, and in my mind, it seemed to sparkle in a way mine didn't. Then he closed his eyes and rolled it between his fingers. "I wish I had a magnifying glass," he muttered as he held it close to his eyes.

"There's one on my desk," the sergeant said, awakening from the trance all four of us had fallen into watching Jake.

We waited for him to return but Jake didn't put the ring down. He peered at the interior as if trying to find some kind of markings. When the sergeant returned, Jake gave him a silent head nod as he took the magnifying glass.

He reminded me of drawings of Sherlock Holmes as he examined the ring. All he needed was a pipe, a cape, and a deerstalker hat. He put down the magnifying glass and held the ring up to the light again.

"Well?" Freddie asked.

Jake put the ring on the table and stuffed his hands in his pockets. "It's not what I anticipated," he answered.

I was crushed. I'd hoped he'd identify the ring as a long-lost prized historical treasure.

"It's a phony?" Felton asked.

Jake backed away from the table as if resisting the urge to pick the ring up again.

"No. It's real. I expected another copy of a copy like the one Harmony has. But this ring…" His voice trailed off.

I wanted to punch him for leaving us in suspense.

"This ring," he continued, "Is an absolutely perfect example of a hand-crafted work of art. I can't imagine how many hours went into creating the mold this ring was cast from." He looked at the other men. "Did you see the fine lines and markings in the design? And did you notice the way it sparkles? I suspect the mold was coated in diamond dust before the gold was poured. This ring, gentlemen and lady, was someone's treasured expression of love to their bride. And how it got into the hands of someone like your suspect, I can't imagine."

We' crowded into Freddie's office. "None of this makes any sense," I complained. "I mean, if my ring was the expensive one, I could see someone wanting to steal it and leave me with the cheap one, hoping I wouldn't notice. Are you sure there isn't something special about my ring, Jake?"

He smiled at me and shook his head. "Not that I can see. Agent Felton, does the FBI maintain a database dealing with stolen jewelry? I read there was one for artwork." He picked at the bandage on his arm covering the spot where blood had been drawn.

"Nothing specific. The NCIC system tracks stolen items for two years tops. So if either of those rings went missing before that, chances are the files have been wiped," Felton explained.

"The clerk in the pawn shop told me my ring had been in stock for a couple of years," I said glumly. "So I guess that eliminates any chance of tracking it. It might not have been stolen anyway." Although I had to wonder how Jake had known where I got it. "So where does that leave us?"

Felton asked "Have your guys had any luck getting the suspect to talk?"

"No. He appears to be an old hand at this," Freddie answered. "We're still waiting for the report on his prints to come back. We might find another state that wants him for something bigtime so we can use those charges as a negotiating tool."

"Has anyone interviewed his partner?" I asked. Agent Felton had left the room several times, and I assumed he'd been conversing with his office.

He smiled grimly. "The allegedly bogus Orson Wallington skipped town before we could bring him in for questioning. We already notified local officials in the next few stops in his book tour, but I doubt he'll show up for any of them." He grinned. "We also reopened a number of cases that appear to fit the *modus operandi* of the real Orson Wallington."

That was good to know, but I wondered where it left me. Would both of the Orson's want to punish me for ruining their arrangement?

Felton must have read my thoughts. "I suggest you take extra safety precautions until we can arrest the fake Wallington. Lock your doors when you're home, vary your schedule, ask your friends to go with you to the store, that sort of thing."

With a snort, Freddie said "You've heard that advice before, Harmony. Maybe you'll listen to it this time."

I doubted it.

On the way out of the station, we ran into Dan and Lori. She wasn't wearing cuffs and I took it as a good sign.

"You're not in trouble, are you?" Dan asked anxiously.

"I would have called if I was," I answered. "No, this time I'm the witness to a crime. How are you doing, Lori?"

Her clothes were wrinkled, and she looked tired and stressed. "Better now that Dan convinced them to release me. The DA decided they didn't have enough evidence to charge me with anything. And Dan has been great. I got really lucky to get him assigned as my public defender."

Dan and I exchanged the smallest of glances. I knew I could count on him not to tell her who was paying the bills.

"I've talked to the school district," Dan said. "Lori won't be able to go back to teaching until things get cleared up, but they're willing to put her in an administrative position for the time being."

Just another reason for me to do what I could to help the police solve the murder. I gave her a squeeze before I went outside where Jake and Freddie waited for me.

In the car on the way home, Freddie said "There's one thing that's been bothering me."

I took a quick glance at his face. Yep, he was in cop mode.

"The officers last night said that the suspect kept mumbling something about a Martha on the way to booking. Any idea what that might have been about, Harmony?"

Chapter 20

I kept my eyes on the road in front of us, and ignored the strangled laugh from Jake in the back seat. "You remember Aunt Martha?" I asked. "You met her last fall after my kidnapping. She made a re-appearance when we went to Pittsburgh, minus the costume."

"Good idea." Freddie tapped his fingers against the steering wheel as he waited for a traffic light to turn green.

"I still don't get how this all ties together," I complained.

Freddie shook his head. "Neither do I."

I expected to see a rental car on the street outside the house when Freddie pulled up to let Jake and me out, but nothing. It made me worry that Eli was sick, or that something bad had happened to him. I checked my phone one more time. No messages.

There must have been some communication

between Jake and Freddie that I missed, because as I stood there with my mind elsewhere, Jake extracted himself from the rear seat of the Mustang. I thought Freddie planned to take him back to the hotel.

"What are you doing?" I asked as Freddie drove off.

He smiled insolently. "Hanging out. Helping you do stuff."

I remembered the morning's conversation. "Seriously? You think you can be my bodyguard? Hell, no. How's that going to work? You can't carry a gun."

He winced. It had been a cheap shot on my part.

"I'm sorry, Jake," I touched his arm.

"Detective Thomason and I talked about it. You know how you get wrapped up in your work. You don't pay attention to anything but your computer and your books. You wouldn't notice someone sneaking up on you until too late."

Shit. He was right.

"So I'll keep track of things going on around you. I'll be your early warning system. Let me do this for you. Please?" he asked earnestly. "It will only be until the cops get this mess figured out."

What was I going to do?

"I'll make myself useful. Like I did in the library. I'll even help you clean house if that's what you want."

I caved. Since his re-appearance in my life, he'd been trying to help me out.

"Okay. Jake, but you aren't going to spend nights here."

Was that a flicker of disappointment in his eyes?

He rubbed his hands together. "So where do we start?"

I had the awful feeling I'd regret this.

He insisted on entering the apartment first, and peering into each room before he let me come in. Since Piper was in the yard, rolling in one of the few spots where the snow had melted, I already knew it would be safe. In the past few days, Piper had given up barking at Jake when he was with me. I put him back to work cleaning the front door—the job hadn't got finished—while I started in on my work email.

Work email, right. The only thing I was looking for was an email from Eli. Although I had several new emails, none were from him.

As I grabbed my cell phone and headed to the bedroom to call him, the thought suddenly occurred to me. Maybe the Oak Grove police had finally installed the updated system and Eli couldn't hack in anymore. And while the break-in rated local news, it certainly wouldn't make national news. So he just didn't know about it. Yeah, that made sense. So I would call to say hello and hear his voice and all would be right in my little world again.

Except that didn't work out either. I stared at the phone in frustration when all I got was those "trying to locate subscriber" and "subscriber couldn't be located" messages. And when the voice suggested I check the number I had dialed, I wanted to throw the phone against the wall.

I might have done just that, except Jake picked that moment to yell from the front room. "You have company, Angel."

Could it be? Pretending indifference, I took my time coming out of the bedroom. "Oh, hey Luke," I said, spotting who it was.

He wore his tool belt and a worried expression on his face. "Why didn't you call us?"

If it wasn't one man yelling at me, it was another.

"It was a coin toss between you and 911. 911 won." I kissed him on the cheek. "I presume you're here to take a look at the door?"

"Yeah. Joe and I can't figure out how it got locked."

"Did one of you bump it the last time you stuck another box on the stairs?"

Luke shook his head. "We've been making sure we don't pile too much stuff in there." By then we had reached the door to the interior stairway. Luke twisted the door knob, and looked perplexed when it didn't respond. He pulled a skeleton key out of his pocket, stuck it in the lock and twisted it, and tried again. Then he threw his weight against the door and tried again. Still no luck.

"Are you sure there's not something blocking it from the other side?" I asked.

There were footsteps on the other side. "It's all clear here," Joe's muffled voice said. I saw the knob on our side moving slightly as he tried twisting it from his.

"Well, it's easy enough to replace," Luke said.

He pressed his face against the door. "Joe, do we have a spare somewhere?"

"No, we'll need to make a trip to the hardware store."

Luke looked at me apologetically. "This shouldn't take long. Back in a few. You want to go, Hennessey?"

"No, but if you leave me the tools, I'll get started on taking this one off," Jake said.

"You could have gone with them," I said once Luke and Joe left for their favorite store. I figured it would be a couple of hours before they got back. I went with them once, and spent my time wandering through the garden shop while they went to pick out a new set of screwdrivers. By the time they got done, I'd fallen asleep on one of the outdoor swings set up as a display.

Jake made quick work of removing the metal plate from both sides and sliding the mechanism attached to the knob out of its place. He carried the whole contraption into the kitchen and put it on the counter. The he started undoing various screws to take apart the insides.

"Normally when old hardware breaks," he said, not looking at me, "the knob turns and nothing happens. I've never seen one break like this."

I'd almost forgotten Jake was an expert at locks.

"So what happened?" I asked.

He ignored my question as he concentrated on the pile of metal in front of him, removing screw after tiny screw. Suddenly the whole thing fell apart. He used the screw driver to poke the many pieces.

"Huh," he said finally.

"Huh what?" came my witty response.

"Metal fatigue. Not what I expected. I figured someone had sabotaged the mechanism. But it looks as if this piece snapped and slipped into just the wrong spot." He picked up a small piece of metal and showed it to me. It looked like every other piece of metal I'd ever seen.

"If you say so." Made me feel better knowing it wasn't a deliberate act by unknown enemies.

Jake dumped the bits and pieces into a plastic bag. "I haven't lost my touch," he said quietly.

But not quietly enough.

It seemed like a lost cause to go to the library for what remained of the day. I opted to concentrate on those jobs I could research exclusively on the internet. While Jake and the boys repaired the stairway door, I dug into the incidents that ultimately led to the beginning of the Vietnam War. I vaguely remembered when it ended, but the topic was not allowed in our house when I grew up. My parents were on opposite sides of the political spectrum, and rather than have heated discussions in front of me, they just didn't talk about it.

I buried myself in old and re-occurring discussions, trying to sort out fact from supposition. Still, I peeked at my cell phone every so often, as if that would somehow force it to ring.

I have no idea what Jake did the whole time. Maybe he took a nap or read one of my many books. Whatever it was, he was so quiet I forgot about him being there. So I jumped when he said "You getting hungry?"

A look out the window showed it was dark. "Geesh, you scared me."

He grinned. "I should have said something earlier, but you were in a zone."

"Occupational hazard." I stood and stretched. "Let me see what I can throw together for supper."

"No need. Luke and Joe invited us to join them."

That was sweet of them, but I wondered what they were up to. There was only one way to find out.

Joe had made his mother's beef stew. It took all day, so any guilt I might have about creating extra work dissolved away as Jake and I walked in the door and the smell reached me.

"So have you heard from Eli today?" Luke asked casually as he filled my bowl for the second time. They were aware of his habit of showing up whenever something happened to me that involved the police.

I took my time swallowing before I answered. "No. I tried calling him but didn't even get his voice mail. I wonder if his cell phone broke or something."

"Is that why you kept checking your phone while you were working?" Jake asked.

I didn't think anyone had caught me. "Did I?" I asked, playing it off. "Habit, I guess."

"Surprised he didn't show up on your doorstep this morning," Joe said.

"He's been busy lately. I guess he couldn't get away." It didn't sound any truer saying it out loud than it did when I tried the line in my thoughts. On to something else. "Luke, will you give Jake a ride back to the hotel after supper? I found a great site for my research and I'm eager to get back to it."

The exchange of glances around the table confused me. "What?" I asked.

"I'm staying here tonight," Jake said. "And by here I don't mean your place. I mean the closed-in porch. I can keep an eye on your steps and Luke has put a heater out there, plus they retrieved my sleeping bag from the Aldridge house. That and a thermos of coffee and I'll be good for the night, especially after my nap this afternoon."

My mouth dropped open. "And tomorrow, Joe and I will take turns watching while Jake sleeps. That way you won't ever be alone." Luke added.

"No," I said sharply. "In fact, not just no, hell no. What makes you think I'd agree to this scheme of yours? Been there, done that. Remember the professional bodyguard Eli hired last year? I'm not going there again, even for you guys."

"Told you she wouldn't like it," Joe said.

"Look, I appreciate the thought. But nothing's going to happen. The bad guy is in jail and he's not going anywhere."

More glances. "He's not the one we're worried about," Jake said.

"Oh? So who are you worried about?"

"The fake Orson Wallington. The police still haven't caught him."

I snorted into the glass of soda I'd just raised to my lips, got carbonation up my nose and started coughing. It turned into laughter that wouldn't stop. Jake finally pounded me on my back and I caught my breath.

"You think that old guy is a threat to me? Really, guys, that's the best joke I've heard all week!"

"You said it yourself," Jake said. "You can disguise your hair, your weight, your age. How do you know that Wallington wasn't a young guy in costume?"

Fuck. He was right. Again.

He said the easy chair wasn't comfortable enough, so Jake spread the sleeping bag out on the floor of my front room. There wasn't any way I would make him sleep in the sunroom, even with a heater, while he was still recovering from whatever had made him so sick. Not with nighttime temperatures dropping into the teens. And between the three of them, they out-stubborned me into making a deal. Jake would spend the nights on my apartment floor, but during the day I'd be on my own. It was a compromise I wasn't happy with, but neither were they.

He seemed tired, so I took my laptop into the

bedroom with me. I wasn't ready to call it a night. There was still a lot of work to be done. In fact, I anticipated working through the weekend to get caught up.

I should have been tired too, with the lack of sleep all week long, but I was wide awake as I rearranged my pillows to make a backrest. It took only seconds for me to get back to the last web page that I'd bookmarked, and the stories of the men who'd served in Vietnam.

I hadn't gotten very far when there was a knock on my door. "Can I talk to you for a sec?" Jake asked, opening it a crack.

I sighed and put down the laptop. "Come in."

He sat on the edge of the bed. "How much do you know about what Eli does?" he asked.

"What?"

"His job. What has he told you about his job?" Jake repeated.

I pushed my glasses higher on my nose and thought. Eli never shared any details. "He does programming for a company in Florida," I answered. "Shifter Technologies or something like that. He doesn't talk a lot about it, and when he does, I don't understand most of what he's saying. Why?"

"And that's all he's told you?"

"Yes, but how much more could there be? Although he seems to spend a lot of time in meetings. And work a lot of nights. Is that normal for a programmer?"

One side of Jake's mouth lifted. "I'm not an

expert in that subject, but you should ask him what he does. There's more to the story."

Jake had my total attention. "What do you mean by that? What do you know that I don't?"

He shook his head. "It's not my place to tell you. Ask him the next time you talk to him. I don't know all the details either." He leaned over and placed a kiss on my forehead. "Don't stay up too late, Angel. And if you have any trouble getting to sleep, I might have just the thing to help you." He winked and swaggered out of the room, closing the door behind him.

All thoughts of Vietnam rushed from my head. I started Googling Eli under various configurations of his name. He didn't do social media, so I wasn't surprised by the lack of listings for those sites. When I checked before, I'd found him on the typical sites for address listings, so I didn't bother with those.

Other than that, all I found was a black hole of nothingness. So I dug deeper and added the name of the company he worked for, Shifter Technologies, into my searches. That gave me pages and pages of results. Some of them led me right to the website of the company which I'd already explored, and a few took me to pages of books featuring werewolves. I got distracted looking at the pictures of nearly naked men featured there. Large, muscular men with marvelous tattoos.

When I finally got back to work, I came across what claimed to be a personnel list from the company. It looked real, and I spotted Scotty's name, but not Lando's. And it clearly wasn't complete because Eli's name didn't show up either.

I changed tactics once again because I was getting nowhere fast. Maybe researching the company instead of researching Eli would produce interesting information. I planned on skipping the official company website, and see what dirt the internet held.

About this time in a project, it was my habit to put on a pot of coffee and settle in for a long session. But with Jake hopefully sound asleep, I couldn't get to the kitchen without waking him up. The arrangement wasn't going to work out if it cramped my style. I'd have to negotiate something new in the morning.

My cell phone rang at the same time as I slowly opened the bedroom door, headed for the bathroom. To silence the ringer, I answered without looking at the screen first to see who was calling so late. Somewhere in the distance, sirens wailed, never a good thing.

"Hello?"

"Harmony. You're awake. Good. I'm on my way."

Chapter 21

"Who is this?" The woman's voice was familiar, but my brain wasn't functioning rapidly enough to identify who was speaking. Plus she talked so fast I didn't have time to process what she said.

But the lack of response made me realize the conversation was over. I checked my recent calls, Sarah. Now why was Sarah coming at this time of the night?

I hated to do it, but I turned on the light in the hallway and softly called Jake's name. "Wake up, Jake. Company's on its way."

"Who the hell is coming this time of night?" He crawled out of the sleeping bag clad only in a pair of black boxers.

"Sarah, and she'll be here any minute. So get dressed." His clothes were in a neat pile on the floor beside him. "And before you ask, I don't know why."

"You want to help me?" he leered.

He was definitely recuperating from whatever

he'd had. I yearned to tell him to get over himself, but instead I said "There's no time for that."

With a cocky grin, he grabbed his clothes, stood, and strutted towards the bedroom. I was still standing in the hallway, and as he walked by me, his elbow bumped my breast.

"Oops, sorry about that," he said, but not for a second did I believe he meant it. Still, it wouldn't do any good to call him out on it, so I pretended to study my cell phone and ignored him.

In the kitchen, I reached for the canister of coffee, and then stopped. Was this going to be a caffeine or alcohol type of visit? Or, in a worst case scenario, both? I decided to play it safe and started the coffee maker before grabbing the wine glasses out of the cupboard.

Jake, fully dressed, came out of the bedroom at the same time there was a knock on my door. When I rushed to open it, he yelled "Stop!"

Startled, I shot him a dirty look. He gave me one back. "That's my job," he said, as he pushed by me. He leaned against the door and checked to see who was there before opening it.

"Hi, Sarah," he said casually.

She looked at Jake, then at me, then back at him and said "I'm sorry, did I interrupt something?"

Shit. The Olde Gossipe network would be going full force tomorrow. I rushed to explain. "Jake got it into his head I needed a bodyguard so he's camping out on my floor." I bent over and gathered up the sleeping bag he'd been using and tossed it into the one corner of the room not already filled up with a bookshelf. "What's going on?"

Sarah sank into my recliner. "What do you have to drink?"

"Coffee, wine, water?"

"How about a beer?"

Sarah never drank beer. "Jake, grab a beer for Sarah, please?"

"You want one?" he asked. It sounded like a good idea.

"Yes, please."

"Three beers coming up."

That would kill my beer supply, but this seemed like an emergency.

"What's going on?" I repeated, settling into the loveseat.

She wrung her hands. I thought that only happened in books. Jake handed her a beer, and she looked up and gave him a tentative smile as she grasped it with both hands. At least she had something to occupy them now.

While I waited for her to start talking, I gave her the once-over. Being in real estate, she made a point of dressing professionally even for her frequent trips to the gas station. So the fact that her blouse was untucked from her slacks and looked rumpled made me suspicious.

"Freddie had the night off," she said. Jake handed me my beer and sat next to me. He flung one arm along the back of the loveseat. "We were at his place watching a movie." Right. Good cover story. My bet was that they were busy doing something else.

"He got called in to work. From what little he said, every cop in town got called in."

This had to be big.

Sarah bit her bottom lip. "I didn't want to be alone. You don't mind that I came here, do you?"

"Of course I don't mind. I wasn't getting anywhere with my research." That much was true, although the research I'd been doing was to satisfy my personal curiosity. "So what's going on?"

"I really shouldn't say anything." She lifted her beer to her lips and tipped her head back. The gulp she took was worthy of a personal record. "Privileged info and all that," she added as she set the bottle down on the coffee table with a thunk.

"You can't tell me Freddie got called in on an emergency and not tell me what the emergency is," I said.

Sarah stared at the half-empty bottle for a long moment. "Somebody shot Lori."

Jake was out of the loveseat and at the front door, swearing under his breath as he locked it. Sarah picked up her beer and finished the rest of it, an amazing feat for someone who takes half an hour to drink a glass of wine.

"And that's it," she said. "I don't know how bad she's hurt or," and she sniffed, "If she's even alive."

I reached for the box of tissues I kept handy for when I'm reading the sad parts of a book and plopped them in front of her. She grabbed several and blew her nose noisily.

"So you can understand why I wanted company," she said, looking at me with reddened eyes.

My bottle of beer sat untouched in front of me. Sarah needed it more than I did, so I swapped my full one for her empty. "You can spend the night here," I volunteered. "It'll be like when we were in college and studying for finals."

"Are you sure?" She glanced at Jake, still hovering in the entryway. "I don't want to be in the way."

"You won't be." In fact, she'd be an added deterrent to keep Jake out of my bedroom. "Although I hope you don't mind sharing my bed."

"I'll warn you, she snores," Jake said. I wanted to kill him. Not a good time to be thinking that way. I stifled the thought.

Sarah giggled. "Yeah," she said. "But I can put up with it for one night."

She didn't have to worry about me snoring because she fell asleep before I did. It must have been that second beer. I woke up before her too, and tiptoed my way to the kitchen to make coffee. But Jake had beaten me to it and sat at the table with a cup in one hand and the newspaper open on the table in front of him.

"Any information?" I whispered.

He shook his head. "No, but they probably printed the paper before it happened."

"Yeah." I poured a cup and sat at the table across from him. "I sent Freddie a text message to tell him Sarah is here. Didn't want him to worry."

"So he'll show up here?"

"Depends. He may just head home and crash."

"You know, when I was a little kid, I wanted to be a cop when I grew up." He glared at me. "Don't laugh."

I swallowed my chuckle with a sip of coffee. "What happened?"

He grimaced. "Life, I guess. I still think I would have been a good one."

It was surreal, having a conversation with a renowned jewel thief about being a police officer. "Sometimes dreams just don't work out," I said, thinking about Janine and the library job.

"What dream hasn't worked out for you?"

I picked up a section of the newspaper so he couldn't see my eyes. "It's not important. I've got a good life and good friends and that's what matters."

"Let me guess, you wanted to be an astronaut but your eyesight's not good enough."

"Worse. I wanted to be a cowboy. Not a cowgirl, mind you, but a cowboy."

Jake snorted into his cup, spraying coffee everywhere. He snatched a handful of napkins from the holder and blotted the liquid from the newspaper. "Yeah, I can see where that might be a little hard to accomplish." He eyed me. "You don't have the right parts. But I must say, I like the parts you have."

I crumpled up an insert from the paper and hurled it at him. I needed to find a way to keep him busy and out of my hair, and soon.

Despite its size, my apartment got transformed into meeting central. Sarah had gone home and then to work—Saturdays are hot for real estate showings—but Merrilee and Lori had shown up mid-morning. Yes, Lori. The bullet, thankfully, had only grazed her arm. Jake disappeared, probably to get some sleep because Sarah and I kept him awake most of the night. Luke and Joe were hanging around, trying to look useful, as if I wouldn't notice them "fixing" the gutters outside my front window. The same gutters they'd replaced a year earlier.

With the pain medication and antibiotics Lori was on, as well as the time of day, alcohol was out of the equation. Thank heavens, because my stock was getting low. Instead, we were drinking coffee or hot chocolate or, in Merrilee's case, a mix of the two.

"I assumed it would be safer going to the grocery store that late," Lori said. "Because there would be fewer people. Detective Thomason warned me that people might be upset I was out of jail, but to shoot me?"

"Are you sure that's why he took a shot at you?" I asked. She'd already told us the police were almost positive the shooter had been male from the store's surveillance video.

Lori shuddered, and Merrilee, seated on the loveseat beside her, wrapped an arm around her. "The police asked me the same thing. And I can't think of any other reason. I haven't hurt anyone here, heck, I hardly know anyone." She thought about it and grimaced. "Well, except the other teachers at the school. And I've met a lot of parents as well."

That doesn't help to shrink the pool of suspects at all. But I couldn't imagine anyone in Oak Grove shooting Lori. Giving her dirty looks was more the speed of most of the local citizens. I'd suffered through plenty of those myself.

Lori sniffed. "I moved here to get away from my past and start over again. But it looks like Calib has managed to screw things up for me even by dying."

No words I could say would fix the problem. "I'm sure things will work out. We have some real smart guys on the police force. They'll figure out what's going on." And I'd be doing everything I could to help them. I wondered if I could get Scotty or Lando to check out the police reports since Eli seemed to be missing in action. Despite the lessons Scotty had given me, I didn't feel confident enough to try to hack the system myself.

Fortunately for me, Lori wanted to talk. "Detective Thomason said I was lucky. I'd been trying to figure out whether I needed fresh milk, and just opened the cooler door when the shot was fired. The bullet hit the metal frame before it hit me."

"Did they recover the bullet?" I asked, recalling what had happened to me.

"I don't know. I wasn't in any shape to ask questions." She gave me a halfhearted smile. "I fainted."

Merrilee rubbed her arm. "Don't be ashamed. I would have too. Harmony's the only woman I know who can face death and just keep going."

My face got hot.

"Ask her about the crime lord she captured," Merrilee went on, grinning like a banshee.

Lori looked at me expectantly. "Merrilee's exaggerating," I said. "I didn't do it by myself. The police did most of it. I just happened to be there."

"That's not the story I heard," Merrilee said. "Let me tell you what *really* happened."

If she told the trumped-up version that not only had me single-handedly breaking up an international crime ring, but rescuing an entire orphanage from a burning building at the same time, there would be serious hell to pay.

"More hot chocolate?" I asked both of them in an obvious ploy to divert their attention elsewhere. "Someday, I'm going to have to dig out my mother's recipe for making it from scratch." Much to my surprise, it worked and we switched topics to which brand of commercial hot chocolate was our favorite.

I wondered about the bullet. Had they been able to identify what kind of gun it had been shot from?

And would that help narrow down the pool of suspects? After lunch, when Merrilee and Lori *finally* left, I pulled out one of my burner phones and called Lando.

After the third ring, I thought he might not pick up because the number would show up as one he didn't recognize. As I prepared to leave him a voice mail, he answered, "Yo?"

"Lando!" I gushed. "I'm glad you answered!"

"Harmony?" he asked, confusion evident in his voice. "Where are you calling from?"

"Throw-away cell," I explained. "I didn't want the call traced."

"I'm glad you learned a few tricks, but what are you up to, girl?"

"Eli tell you about the murder here a couple of weeks ago?"

"No. Hold on." I heard the sound of fingers typing away on a noisy keyboard and Lando humming quietly as he worked. "You said a couple of weeks ago? Not last night?"

"Yes. That's why I called. Any chance the bullet from last night was fired from the same gun?"

"What makes you ask?"

"The lady who got shot last night is the ex-wife, no, legally the widow of the dead guy. They were separated, but not divorced."

Lando whistled softly. "They recovered the bullet, but the ballistics tests aren't in yet."

Whatever that meant.

"In other words, it's too soon to tell." He fell silent, and I assumed he was reading. "You didn't mention you were shot at. Is that why Eli went flying out of here a couple of weeks ago?"

"The police decided that it was coincidence that I happened to be cleaning when the window was shot."

"Uh-huh. I see the victim was killed with a 45 caliber handgun while the window was struck by shotgun pellets. No link there. You want me to email copies of the reports to you?"

"Can you send them encrypted? The FBI has been nosing around and I don't want to take any unnecessary chances."

"The feds, eh?" More clicks as his fingers raced across the keyboard. "Done, and on their way. And as much fun as this has been, I have to ask, why didn't you ask Eli to do this for you?"

Good question. "He's not talking to me. Has me blocked or something." That's the only thing I could figure out. It hurt he hadn't told me he was breaking up with me, but I wasn't going to tell *anyone* that. Especially not one of the guys he worked with. Not when *someone* might tell Eli. Or Jake.

"You want me to wring his neck for you? Or hold him down and torture him until he calls?"

Both sounded like good ideas. "No, you better not," I said regretfully.

"Come to think about it, I haven't seen him the last few days. But he does that once in a while. Works from home where he won't be distracted. I'll ask around on Monday and see what I can find out."

"I appreciate it."

"So you going to go to the Con with me and Scotty? We'd have to hustle to pull you a costume together, but we can do it."

The temptation was strong. Maybe it would make Eli jealous. But I didn't operate that way.

"You're going to tell me no, aren't you?" I could hear the grin in Lando's voice. "Can't blame me for trying, Spitfire. But no worries, I love ya' anyway."

I was glad I didn't have to answer.

"Tell you what, I'll keep an eye on things the next few days. If anything pops up, I'll give you a buzz. You want me to call this number?"

"No, text me and I'll call you back. It won't necessarily be from this phone."

"You have learned well, grasshopper," he chuckled.

Silly, but I felt like I did when I earned a gold star for my work back in first grade.

Jake showed up after supper. I was finally getting somewhere in my back log of research, and his presence was an unwelcome distraction. Doubly so, because he wanted to talk. And watch TV. And sit next to me and run his fingers through my hair. I wasn't sure which was worse—the professional bodyguard who was the silent type I'd dealt with last fall, or the gregarious amateur, Jake.

Who, at the moment, was rubbing the back of my neck, easing the tension caused by leaning forward and peering at small print on my laptop screen. As much as I hated to admit it, I was enjoying it.

But when my phone rang, I was glad of the excuse to move away. Part of me hoped it was Eli calling, but another part of me dreaded the time when he finally called.

"Hey, Merrilee," I said cheerfully after checking caller ID.

"I'm glad you're home," she said without even a "hello." "I need your help."

She sounded more plaintive than desperate, so I decided it couldn't be too bad.

"What's up?"

"Lori's staying with me because she doesn't feel safe being alone."

Made sense.

"But the thing is," Merrilee continued, "I have a date tonight, and it will be weird having her along. Is there any way you could come over and stay with her?"

The idea came in a flash. An absolutely brilliant idea that killed two birds with one stone. "You know what Lori needs?" I asked. I answered my own question without giving Merrilee a chance to respond. "A bodyguard. And I know just the man for

the job."

"Are you kidding me?" Jake sputtered after I hung up. "It's one thing keeping an eye on you, but I'm no bodyguard. Hell, I'm not allowed to carry a gun."

"So you're just hanging out here as eye-candy? Or was it a ploy to get me in the sack with you? Gee, thanks. I thought for a minute you were actually concerned about my safety."

His eyes narrowed and his mouth formed a thin line. A smart woman would have shut up. Sometimes, I wasn't very smart.

"Or are you too busy planning your next heist and I'm your cover story?"

Jake stood abruptly, almost knocking over the beer he'd been drinking when he bumped the coffee table.

"The guys in prison told me people would act this way. Once a felon, always a felon," he said, clenching and unclenching his fists. "No matter what I did when I got out, no matter how hard I tried. But I didn't expect it from you." He started toward the door.

But I was faster than him. He had to work his way over the power cord for the laptop and I had a straight shot. I got between him and his destination and stood there, feet planted firmly. He was going to have to move me to leave.

"So what are you going to do about it, Hennessey?" With one finger, I jabbed him in the chest and kept pushing. "Run away like a scared little boy? Or prove yourself and become a hero?"

He backed away. "Hero? Are you crazy? I'm nobody's hero, and never will be. More like the classic villain." He swirled an imaginary mustache.

"You were Eli's hero, once upon a time," I said softly.

Chapter 22

"That proves even smart guys can be idiots sometimes," Jake said with a strangled laugh. "He was a pain in the neck, following me around like a lost puppy. If Aunt Tillie hadn't been so nice to me, I would have dumped his scrawny ass."

I remembered Eli mentioning his mother's name was Tillie. I closed the gap between me and Jake and poked him in the chest again.

"So forget Eli. What would your aunt say about you throwing away this opportunity?"

Jake's eyes widened. "You don't play fair," he said as he gently moved my finger away from his chest. He didn't let go of my hand, but clutched it in his.

"I've been watching you, Jake. Ever since the moment you laid down your shovel when Freddie confronted you." I took a step forward and he took a step away. "You read people's body language and change your response based on their reactions to you. I can't tell if it's instinct or if you trained yourself, but it's invisible unless someone looks for it. And you're good, Jake, damned good."

"You know who I can't read?" Jake's breathing was rapid and shallow. "You. I can't read you. Little innocent you, who is as easy to read as an open book. And then you go and come up with something like this. You ambushed me and I never saw it coming. I can't figure you out and it drives me crazy."

"Tell me you don't want to give this a shot," I challenged him. "Isn't that what a bodyguard does? Studies everyone and everything looking for any signs of potential trouble? The only difference is you'd be watching to see how people are looking at Lori, not you."

He didn't know it yet, but I had reeled him in, hook, line and sinker.

"But what about you? Who'll keep an eye out for you?" he asked.

I bit my lower lip so I wouldn't tell him I could look after myself. "I'll buy a gun. I've been meaning to do it anyway. And I have Luke and Joe watching out for me."

He'd almost bought it. Just a little bit more. I brought out the big guns, pouted and fluttered my eyelashes.

"Hell, half the city cops are keeping an eye on me. They show up wherever I go. Besides, I'm sure it'll only be for a day or two, until they arrest whoever shot her."

And sold. Jake nodded slowly.

"I'll give it a try," he said.

There was one more piece to the puzzle. I called Dan on his private number and explained what I was up to. Lori would take the bait easier if I told her the use of Jake as a bodyguard was arranged through her public defender. If she knew anything about public defenders she'd realize it was bogus, but I was willing to take the risk.

To make it more legit, Dan would unofficially hire Jake and pay him. It would be our secret that the money would come out of Lori's fees. Paid for, of course, by me.

Now I needed to sell the scheme to Lori. I thought that might be harder. When I saw her giving Jake the old once-over as we got out of the car I smiled, the battle won before it started. It all came together easier than I expected. Jake would stay at Lori's apartment, sleeping on the couch. Since her apartment was on the third floor of the complex, and didn't have a balcony, Jake wasn't worried about someone coming in the window. And with the addition of blackout curtains instead of the thin drapes provided by management, it would be difficult for anyone to track her movements.

Jake would drive Lori to and from work each day, but once at work the school's on-site security officers would take over guard duties. That gave Jake time to take a nap or whatever else he wanted to do. And after work, he'd escort her to the store to do her shopping, visit friends, or anything else she planned.

The best part was I'd be able to get back to my daily routine. Pat Piper and collect the newspaper, read it while drinking my coffee, go to the library and do research, head home and enjoy supper while listening to a favorite band. Heck, maybe I'd dig out my mother's John Denver CD's. Hadn't listened to any of them for a while.

It was a good plan. At least on paper.

Sundays were my days off. And though I was still far behind in my work, I decided to make that Sunday no different. With blue skies predicted and the major roads cleared, it would be a good day to go for a drive. I told Joe and Luke my plans and Joe muttered something about going with me. But he and Luke had a previous commitment and how much trouble could I get into just going for a drive? I hummed a cheerful tune as I pulled Dolores out of the garage.

As I waited for a lone car cruising down the street to get by me, I debated which direction I wanted to go. But with the Jag low on gas, the decision was made for me. The gas station I liked was north, so north it was. I could grab a sandwich and go sit on the shores of Lake Erie and watch the waves.

The plan didn't work the way I wanted. The bitterly cold wind blowing across the lake from Canada made it too cold to sit on the beach. Worse,

I ended up in the same spot I'd brought Eli to last fall. It must have been a sign, I thought, and I tried to reach him again. With no luck.

With the heater on full blast and the window down, I allowed myself to cry. More than a few tears. No one was around to see me or hear me, and I let go of everything that I'd been holding in. When I got back to Oak Grove, I'd carry on and no one would ever know.

Before I headed home, I stopped at the same restaurant Eli and I ate at on our trip, to test myself. I didn't feel like eating, but if I could sit there and drink a cup of coffee without crying, I'd call myself officially cured. I avoided the waitress's eyes when I placed my order because I didn't want her to see the puffiness around my eyes.

While waiting for my coffee, I pretended to be occupied with reading a book I'd taken out of my purse, but in reality, I was checking out the other customers. When a familiar man walked in, I scooted down in my seat, and studied him. His hair was brown instead of gray and he'd lost weight, but it was hard to disguise the crooked nose. Orson Wallington.

The waitress brought me my coffee, and I barely took my eyes off the man seated at the counter while I sipped it. He exchanged a few words with the customer next to him, but it seemed to be nothing more than polite acknowledgment of each other. My fingers itched to reach for my cell phone but I doubted the local police would respond quickly to a non-emergency. As I debated what to do, the waitress handed him a foam cup. He paid her and took a moment to add a spoonful of sugar to its contents before he left.

The brief pause gave me time to put a couple of ones on the table. In every game of tailing someone I'd ever played, I was the one being followed. Now it was time to turn the tables.

I prayed that he would be traveling by foot. Dolores wasn't made for unobtrusive surveillance. Outside, I spotted him a few feet down the sidewalk, alternating between puffing on a cigarette and taking sips from his cup.

Pulling my collar up around my neck as if to ward off the cold wind, I headed the opposite direction. The windows of a second-hand store next to the restaurant gave me the opportunity to stop and study the items displayed while watching him. When he glanced my way, I stepped into the recessed entryway of the store, as if going inside. In reality, I scrolled through my contacts and dialed the only person I could think of who would have the proper contacts to handle the situation.

"FBI, Pittsburgh office, Agent Felton speaking," he answered.

I breathed easier. With it being Sunday, I didn't think I'd reach him. He must have been behind on his paperwork or something.

"This is Harmony Duprie," I whispered.

"Miss Duprie? Where are you? Are you all right?"

"The outskirts of Erie. Hold on."

Wallington started walking away from me. I

should have crossed the street, but the traffic was too heavy, so I let him get halfway down the block before I moved. He tossed his cup towards a trash can, but missed. He kept on walking and it got caught by a gust of wind and tossed into the street. It shouldn't have surprised me the con man was also a litter bug.

"Miss Duprie?" Felton said again, with more urgency in his voice.

"I'm tailing Orson Wallington or whatever his name is," I said. "For your records, his hair is dark brown now, and he's lost about twenty-five pounds." Which told me he'd been wearing padding in Pittsburgh.

"Stop right now," Felton ordered. "We'll take it from here."

I ignored him, and when I got to the corner where Wallington made a right-hand turn, I crossed the street. The move had the potential to be a game-ender, but I got lucky and the walk signal turned white just as I got to the intersection.

Once safely on the other side, tailing him was easier. Although he looked behind once in a while, he never looked my direction. The trunks of the old trees that lined my side of the street made the job easier.

"Miss Duprie!" Felton yelled.

"Corner of Fifth and Sycamore," I said as I stood under the street signs. "I think this is part of Watersford."

Wallington waited for the walk signal on his side of the street while I waited on mine. I took the opportunity to study the area. It looked like it turned into an older residential area a block in front of me, but there appeared to be mostly businesses on his side. There were a lot of vehicles using the road, but next to no pedestrians on the sidewalk which made me easily noticeable. On the other hand, if Orson saw me, he might assume I was heading towards one of the houses.

"Turn around. Turn around now and go back to wherever you started from," Felton commanded.

That was a good idea, so of course I ignored it. I crossed when the light turned and stopped on the other side to retrieve a real estate guide from a kiosk on the corner.

"He's heading into a used car dealership," I said into the phone. "Larry's Used Cars." I snorted. "Larry must get his cars from a junkyard."

"This is not a game!" Felton shouted into my ear. "Break off!"

I had the sudden urge to buy a used car. A blue Pinto sat on the lot.

"Like anything you see?" a voice asked in my ear.

I jumped, startled, but quickly recovered. "Actually, yes," I said. "That blue car. Reminds me of a car a friend owned years ago." I tried to sound like I didn't know what I was talking about. The real challenge was keeping my voice steady to cover my nervousness. "I wonder how hard it would be to fix it up?"

I turned around to face the man who'd snuck up on me. In my quest to track Orson, I'd forgotten to pay attention and see if someone followed me. "You're not a salesman for them, are you?" I asked, batting my eyelashes. I knew better. He was the man Orson talked to at the restaurant.

A quick analysis assured me I had a fair shot at taking my accoster down if I needed to. He was shorter than me, older, weighed less, and unless he had muscles hidden under his coat, I was probably stronger than him as well. I hoped he didn't have a weapon. I also prayed he wouldn't notice my connection to Agent Felton was still active, and that Felton was smart enough to shut up and just listen.

"No, but you and I should go take a look at it." It didn't sound like an invitation.

I sighed loudly. "No, I can't swing it right now." Since I was wearing worn-out jeans and an old coat, I didn't look like I had money. "It's too tempting." I sniffed loudly, hoping he'd think I had a cold and keep his distance.

It didn't work. The man grabbed my arm. "Let's go."

"Don't touch me!" I squealed, trying to pull away. I didn't try very hard. In reality, I was testing his strength. He was stronger than I had guessed. Time to re-calculate.

He pushed me. "Get going."

I stumbled a few steps, doing everything I could to convince him I was a weakling, and used it as a cover to drop my cell phone into my pocket. "That hurt!" I complained. "What's your problem?" We were standing on the curb, and cars whizzed by. No one, however, seemed to be paying any attention to us.

"You're my problem. Sticking your nose where it doesn't belong." He gripped my arm tightly, while he waited for the traffic signal to change. "And don't even think about screaming," he said. "Unless you want to get hurt."

When the time came, I would scream all right. So far, there had been no sign of a gun, and the odds were going up in my favor. I needed to remain patient and wait for the right moment.

"What are you talking about?" I fake-whimpered. "Who are you?"

He grinned, pulled me close, and whispered into my ear.

"You may have heard of me. I'm Orson Wallington."

Chapter 23

Holy crap. When Orson released me, I almost fell, as much from the shock as from being temporarily off-balance. If he hadn't reached out to steady me, I would have ended up in front of a car driving by.

"Shall we go talk Martha, or whoever you are?" he said, indicating the run-down building that served as the office for Larry's.

I pulled myself free again. "Not there. Back at the coffee shop or someplace more public."

"And what are you going to do about it?" he grinned as he slipped his hand inside his jacket. When he took it back out, I caught the glint of metal.

The first choice was always to run. I didn't, naturally. If he didn't know who I really was, he wouldn't know anything else about me. I grabbed the arm not holding the knife and pulled, throwing him off balance, just slightly, but enough to make the next move effective.

Still holding his arm, I swiveled so I was behind him, bringing his arm with me. Then I kicked the back of one of his knees. It was enough to drop him to the ground.

I'd hoped for the clang of metal on concrete, but didn't get it. He slowly rose and turned around. I took several steps backwards.

"Do you still want to have that conversation?" I asked, my voice dripping with sugar.

"Who *are* you?" he asked. For the briefest of moments, I caught a glimpse of wonder in his face, but he quickly reverted to an expression of almost boredom.

"Martha works for now. How about you lose the knife and we'll just stroll back and sit in a quiet booth and talk?" I wondered if Felton was getting any of this or if the connection had dropped.

The ghost of a smile flitted across his face. "You're not what I expected. That amuses me." He tossed the knife under the stand holding the real estate guides. "I can retrieve that later."

I crossed my arms and stared at him. "Got any more?"

He raised one pant leg. "You ditch the cell phone and I'll get rid of this."

I eased the cell phone out of my pocket, powered it down, and pulled the battery out. "Good enough?" I asked.

He nodded, and I put the phone into my purse and the battery in my coat pocket. So much for

Felton. I suspected I'd lost him earlier anyway. In return, a second knife joined the first in its hiding place.

"You got any pepper spray in that purse?" he asked.

"Nope. My instructor says it's a crutch."

He extended his elbow. "Shall we walk?"

We walked the first block in silence. At the corner, while we waited to cross the street, a police car went screaming by, sirens wailing and lights ablaze. Orson casually put his arm around me as if we were a couple, and I let him. Once across, he dropped the pretense and asked "So what is it you do?"

"Research." I could answer the question honestly. "People pay me to do research."

"Sweet gig."

"It's not bad. The hard part is deciding which projects I can finish in a reasonable amount of time for a reasonable price."

"And who's paying you to research me?"

"No one. Sometimes I come across topics that I look into to satisfy my personal curiosity. You were an interesting side note to a different project."

Orson held the door to the restaurant open for me. I nodded at the waitress, who, with a puzzled expression on her face, nodded back. I think she recognized both of us, but couldn't place why. If I wanted to scream, this was my chance. But for whatever reason, I no longer felt threatened by

Orson, and led the way to an empty booth. I slid onto the bench so my back was to the door, figuring he'd be more comfortable being able to watch who came in.

"I'm going to get dessert," I told him as I took a menu from the holder. "Their pies looked delicious."

"Ice cream or whipped cream?" he asked.

"Depends. Berry pies are whipped cream, apple are ice cream, and what goes with cherry changes with my mood. How about you?" This seemed more like speed dating than an interview with a famous thief.

"Ice cream. Always."

Conversation lagged until the waitress came and took our orders. Blueberry pie and coffee for me while he got the traditional apple pie to go with his coffee. I mentally filed away the factoid that he took his coffee black. Orson watched with interest when another police car flew down the street in front of the restaurant. "Must have been an accident or something," he said.

The waitress brought our orders so I didn't need to respond. In between bites, I studied him.

He still had a full head of hair, although it was totally gray. His body was on the thin side, but there was plenty of muscle built into that spare frame. The most interesting part of all was his face.

Based on the number of wrinkles that marked his face, he'd spent too much time in the sun at some point. I wondered if he'd grown up in the South or the West, but he didn't speak with an accent that would identify where he had lived. He appeared to be in his seventies, but still had a handsome face.

He was looking me over, too. I tried not to notice.

"What did you want to 'talk' about?" I asked finally. "It's not ice cream."

He leaned towards me, his eyes inquisitive. "Who told you we would be here?"

I shrugged. "No one. It was purely coincidence. I meant to spend the day on the peninsula, but it's too dang cold. I needed to get away, and I've always found the sound of the waves rolling in over the sand soothing. Not today." I took a sip of my coffee, its warmth wiping away the memory of how cold I'd been earlier.

Orson nodded, apparently satisfied by my answer. But he wasn't done yet.

"Why have you been crying?" he asked.

I almost teared up again. I could have denied it, but I didn't. "Man troubles." I bent my head and used my fork to play with a loose blueberry so he wouldn't see the moisture that gathered in my eyes.

He nodded. "Men are pigs."

His unexpected response made me smile. "Some of them. I have a feeling you've broken a few hearts along the way."

"A few," he agreed. "Mostly I tried to avoid getting mixed up with women who might expect anything more than a good night."

"I suppose a long-term relationship would be impossible for a man in your profession."

"What do you know of my profession, Martha?" he asked sharply.

"Mostly what I've found on the internet. And I don't believe half of what I read. Anything you want to share with me?"

"And how much has Hennessey told you?"

If he expected me to deny knowing Jake, it wasn't going to happen. "He doesn't talk about it."

"And neither will I."

"Fair enough." I concentrated on my pie while the waitress refilled our coffees. "There is one thing I wonder if you'd clear up for me," I said. "There's a raging debate in the forums if you're responsible for the theft of the Marquesa's Necklace. Your fans say you are, but other people seem to think Hennessey did it. He denies it."

"So that's what has your panties in a bunch." Orson set his fork down abruptly and it clanged against the plastic plate. "What do you think?"

"If he didn't do it, someone went to a lot of effort to make it look like he did. I can't figure out what the motive for that would be and it bothers me. I hoped you would have some insight into the whole thing."

"Are you wearing a wire?"

"Ha. The FBI has tried to convince me to participate in a scheme to entrap Hennessey, and I've turned them down, much to their displeasure. No, I'm not wired. And I'd offer to let you check me, but I have a thing about letting strange men touch me. Besides, you didn't find anything when you were checking me out earlier." I figured that's one reason he'd been so touchy-feely when we were waiting to cross the street.

"You caught that." He grinned. "You are an

interesting woman, Martha. And I've got an idea who had it in for Hennessey." He looked up and stiffened. With my back to the door I couldn't see what he was reacting to.

"What?" I asked.

"A couple of cops just walked in. There seems to be a lot of them around this afternoon."

"I suspect they're busy chasing the guy posing as you. Not the normal course of affairs for the cops around here, I imagine."

Like a cornered stray dog, he eyed me. "You knew, and you didn't let me walk into it."

"I won't admit to anything. You're not mad at me, are you?" I asked.

He relaxed. "No, he was getting to be a liability. But you'll understand if I don't want to hang out here any longer."

I jerked my head towards the kitchen. "There's a back door. I'll get the bill."

"Why are you doing this?"

"I'm trying to help a friend get her life back. Hennessey's ex-girlfriend. Until we can figure out who's behind the attacks on Hennessey, she won't be safe."

"I owe you," he said, as he stood up. "I don't like owing people." He stood beside the table, leaned over and kissed me on the cheek. "Give Hennessey my regards. I wish I'd met you about 30 years ago, Martha. I'll be in touch." With one last crooked grin, he was gone.

I took my time finishing my pie and allowed the waitress to refill my coffee while I listened to bits and pieces of the cops' conversation. Someone had been arrested, unfortunately, I didn't catch who.

It wasn't until I was headed back to the parking lot that I remembered to stick the battery back into my phone and turn it on. Then, I wished I hadn't, because it started beeping like crazy as messages rolled in. I waited until I plugged the phone into the charger in the car and was driving home before I called Agent Felton back, breaking my rule of no calls while driving.

"Duprie!" he spat. "Where are you?"

"A few miles from Interstate 75 and headed home," I answered. "Sorry about the dropped call. My battery died, and I just barely got it charged up enough to call you. And don't worry, I'm talking hands free. Did you catch him?"

"No, he managed to get away. Where did you go?"

I channeled the innocence of a Girl Scout. "Back to the restaurant, like you told me to. Once my phone didn't work, I figured I couldn't help anymore and I should get out of the way."

The garbled noise I heard from the other end of the call made me want to giggle. Had Felton actually put his hand over the receiver to swear? I struggled to maintain my composure.

"I may need to talk to you in the next few days."

I caught my breath. "No one will find out it was me that tipped you off?"

"No. I'm listing you as anonymous. There are no rewards for this guy if he turns up, so you aren't missing out on anything."

Huh. I'd forgotten about my quest to become a bounty hunter. I wonder how many rewards I'd lost out on by letting the real Orson go free.

"You know where to find me," I said.

Was that a muffled laugh I heard? Too bad I couldn't see his face. "I'm not so sure about that, Miss Duprie."

Since I had spent the entire afternoon breaking one rule after another, I decided to go ahead and listen to my voice mail once I got on the interstate. I skipped the half-dozen messages from Felton and laughed at the one from Janine about a library volunteer shelving an erotic romance in the medical reference section. I'd call her back later. Jake had called, upset I didn't tell him where I was, surprise, surprise. I'd return his call when I got home. But the one from Lando had me worried. Even though it was the weekend, he'd been trying to find Eli.

No one, and I mean no one, knew where Eli had gone.

Chapter 24

"Everyone figured he was with you," Lando said, I'd called him as soon as I got home, not willing to risk hearing more bad news while driving. The way my heart lurched when I listened to Lando's message made it clear I was fooling myself if I thought I was over Eli. "He's been working too hard for the last couple of weeks, and Darla said he finally got to a point where he could take a break."

"Darla?" I asked casually, despite the twinge of jealousy I felt.

"His admin assistant. Sweet old lady with mad organizational skills."

Why did Eli need a secretary? Why did a programmer need an administrative assistant? But if she was old, I didn't need to be jealous of her. Small consolation.

"He must be a real hotshot to get his own secretary. I thought all programmers do is crunch code for hours and hours."

"Well, see, there's a story behind that." Lando

hesitated. "And he made Scotty and me promise we wouldn't tell you."

I waited, hoping the uncomfortable silence would make Lando reveal the secret.

"Eli's not just a programmer."

I waited some more.

"Remember how Scotty and I call him boss-man?"

I remembered.

"Yeah, so he is our boss. For real. In fact, he's everyone's boss here. He owns the company."

A bunch of pieces fell into place. The meetings he went to, the way he took time off at a moment's notice, how hard he worked. Jake's hints about things he wasn't telling me. It all made sense now.

"Why didn't he want me to know?" I asked.

"Not going there. That's between you and him. I've already told you too much."

If Eli ever showed up, I'd make him tell me.

"Anyway, we all know how crazy he is about you. He talks about you all the time. So when he told Darla he was going to take a few days off, she just figured he was on his way to visit you."

A cold hand wrapped itself around my heart and squeezed it. "If he headed this direction, he never made it."

"Well, he didn't take the company jet. I'll check commercial airlines and see if I can find out if he booked a flight."

Company jet? No wonder he could get here so quickly. Usually. "Did you call his parents?"

"No." Lando blew out a deep breath. "And I don't want to worry them, so I won't. I'll drive by their place tomorrow and make sure his car's not there."

"And check with the airports to make sure his car isn't parked at any of them."

"Good idea, I assume they maintain a database that tracks license plates. And he has a personalized plate, so it'll stand out."

"Let me guess. CDMNKY."

Lando laughed. "No, but I might steal that the next time I renew my tag. No, his is SHIFT."

Made sense. Especially since his company was named "Shifter Technologies." *His* company. That would take some getting used to.

"Someone should go by his house too. Make sure he's not there and sick or hurt or something."

"I already did that. Eli gave me his spare key. Everything looks normal and his car's not there."

A few more ideas floated around in my head, but I kept them to myself. "Call me as soon as you hear anything. Good or..." I couldn't say it.

"I will. And Harmony? Keep it a secret, will you? We don't want the news leaking out yet."

To my relief, the federal databases I'd pulled up

on plane crashes didn't reveal anything relevant, but I continued to scroll through them as I called Jake. While he rattled on about how boring his day had been, I sifted through the official reports for every airplane incident that happened anywhere between Florida and the Great Lakes. Unless Eli had hitched a ride with a hobbyist, he hadn't been on any of them.

"So what are your plans for tomorrow?" Jake asked. I was only half-listening, so I took a moment to answer.

"Work. Nothing but work."

"Can I take you out for lunch? I owe you. Lori already said she'd eat in the teacher's lounge and not leave the school."

I couldn't come up with a quick excuse to get out of it. "Okay, meet me at the restaurant down the street from the library." I always ate lunch there, and most of the time ordered the daily special.

"I distinctly remember someone advising you to switch up your schedule."

"So make it eleven-thirty instead of noon. Does that satisfy you?"

Jake chuckled. "It's a start. I'll meet you in the library."

Digging into a particular thorny research project normally helped take my mind off my problems. But I was trying to get details on the celebration for Queen Victoria's fortieth birthday for one of my romance novelists. Not exactly the most interesting topic, but it helped pay the bills.

It also gave me too much time to worry about Eli and wonder why Lando hadn't called. I kept looking at my phone to check for missed calls. But *not* hearing anything also meant there was no bad news.

Jake showed up early, a welcome distraction. We took Dolores and got to Mama D's before the lunch crowd hit. Jake was funny and courteous and told me stories about the trouble he got into as a kid, and I remembered why I'd fallen in love with him. But I'd never be able to fix him up with anyone in Oak Grove, and most of my out-of-town friends were already married.

His plans for the rest of the afternoon included a nap before Lori finished work. So after the normal implied invitations to join him in his bed, and my standard rejections, we went back to the library. He took off for the hotel, and I returned to my job.

As typical for Oak Grove, nothing happened for the rest of the afternoon. Until, that was, one of our high school volunteers came and sat down at my table. Cute little thing, impossibly young, she went by the nickname Sam.

No matter how deeply I was buried in books, I always made time to talk to the teenagers who help out at the library. They came to ask the questions that the librarians don't have time to answer or that might sound dumb. I did my best to help them out.

Sam usually didn't ask dumb questions, but she seemed uneasy. We chit-chatted for a while about how her classes were going, and how she didn't have a date for the prom yet. I let her lead the conversation, figuring she'd get to the point when she was ready.

"How scary was it when you got shot?" she asked eventually.

That threw me for a loop. I thought she was going to ask something about boys. "I didn't actually get shot," I answered.

"You know what I meant. You were shot at. It must have been scary."

"Have you ever been to one of those spooky Halloween houses?" I asked. Granted, the ones in Oak Grove were pretty lame.

She nodded.

"So take the scariest one you've been to and double how scared you were. Now double it again." Her eyes got bigger. "Now double it again. And that might be almost as scary."

"Wow," Sam said. "Did you faint?"

"No, but I hit the floor so fast it would make your head swim, in case whoever was shooting fired a second time."

"The police haven't figured out who did it yet, have they?" she asked.

"No."

"And they don't know who killed that guy they found either, right?"

"Right. And that's more important."

She bit at a hangnail. "The kids at school say the police are hoping to find whoever shot out the window at the house, thinking they might have seen something."

It was comforting knowing the Oak Grove gossip grapevine thrived among its teenagers as well.

"A couple of days ago some guys were talking about seeing something strange over by the house you're fixing up," she said.

"Do they think it had something to do with the murder?"

"Yeah." She poked at the spot where she'd torn off a piece of skin, and I spotted a drop of blood. I dug into my purse and handed her a bandage. "They have a video of a guy out in the woods. They were hanging out, goofing off and making stupid videos."

I wondered if it was Jake. "Anyway they'd be willing to show the police?"

"Here's the thing." She wrapped her finger in the bandage. "The kid who took it has been in trouble before. He's afraid the cops may try to blame the shot-out window on him."

"I understand that. But the video might be important to figuring out who really did it."

"Yeah, that's what his friends tried to tell him. He wasn't listening."

I was running out of ideas. "How about sending it using a fake email address?"

"He's paranoid. Thinks the cops will trace it back to him."

How much should I tell her? "I might know someone who knows how to get the video to the police anonymously. But if it helps the police identify the murderer, they'll need the original eventually."

Sam played with the bandage, realized what she was doing, and stuck her hands into her lap. "I'll pass the word along," she said. She got up to go back to work. "I'm not making any promises."

I nodded in understanding.

My Monday night self-defense class had been canceled and I didn't want to go home. So I stayed past my normal time and kept on working. Janine stopped by my table before she left to make sure I was all right. I gave her the excuse about being so far behind I was putting in extra hours. The reality was I didn't want to be by myself. Lando hadn't called, not even to update me. That left me imagining all kinds of horrendous scenarios.

Had Eli been kidnapped and dragged off to an old shack in the middle of a swamp? If so, why hadn't a ransom demand surfaced yet? Maybe he'd decided to chuck it all and was hitchhiking his way to the West Coast to take up surfing. Or was he off in a remote mountain lodge with a beautiful spy who was trying to extract his business secrets from him? How would I find him to rescue him? Did I want to rescue him anyway in that case? He was a Hennessey after all, and I couldn't trust a Hennessey.

Around eight-thirty, as I gathered up my books to re-shelve them before the library closed, I saw Jake stride in through the front doors. Without Lori. Had he gotten tired of being her bodyguard already?

He spotted me, and relief flashed across his face. "There you are," he said when he reached me. He took my pile of books out of my arms. "Let me help you with those. I got worried when I went by your place and you weren't there."

"Yeah, I lost track of time when I rendezvoused with Hans at the motel." Jake almost dropped the books, and I laughed at the look of shock on his face. When he realized I was teasing him, he grinned and shook his head. "I stayed late. Had work to do," I said. I guess I should have called Luke or Joe, but I normally didn't have to answer to anyone. "Where's Lori?"

He followed me up the stairs to the second level, handing me a book at a time for me to put away. "She's down at the cop shop," he said. "Reviewing the surveillance video from the store. The cops want to see if she can identify the shooter before they release it to TV stations."

I wanted to see the video too. If Eli were around, he could have gotten it for me. "Have you heard from Eli?" I asked Jake as he handed me the last book.

"No. Why?"

"No reason," I lied. The last book had been on the lowest shelf, and Jake offered me his hand to help me get up. I wasn't expecting him to pull me to his chest.

"Why are you so worried about him?" He rubbed my back and unexpectedly, it felt like a dear friend's touch.

I pushed away from him and studied his face.

"I figured it out, Angel. You kept telling me, but I didn't want to hear it. I've lost you, and it was my own fault."

I just stared at him, unable to form coherent thoughts.

"But I'm willing to try being your friend instead. It's only fair after everything you've done for me. So tell me what's going on with Eli?"

"I don't get it. What changed between lunch and now?" I asked, finally getting something to come out of my mouth.

Chapter 25

"I was sitting in the excuse of a waiting room at the police station," Jake explained, "and the cop at the front desk must have been bored, because he started talking to me. He and his buddies have a pool going, betting on how soon I'll mess up and get busted again. Then the topic switched to the excitement last fall. I got the whole story out of him."

We'd gone back to my place to talk while he waited for Lori's call. He turned down a beer, to my surprise, but took me up on my offer of coffee. Said he needed the caffeine to stay sharp.

"It's a wonder you talk to me after all the crap you went through. And I'm glad Eli was here for you. He's a good guy, and I can understand why you fell for him. Doesn't make it any easier for me to let you go, but at least it doesn't hurt as bad."

He'd been staring into his coffee cup, and at the end of his speech he looked up and gave me a crooked grin. "So friend, what's bothering you? If Eli hurt you, I'll take him down a peg or two."

I hesitated, not sure whether to tell Jake or not. But he was family, and family trumped the need for secrecy.

"Eli's missing."

Naturally, that's when Lori called, ready to go home. I rode with Jake to pick her up, and we talked on the way.

"I used to know everything about Eli," Jake said. "We hung out at the same places, had the same friends, did the same things. Then I went away to college—yes, I actually went to college for a couple of years, majored in sociology—and we drifted apart.

"When Eli graduated high school, he went the military route. We saw each other once or twice a year, if that. The last few years we didn't keep in touch at all. My fault. Then he showed up out of the blue at my trial. So I don't have any idea where he might have gone. If you want me to help search for him, I'm all in."

"I'm waiting to hear back from one of his guys," I said as we pulled into a parking spot in front of the police station. "It bugs me that I haven't gotten a call yet."

"So that's why you keep checking your phone."

So much for trying to hide my obsession. "Yeah, I guess I've been hoping if I glare at it enough, it'll ring."

"Maybe it's the watched pot effect," he said.

We climbed out of the car and headed inside where Lori waited.

"Any luck?" I asked.

She shook her head. "No, the video was pretty grainy, and I couldn't see much of anything."

"Don't feel bad. None of us were able to tell much from it either," said the officer manning the front desk.

"Can I see it?" I asked, checking out his name tag. McReedy. I memorized the name and face for future reference.

"I don't see why not. It'll be all over the news tomorrow. Here, I'll show you."

The whole station must have had access to the video because it only took McReedy two clicks to pull it up on his screen. "We don't recognize this guy as being from around here," he said as I walked behind the desk. "We're hoping the TV stations in the bigger cities nearby will run this."

The computer screen was small, the lighting in the video crummy, the film low resolution and the person in the video wore a hat to hide his face. At least, I assumed it was a he, based on the way he walked. But the figure on the screen seemed familiar. The why and the who stayed just out of my reach, however.

The clip played through twice. After the second showing I stood up and shook my head. "Sorry, I gave it a shot." Oops, bad choice of words.

"Ready to go then?" Jake asked. "We need to get Lori home."

"Can we go get something to eat first?" Lori asked. "I missed supper."

Me too. "Burger Barn?" I suggested. "There's not much open this time of night."

With what was left of my peppermint-chocolate milkshake in my hand, Lori and I headed back to her car. The plan was to drop me off first, and then for Lori and Jake to head back to her place. I'd been watching Jake while we ate, and his diligence impressed me. Even as he ate and joked with us, his eyes constantly roved the restaurant, looking for anything that might be out of place. He caught me checking my cell phone a couple of times, but each time I shook my head slightly and he'd give me the barest of nods back.

Jake was a couple of feet in front of us. I was laughing at a silly remark Lori made about Jake's ass when I heard the squeal of tires. Jake yelled "Down!" Headlights illuminated us.

Acting on pure instinct, I threw myself at Lori, knocking her to the ground. A fraction of a second later, something large landed on top of both of us. Lori's screams didn't cover the "POPS" of small-arms gunfire. Or the sound of a revved-up engine racing away.

Jake rolled off of me and hissed, "Stay down." I slid off of Lori and watched him snake his way through the sparse coverage of cars in the parking lot. My first thought was to follow him, but with Lori's screams having turned to loud sobs, I decided to stay with her instead. I placed my hand in the middle of her back and rubbed it with light strokes.

The front door of the restaurant burst open and Tony, the owner, came out brandishing a golf club. "Everyone okay?" he asked. "I've already got the cops and paramedics on the way.

In the dim light from the not-so-nearby streetlamps, I crouched beside Lori. "You okay?" I didn't see any fresh blood mixed in with my spilled milkshake. She and her injured arm had been on the bottom of the pile.

"I think so," she managed to get out.

"Stay down until the paramedics get here. No use taking chances."

Like a Buckingham Palace guard, Tony hovered over us, golf club still grasped in his fist. The sounds of sirens in the distance got closer. I hoped Jake hadn't done something foolish, because he wasn't back yet. He wasn't armed, and his quick wit was no match for a handgun.

Several emergency vehicles arrived at the same time, and the scene became more chaotic. EMTs examined Lori and me while police officers scanned the area, searching for evidence and guarding us against any further threat. Even McReedy had left his spot at the desk, and he paced nearby waiting for me to be cleared medically.

But still no Jake.

I was busy reciting my version of the story to McReedy when Freddie's Mustang pulled into the parking lot. I felt sorry for him, getting called in yet again, but I felt sorrier for Sarah. Another date night interrupted. But he wasn't alone.

"Look who I found," Freddie said with a somber face.

Jake was breathing heavily.

"Where the hell did you go?" I snapped. "I was worried about you." I'd been imagining a second Hennessey gone missing in action.

"Found him about a mile down the road." One side of Freddie's lips rose. "He had this crazy notion he'd find the car the shots were fired from along the street somewhere and be able to capture the suspect."

"Hey, I tried," Jake wheezed.

Tony was passing around glasses of ice water, so I snagged one and handed it to Jake. When he dumped it over his head, I got him another.

"Drink this one," I ordered. "Slowly."

"Yes, Mother," he said with a wink, before downing half of it with one gulp,

When we finished telling our stories, Freddie offered to take me home so Jake and Lori could head straight to her place. He offered to walk me up the stairs. I was tired and thought it a gallant gesture, so I accepted. I didn't expect him to blindside me when we got in the door.

"You know," he said as I hung my coat on the rack, "that shot might not have been aimed at Mrs. Booker."

I'd come to that same conclusion but hadn't shared it with anyone. A shiver ran down my spine because hearing him say it made it too real. "I know. All three of us have enemies. Although it's logical to believe the attack was on Lori, I'm not willing to stake my life on it. So I'll be extra careful."

"That's all I ask." Freddie reached out and put a hand on my shoulder. "We may not always agree on things but I care about you, Harmony."

"Thank you," I said and meant it. "Was Jake able to give you a description of the vehicle or its driver?"

"Unfortunately not." Freddie frowned. "Other than an older dark colored sedan with no plates."

"That's about as much help as the security video from the store where Lori was shot," I complained.

"You saw it?"

"Yeah, and the funny thing is, I keep thinking I recognize the guy but I can't place why."

"Someone from the library?" Freddie suggested, immediately switching into cop mode.

"No, I don't think so. If he was a regular I'd know."

"Your gun class? Self-defense class? The Flamingo?"

"No, no and no." Which reminded me, I needed to buy a handgun. It reminded me of something else, too. "Is there any way Jake can legally carry?"

"He has a gun?" Freddie's eyes darkened and he stiffened.

I held up my hands. "No, I was just thinking how

handy it would have been if he'd had one tonight."

The tension in Freddie's shoulders eased. "He did good, but I don't think anyone in Oak Grove would be happy if he was armed."

"Except Lori."

"And people still have doubts about her."

"Yeah. But then, people still have doubts about me too."

❊ ❊ ❊

Maybe I deserved them. The doubts people had about me. But not for the reasons they had. Sure, I'd hidden evidence that tied Jake to some unsolved crimes, and I assisted a known criminal in avoiding the police, but I'd never sold drugs. On the flip side, I'd helped the local police get the glory for arresting a crime boss. And I had helped the FBI get their hands on a couple of con artists. That should count for something.

Despite how late it was—or really, how early—the urge to check my email for news from Lando was too strong to resist. Nothing. Then I checked my burner phone to make sure he hadn't called it. Nothing. Before going to bed, I sent him a one-word message. *Anything?*

I tried to make the day as normal as possible. Got up at the normal time in the morning, made my coffee, took my shower, patted Piper, read the paper. Went to the library, surrounded myself with books. Ate lunch at the little diner down the street. Tried not to look at my phone.

Okay, so that wasn't part of my normal routine. But I couldn't help myself. Why hadn't Lando called or texted or emailed? Granted, I got a lot of work done, and it looked as if I'd meet my self-imposed deadlines. Until school let out, and the kids showed up.

I didn't pay much attention at first to the teenage boys passing by my table. I figured they were working together on a school project, but they acted as if they'd never been in the library before. A little too noisy, wandering in and out of the aisles, carrying books to random tables and setting them down before wandering off. But the prickle at the back of my neck told me I was being watched, and they were the most likely candidates.

Pretending not to notice, I leafed through a book about the birds and animals that live in Central Park. Lots of pictures, very little information. Tired of the game and wanting to get back to work, I decided to leave my table and see what happened.

I headed to the second level to a spot that overlooked the main floor. It didn't take long for one young man to make a loop around to the table I'd taken over for the day. He looked around suspiciously, reached into his pocket, dropped something on my chair, jerked his head at his friends, and quickly headed out the door. His friends scurried behind. All but one. One stayed, trying to hide behind a nearby carrel.

Very interesting. I waited a few minutes to make sure they were gone and then returned to my "office." There, almost hidden in the shadow created by my coat hanging on the back of the chair, was a small black object.

I swooped up the thumb drive before sitting, wishing I knew the local teenagers better. The last boy exited by the main library doors as I studied the device. Unmarked, no label, nothing to tell me what it contained. Exactly what I'd expected. The only way to find out was to stick it in the USB slot of my laptop and open it. If it was a practical joke, my laptop could get infected by some nefarious virus. Or, it could hold the video that would either clear Jake or damn him back to prison.

It was a risk I needed to take.

Nothing exploded when I plugged the drive in. Good start. The only file listed on it had a string of numbers for the name. Not exactly confidence-boosting, but I'd already made up my mind. With a deep breath, I double-clicked and waited for my laptop to do its thing.

The video—and it was a video, not a virus—started with a scan of the woods, while unseen people, seemingly all male, joked with each other in the background. A row of cans on a fallen tree in the frame appeared as if they'd been used for targets. Occasionally, a puff of smoke would float into the range of the camera. I refused to make any assumptions as to what they were smoking.

The person with the camera played with his zoom feature, and I got the beginnings of a headache as the display moved in and out, in and out. Faintly, in the background, I heard a noise that sounded like a gun being fired. The boy closest to the camera whispered "Shh" and when the others didn't immediately respond, "Shut up!" Being typical teenage boys, they didn't. As the camera zoomed in, the same boy said "Who's that?"

I strained my eyes trying to identify the distant figure. Even zoomed in, I couldn't tell who it was. I flipped the display to full size and wished I'd sprung for a laptop with a bigger screen.

It didn't look like Jake. The man on the film had a heavier build. Not fat, but not trim like Jake, Shorter, too. I sent a silent "thank you" to whichever spirit of goodness listened.

The next few seconds all I saw was the ground passing by as the boy walked. I guessed he was angling to get closer to the unknown individual. The camera was raised again and it rapidly panned the area. My headache worsened. The movement stopped, and the picture blurred as the camera lens zoomed in again.

When it settled, the view of the man was much clearer. Definitely not Jake. And I knew who it was.

Chapter 26

While waiting for Freddie to answer his phone, I shut down my laptop and stuck the thumb drive in my pocket.

"Harmony." He didn't sound happy. I'd interrupted something important, but at the moment, I didn't care.

"Are you in your office?"

"Yes, but I'm busy right now. Can it wait?"

Already on my way out the door, I mouthed my apologies to the lady at the front desk for leaving my stack of books on the table. "I'll be there in five minutes."

"What…" was all he got out of his mouth before I ended the call.

He tried to call me back. I looked at my phone screen long enough to check who was calling and ignored him. He could wait until I got there.

I felt no guilt for what I was about to do. There would be no anonymous email to Freddie or someone else on the force. Okay, a twinge of guilt. I knew there were ways to identify who had taken the video from attached "tags" or whatever they were, but there was no time to get Lando to strip them from the file.

All the parking spots in front of the station were full, and I had to snag one in the lot behind the building. Freddie was impatiently waiting for me in the reception area. "What's so important? I'm busy trying to follow up on the leads we got when the local station aired the video from Mrs. Booker's shooting. Although most of them are useless. Did you remember who it was?"

I pulled the flash drive out of my pocket and waved it in his face. "Better yet. I know who killed Calib Booker."

❋ ❋ ❋

The police chief's office wasn't much fancier than Freddie's. I found that comforting, knowing he wasn't wasting my tax dollars on fancy furniture and ornate decorations. As a matter of fact, his desk appeared to be more beat up than any other one I'd seen in the station.

Freddie always called him "Chief" but luckily the nameplate on his desk faced my direction. Sorenson. I filed the information away.

I'd seen the chief before, but never talked to him.

His job didn't include interviewing librarians with drug trafficking charges. When he walked into his office, I immediately figured out why he was the chief.

The term "command presence" described Sorenson perfectly. He filled the entire room just walking to his chair. I consciously sat up straighter as he took his seat, and so did Freddie. Sorenson folded his hands together on his desk and studied me.

"Miss Duprie," he said with the slightest of nods and absolutely no smile. "What trouble have you brought with you?"

If he wanted to intimidate me, it didn't work. I met his gaze and put the thumb drive on top of a stack of paperwork, careful not to disturb it too much. "The evidence you need to arrest the killer of Calib Booker," I said.

He leaned back, but didn't remove his eyes from my face. I wondered who would win in a stare-down. "Thomason?"

"It's a video supposedly taken the day of the murder. I haven't watched it yet. I brought Harmony and it straight to you."

The chief blinked. I won. "Well, let's take a look."

Freddie joined the chief on the other side of the desk to watch. I studied their reactions as the video played. Rather, I watched Freddie's reactions. The chief's face never changed expression the whole time. When the playback completed, he rubbed his forehead. It must have given him a headache too.

"Where did you get this?" he asked.

"Some boys dropped it in my chair at the library." I grinned apologetically. "I don't know their names."

He closed his eyes for a moment. "But you know how to find out who they are?"

"Yes. At least, I know someone who knows who they are."

He opened his eyes. "The old 'I know someone who knows someone' line?" he asked dryly.

"Something like that. The boys involved don't want to get in trouble."

"I'll deal with that later. And how is this connected to the murder, Miss Duprie?"

"The man in the video? I know who it is."

Sorenson rubbed his forehead again. "Are you going to tell us? Or do you want to play twenty questions?"

As much as I wanted to draw the moment out, I didn't want Sorenson's headache to get any worse. "Eric," I said. "His name is Eric. He works at one of the pawn shops that Calib Booker owns—owned. I didn't catch his last name."

"I'm almost afraid to ask—how do you know?"

Freddie jumped in. "Is that where you bought the ring?"

"Yes, and Eric is the one who sold it to me."

"So let me get this straight. You just happened to

go to a pawn shop owned by a guy murdered on your property, buy a ring from the guy who appears in this video, and later someone breaks into your apartment with an almost identical ring." Sorenson frowned.

"Right." Well, maybe I didn't just "happen" to go to that particular pawnshop, but that was my secret.

"And you just happened to be friends with his wife. Or ex-wife. No, widow."

Now that was truly circumstantial. "Right."

Sorenson looked as if he was in pain. "And you just happened to be with her last night when somebody shot at her again. You and your boyfriend."

"Ex-boyfriend. Other than that, right."

Sorenson opened a drawer, ripped open a package of headache powders and dumped them in his mouth, followed by a swig of coffee. "And is there any chance you saw the video from the store the night Mrs. Booker got shot?"

"I did. But I didn't recognize the guy. Although I suppose it's possible it was the same person. I thought he looked familiar, but I couldn't figure out why."

The crumpled wrapper from the medicine made a perfect arc in the air and landed squarely in the waste-paper basket. "Thomason, did they recover shell casings from all three crime scenes?"

"I haven't seen a report on last night's yet," Freddie said. "But the guns used in the murder and the first shooting were both .45 calibers."

"Miss Duprie, can you provide us with the address of the pawn shop?" Sorenson asked, the lines on his forehead getting deeper.

"Absolutely. It's still programmed into my phone."

"I'll get it from her," Freddie said. "Then I'll call local law enforcement."

"This doesn't solve the case, Miss Duprie."

"No, but it gives you a place to start. Once you find out what Eric's last name is, you'll need to figure out motive and opportunity. Of course, you'll want other witnesses. Find the kid who made the video and question him and his friends. Try to find out if he owns a gun that matches the bullets recovered at the scene. Get a subpoena for Eric's phone records so you can place him here at the time of the murder," I rattled off. I'd been thinking about it on the way.

Sorenson held up one hand. I closed my mouth. "You've been very helpful, now let us take over and do our jobs," he said. "Please?"

I told him I would. And I meant to keep my word, really I did.

The long-overdue trip to Gary's pawn shop was next on the agenda. Jake might not be able to carry, but I could. I don't know whether I'd be able to shoot to kill, but I could certainly shoot to scare. While he waited on other customers, I glanced through the piles of used books, not spotting anything of interest.

"No new books," he said when everyone else left. "I would have called you if there was anything exciting."

"That's not why I'm here. I'm looking for a gun."

His right eyebrow shot up. "You too? You wouldn't believe how many people have been in here looking for a handgun in the last week or so. I bet half of them return them in six months."

Darn, that meant the bargains would be gone.

"I've been thinking about getting one for a while and now seemed as good of a time as any." I sighed. "But if your selection is limited, I'll come back later."

"There're still a few in stock." He jerked his head towards the back room where his firearms were kept in locked cases. "Come take a gander."

"All the shootings around here got you scared?" Gary asked as he laid a couple of handguns on the counter for me to examine.

"The one last night did." I shook my head at the pink derringer he added to the display. So not my style. He grinned and put it back.

"I didn't think so. Never should have bought this one, but the lady traded up. So what happened last night that was any different?"

The grapevine must have broken. "I was there. I don't think I was the target, but I don't want to assume the best and discover the worst."

Gary whistled a low note. "You going to leave it at your place or are you planning to haul it around in that fancy car of yours?"

"I already have a concealed-carry permit, so I want one I can tuck under the seat. I can't get a gun small enough to fit in the glove compartment that holds more than one or two rounds." I eyed the ones he'd chosen. "What do you have in a .9mm?"

An hour and a boatload of paperwork later, I walked out with a sweet little Beretta and cleaning kit. Yeah, like the original James Bond gun. It didn't have enough firepower to rescue Eli from the clutches of the mad scientist who'd kidnapped him, but for personal defense, it was just right.

While my supper warmed up in the oven, and as I cleaned my new possession, I called Lando, not willing to sit and wait for him to call me.

"Any word?" I asked as a greeting.

"None," he answered glumly. "Darla is going to go talk to his parents tomorrow. It's like he dropped off the face of the earth. We're hoping they have some clue where he might be."

"You tried tracking his cell phone?"

"It's either out of range of a cell tower or turned off."

"He didn't buy an airline ticket?"

"Not that I can find. And his bank account is locked down so tight I can't access it."

Made sense, with Eli being a security guru.

Having almost singlehandedly solved the murder

of Calib Booker, I felt like I should be able to solve the disappearance of Eli Hennessey. Maybe I should become a private investigator after all. "You checked local hospitals?"

"Yes, but if he was admitted as a privacy patient the staff wouldn't be able to tell me anything. I asked, and none of the medical centers here have any patients with loss of memory at the moment."

That gave me a new idea for research. Check news reports along the East Coast for accident victims with amnesia.

"I don't get it," Lando admitted. "There's a lot I don't know about Eli, but this isn't like him at all."

That's what worried me.

Chapter 27

Wednesday morning found me back at the library, pretending everything was back to normal. Which it wasn't. I'd packed a suitcase and stashed it in my trunk, ready to head south and look for Eli. My new "toy" lay nestled under the driver's seat. But Freddie called me before I left my place to see if I'd be available to take a look at pictures of boys from the high school. I cursed at the bad timing but I was glad the police moved quickly with the investigation. Jake called shortly after that to take me to lunch. He wanted to talk privately, and there would be no chance to do that at Girls' Night Out with his attention focused on Lori. And Will, the electrician, wanted me to check the progress of the wiring job at the old house.

So I was stuck in Oak Grove for another day. Besides, I needed to call Lando and get the make, model, color and tag of Eli's car so I'd know what to hunt for. And to ask for a head shot of Eli. The pictures I had were profile shots, taken on the sly. He claimed to have an allergy to cameras.

It was surprisingly hard to find reports of patients without names. Patient privacy restrictions and all that, I guessed. And in the sparse newspaper reports I found, the patients had been there for weeks. Not Eli.

The next step would be to alert law enforcement in all the states between Orlando and Oak Grove. That was a decision for Eli's parents to make, not me.

Freddie showed up mid-morning, carrying several books. I cleared a spot for him to put them down. "Didn't want to make you come to the station for this," he said. "These are yearbooks from the high school. Can you go through them and see if you recognize the boy who left the flash drive for you?"

"I'm not sure he'll admit to leaving it," I said, leafing through the top book. They all looked so young, and I wondered when I'd gotten old.

Leaning over my shoulder, Freddie watched as I ran my finger across the rows of pictures. I stopped at the image of a boy with a rakish smile and looked at the name underneath. "Is that the kid?" Freddie asked.

"No, that's Janine's sister's boy, Rafael. I guess good looks run in the family."

The next photo I stopped at was Sam's. Between her hair being done up in ringlets and the lacy black blouse she wore, she reminded me of a heroine on the cover of a romance book. "One of the volunteers here," I explained to Freddie's sigh.

It didn't take long to move through the seniors and onto the juniors. That's where the faces became familiar. I took my time studying two boys with similar haircuts and clothing, and wished the pictures were in color instead of black and white.

"That's him," I said finally, tapping the picture. The name underneath read "George Maracle."

"No wonder he didn't want to be identified," Freddie muttered.

I turned and raised an inquiring eyebrow at him.

He shook his head. "There *are* things I can't tell you."

I was good with that. As long as he realized there were things I couldn't tell him either. I closed the book and handed it back to him. "Anything else?"

"Not now. I appreciate the information." He took a few steps towards the door, then came back. "By the way, I might see you tonight. Sarah's after me to come to Girls' Night out."

Girls' Night out was quickly becoming no such thing. It might be time to revisit the unwritten rules. Sure, I'd broken them a couple of times myself, but the exceptions were becoming the norm. "Later then," I said with a polite smile.

Jake arrived around eleven-thirty. I played with, and discarded, the concept of buying an appointment book to schedule my visitors. But he did offer to pay for lunch, and I'd accepted, so I had no right to complain. I even let him drive Dolores to the restaurant at the edge of town, one of the national chains. Not my normal pick, but his treat, his choice. He waited until we were almost finished eating to reveal what was on his mind.

"Any word on Eli?" he asked. The expression on my face was the only answer he needed, I guess, because he reached across the table and patted my hand. "He'll be okay."

"How can you be so sure?" I asked setting down my fork, no longer hungry.

"You do any research on him?"

"Didn't do any good. There's next to nothing out there about him on the internet. He keeps a low profile."

The discussion didn't bother Jake's appetite any, and the conversation lagged while he finished his chicken. "I mentioned he served in the military, didn't I?" he asked as he pushed his plate towards the edge of the table.

"Yes, but I have no way of accessing those records. Besides, you didn't say which branch."

"Army. Ranger. Look it up," Jake said as he finished off the last breadstick. "He was involved in some serious shit. Classified stuff. Probably where he got his interest in security."

"Why are you telling me?"

"Because he can take care of himself. You're worrying too much."

Maybe and maybe not. I reminded myself to fill the gas tank before my meeting with Will. I'd leave my suitcase in the trunk overnight.

❋ ❋ ❋

A booth wouldn't hold everyone, so we pushed a couple of tables together. Al didn't mind because the restaurant had fewer customers than normal. I wondered if the shootings had anything to do with it.

The odd girl out, I sat at the end of the table. Sarah and Freddie were together, Jake was so attached to Lori that they looked like a couple, and Janine had forced her newest boyfriend, Pete, to come along. Even Merrilee had brought a friend—at least it was a she—Georgette. I wasn't sure if they were a couple or not and didn't have the right opportunity to ask. That left me.

Although we weren't in our normal booth, I made sure I had a seat facing the front door. I tried not to watch each time it opened but Janine caught me as my head twisted enough so I could see past Freddie. "Expecting someone?" She grinned. "Eli?"

No matter how much I wished otherwise, I didn't expect him. "No, he only shows up in the mornings," I told her nonchalantly. But something felt out of kilter, like the stars weren't aligning correctly or life was preparing to send me down a rabbit hole. If trouble walked in the front door, I'd recognize it.

I wasn't the only one keeping an eye out. Both Jake and Freddie were in full on-guard mode. Still, when the party split up early, I blamed myself for being the Downer Debbie responsible. So when Lori waxed poetic in her admiration for Dolores, I offered to take her home. Jake would take her car and we'd meet up at her place. What could go wrong?

* * *

Some rules are made to be broken, but I cursed under my breath as I used voice commands to call Jake's burner phone and prayed he'd answer.

"Harmony."

"Jake. Behind you."

Lori and I had taken the long way to her place to give her a feel for what the Jag could do while Jake took the straightest path. and stopped at a convenience store on the way as planned, so now, about half a mile from her apartment, we'd caught up to him. But he wasn't alone. A dark-colored car was behind him, and its rear lights were out. I suspected the headlights were off as well. I flicked the switch to put Dolores into dark mode. The overhead streetlights radiated enough light for the chase.

"I got it," he responded, the tension in his voice matching mine. "Can you read the plate?"

"No. You headed to the police station?" I asked. I turned to Lori long enough to see her pulling out her cell phone. I mouthed 911 and she nodded.

"That would be the smart move," Jake's voice sounded like he was in a tunnel. He'd put the phone on speaker to free up both hands. "I don't think this car can handle much more than standard stop-and-go driving."

Lori was talking to someone and, assuming it was the police, I blocked her out to concentrate on Jake and the car in front of me. If this was the same guy who'd attacked us the previous night, he was desperate to try again so soon. That made him doubly dangerous.

Jake knew the streets almost as well as I did. When he made an abrupt right hand turn, I knew he'd followed my advice. I had to back off when the second car almost missed the turn and braked sharply. "This guy isn't a trained driver," I said loudly. "That gives you an advantage." Jake would need every bit of skill he had to maintain a safe distance in the underpowered car he drove.

"It also means he's likely to make stupid mistakes. Hang back as far as you can."

"He doesn't know we're here from the looks of things."

"The police want you both to pull over and wait for them," Lori said softly.

I nodded, and asked "Did you catch that, Jake?"

"Yes, and it's not going to happen. We'd be putting Lori in more danger than she is already. The safest place for her to be right now is with you."

Actually, she'd be safer if I abandoned the chase but that might be signing Jake's death certificate. He made another hard right, and again, the driver in between squealed his tires as he changed direction. As I made the turn, I heard a "POP." Whose car backfired?

"Shit!"

"What?" I asked.

"He put a hole in the back window. Sorry, Lori."

"You okay?" she asked.

"Yeah."

I leaned over and reached for my pistol under the seat. Wordlessly, while straightening back up, I laid it in my lap. "Shall we even things up a little?" I asked no one in particular as I rolled down my window.

"What are you talking about?" Jake asked.

"She has a gun!" Lori squeaked.

Jake chuckled as he swung Lori's car to the left. "You keep doing things to make me love you, Angel."

As he passed through a puddle of light cast by a store's marquee, I caught another "POP." The back window of Lori's car shattered.

"Fuck!" There was a pause and then Jake said in a strained voice, "Get out of here! Get Lori someplace safe."

"Are you all right?"

"The engine's overheating."

I knew it was more than that and figured that either the last bullet hit Jake or broken glass from the window had. Time to even the score. I clicked off the safety.

With the Beretta held in my left hand, I didn't expect to hit anything, I stuck it out of the window and squeezed the trigger. If I got lucky I would scare off the assailant. There wasn't any reaction on his part, so I assumed I'd missed. I brought the gun back inside to cock it when a puff of smoke came from the front of Lori's car. Her car jerked to the right and rolled to a stop. The other driver pulled in behind him.

"Get down and stay in the car," I hissed to Lori. Her face paled, but she nodded and slumped as far as the tight quarters allowed.

I threw Dolores into park and jumped out, gun in hand. With the memory of the action scenes in every cop show ever, I used the car door as a shield. "Drop your gun," I ordered, in the deepest voice I could summon.

The man seemed confused as he climbed out of his vehicle, unsure which car to target. I flicked on Dolores' headlights. He raised one hand to shield his eyes in the sudden flood of light. Hearing sirens nearby, I hoped he'd stay confused long enough for them to arrive. No such luck. He raised his gun my direction and fired.

Chapter 28

Thank God for strong doors. I ducked, heard the bullet hit and winced. That would be a hell of a story to explain to the insurance company. He didn't have a car door to hide behind, and I took my time before I shot.

My gun instructor had drilled it into my head to aim for center mass. I must have pulled my shot at the last second when I recognized him. It was tougher to shoot someone you'd talked to before than a paper target. The man's right side jerked and he dropped his weapon. His left hand rose to his right shoulder and he fell to his knees.

"Bitch!" he screamed, scrambling for his gun.

I cocked my .9mm and rose. "Don't move or the next one won't be a shoulder shot," I said smoothly, bluffing as if that's where I'd meant to hit him. "Lori," I called over my shoulder, "Tell them they need an ambulance too."

He glanced at me and took the chance. He reached for his gun and I fired. The bullet hit the pavement and ricocheted, grazing his hand. My headlights illuminated him and showed the blood dripping from the wound as he pulled his hand to his body.

"Who the hell are you?" he yelled.

I couldn't resist. "Your worst enemy." I cocked the Beretta praying I wouldn't need to shoot again. "Back away from the gun or the next shot won't be a warning." I needed to take him out of action. I wasn't sure I could shoot to kill.

"No way in hell am I going to give up to a *girl*," he said, lurching for the gun.

I steadied my breath, preparing to fire. But suddenly the man tumbled forward. Jake had snuck up behind him and kicked him in the back. Another kick sent the gun flying, out of reach of either one of them.

"Don't want to give the cops a chance to think I'm armed and dangerous," he said jokingly, clutching his right arm. I heard the pain through his chuckle.

"How bad is it?" I asked, keeping my eye on the man on the ground.

"I'll survive."

The man on the ground made an attempt to get up, and with a solid kick to his rear, Jake put him down again. Then the light from the first police car flashed on the scene, and Jake backed away, one hand in the air.

Even Chief Sorenson showed up on the scene, a solid pillar among the flashing lights and strobes of police cars, ambulances, and wrecker trucks. "I thought we had an agreement, Miss Duprie," he said, arms crossed and staring down at me.

I was too busy watching the EMT's treat Jake to worry about the chief's anger. "I fully intended to honor the agreement when we made it," I told him. "But circumstances got in the way."

He sighed. "I'll need you down at the station to make a statement." Jake was being forced to lay on a stretcher and Sorenson noticed the focus of my attention. "You can make sure your friend is all right, but don't keep me waiting all night." He turned sharply on one heel and went to talk to his officers on the scene.

I forced a smile onto my face and walked over to where the paramedics were arranging a blanket over Jake's shoulders. His coat had disappeared, and one sleeve of his shirt was cut off and discarded to give the paramedics access to his injury. "How bad is it?" I asked.

"Flesh wound, but he'll need to be in the hospital at least overnight for observation," said one of the medical technicians. "The docs want him on a course of antibiotics to prevent infection, and he'll get dosed up with pain meds too."

"Against my better judgment," Jake grumbled.

I stroked his left cheek. The right one had cuts caused by flying shards of glass, and I wondered if that's what my face had looked like not too long ago.

"Any idea who that guy is?" Jake asked. Even with the blanket, I could tell he was shivering, either from the cold or from shock.

I tucked the blanket around him a little tighter. "His name is Eric. I think he killed the guy they found at the house, too."

Jake's eyes got big. "And you faced him down? Hell, do you realize the risk you took?"

"But here I am."

One of the EMTs coughed. "We need to get him in the ambulance for transport now."

Before I stepped away, I leaned over and kissed Jake. Not a passionate, soul-shaking kiss, but a warm kiss between friends. Sometimes a kiss is just a kiss.

The squeal of tires spinning out on pavement caught my attention. I turned to see a souped-up, bright yellow Dodge Charger roaring down the cross street, just beyond the barricades.

I knew that car like I knew Dolores. And there was only one person who should be driving it.

"Chief Sorenson," I called. "You have a spare officer to follow that car?"

He looked at me questioningly, but Officer McReedy hopped into his patrol car and turned on his light bar. "Why?" the chief asked.

"That's Jake's car," I explained. "And the only person with access to it has been missing for a week."

He nodded, and one of the officers handed him a radio. McReedy was already out of sight. "You want him brought back here?"

I'd had my fill of drama for the night. "If it's Elijah Hennessey driving, tell him to call his mother and his secretary. They're worried about him. If it's anyone else, that's up to you."

He relayed instructions into the radio, then looked at me and shook his head. "You're going to tell me that story too. You need a ride to the station? Or is your car still drivable?"

One bullet hole wasn't enough to put Dolores out of action. "I'll follow you there."

❈ ❈ ❈

No amount of caffeine was going to be enough to keep me awake much longer. My statement was on file, taken by one of the other officers, and now it was a matter of waiting. I'd dosed off several times while Sorenson talked to other people in his office while I waited in his secretary's cubicle. At least it gave me the illusion of privacy when I laid my head on my folded arms on top of her desk.

Lori went with Freddie to give her statement. He'd shown up in the same clothes he's worn at the Flamingo, but rumpled, and I wondered if I'd interrupted him and Sarah again. That had been over an hour ago, and I hoped Freddie or one of the officers had taken Lori home. But the chief wanted to talk to me personally. So I waited, filling the time drinking coffee and dosing off.

If I'd been a little more daring, I would have tried to access the computer that took up half of her desktop. All that information at my fingertips and I couldn't get to any of it. If the chief wanted to punish me, there wasn't a better way to do it. In fact, it counted as cruel and unusual punishment in my opinion, and I bet I could have convinced the Supreme Court to rule in my favor. But I was too tired and too stressed to be daring.

"Sorry to keep you waiting so long, Miss Duprie." Sorenson's deep voice startled me, and I jerked awake. "I'm ready for you now."

I mumbled, "It's okay," and followed him to his office. A coffee-maker had appeared on his desk, along with a stack of foam cups. With an inclination of his head, he indicated the pot and the cups, and with an inclination of mine, I accepted. With his cup full, he opened a desk drawer, took out a package of headache powders, tore open the foil wrapper, and dumped the contents into his mouth, to be followed by a swig of coffee. Then he crumpled the wrapper and, with a perfect arc, tossed it into his trash can. He cleared his throat.

"Now, Miss Duprie," he said, "Let's get down to business, shall we? I've developed a list of potential charges against you. Exhibition driving, ignoring the lawful commands of an officer, discharging a weapon in an unsafe manner, discharging a weapon inside city limits, oh, and my favorite, driving under the influence. I have witnesses that will attest to the fact you were drinking at the Pink Flamingo."

One beer with supper doesn't meet the standards for drinking and driving. I reached for my cell phone. "I'm not saying a word without my lawyer present."

Sorenson rubbed his forehead. "Put away the phone, Miss Duprie, you don't need your lawyer. If I attempted to press a single charge against you, half the force would have my head, the mayor would have my job, and the local press would tar and feather me." His mouth twitched. "As it is, I should offer you a job."

I considered it for a couple of seconds. Officer Harmony Duprie, Or Detective Harmony Duprie. Then I remembered what our police officers do most of the time. Write tickets and follow up reports of loud music. No thank you.

"I've reviewed the statement you gave to Officer McReedy," Sorenson said as he refilled his coffee cup. I wondered if the caffeine was what gave him his headaches. "And your statement is in sync with the other witnesses." So why was I there? "But I have the feeling you know more than what you've told us. Is there anything else you'd like to share?"

It would be nice to have someone to share my secrets with. It was hard keeping them to myself. I caught myself as I opened my mouth and turned it into a yawn.

"I'm sorry, I'm not sure I understand," I said innocently, blinking my eyes.

Sorenson actually smiled for a second. "I tried. How about if I make you a paid consultant? Answering directly to me?"

Maybe it was because I was so tired, or that the offer came out of nowhere, but it took me a while to process what he had asked. "What are you trying to accomplish exactly?" I asked.

"Three things. One, I need a good explanation for the esteemed members of the City Council when they ask why our town's ex-librarian is solving crimes my highly trained law enforcement professionals can't. Two, I want to make use of your sources, whoever they are. Three, and this may be the most important," he leaned forward and stared at me, "I want to be able to offer you training. You keep getting yourself into situations where you need protection, and we can't provide it. If I can make sure you have the tools you need to protect yourself, I'll sleep a little better at nights." He slid my Beretta across the desk to me. It had been taken as part of the investigation. "For one, I need you to learn how to shoot."

I blushed. "I just bought it. Haven't even taken it to the range to sight it in and get used to it."

"And it showed tonight."

He was right and I knew it. I also knew I wouldn't take him up on his offer.

"I'll think about what you said but I can't give you an answer right now. Besides, how many times can lightning hit in the same place?"

"Have you forgotten the man we're holding for breaking into your place? He's still not talking."

Shit, I had forgotten in the night's events. "Is he tied to Eric?" I asked excitedly. "That's the only person who knew about my ring. And did you ever get any more information on the ring he had? Was it stolen?"

Sorenson rubbed his forehead again. "Please consider my offer, Miss Duprie."

"I will," I promised as I re-arranged the things in my purse to make room for the gun.

"Before you go," he said. "What's the story with Elijah Hennessey?"

The tears came too easily and I blinked them away. "I don't have the answer for that. All I know is he wasn't in touch with his friends and co-workers in Florida, he wasn't taking my calls, and no one knew where he was." It was weird he just happened to show up when he did.

The chief took a piece of paper out of his shirt pocket. "According to what he told McReedy, he's employed by a company named Shifter Technologies and they're trying to sell us a new, more secure system for our records."

Owns the company, but I decided not to reveal that bit of information "Yes." In fact, Eli had probably read the report the chief held in his hand.

"The gossip is that the two of you are romantically involved."

"We were," I answered, tight lipped.

"And he's cousin to Jake Hennessey, who you were involved with previously?"

I nodded.

He sighed and shook his head. I imagined my

father reacting the same way. "I'm not even going to try to give you advice about that situation," he said. "My head hurts just thinking about it."

Mine too.

"But there's a good chance Matthew Elijah Hennessey is still in town. McReedy fed him a line about clearly being too tired to drive and threatening him with arrest for impaired driving if he didn't find a place to stay."

My heart leaped, but my head couldn't figure out whether that was good news or bad news.

"There's one more thing that bothers me, Miss Duprie," he said, as he stood, dismissing me. "How the hell did you manage to turn Jake Hennessey, the town's villain, into a hero?"

Chapter 29

If he was still in town, he'd be at the Towers, Eli that was. Hopefully Jake was fast asleep or busy flirting with his nurses. Either one worked for me.

I considered driving by the Towers to see if Jake's car was there. Jake would be thrilled to death to have it back. But I wasn't excited by the concept of Eli spotting me driving through the parking lot, so I chickened out and went straight home. If he wanted to talk, he could come to me. He knew where to find me.

Which is why I half expected to see the yellow Charger parked on the street, in the same place that Jake parked so many times. My heart broke a little more when the spot was empty.

Before crawling into bed to get a few hours' sleep, I sent Lando a text message. *"Eli spotted. Apparently in good health. No guarantee how long said condition will last."* I really didn't expect Lando to answer, but my phone played its notification tune a few minutes later. *"Don't kill him before I do."*

The paper didn't carry it, but the stares I got at the library told me the news was out. So I built my castle of books higher than normal to hide behind them better and buried myself in medieval Europe.

The call from the hospital to pick Jake up timed perfectly with my lunch break. We stopped to fill his prescriptions and for fast food on the way back to the hotel. We ate in his room and I stayed long enough to make sure he fell asleep before leaving. I didn't mention anything about the Charger to Jake, which turned out to be a smart move, because I didn't spot it at the hotel. Had Eli already left town?

There was no doubt in my mind why. He'd been listening to the police scanner and caught my name or Jake's name. Or, he'd spotted Dolores and knew where she was, so was I. Or he tracked me using the app he'd put on my cell phone. Eli had seen that kiss.

But I was too stubborn to track him down and apologize for something I didn't regret doing. Plus, he was the one who had been ignoring me and everyone else. No, he needed to come to me and ask for forgiveness, not the other way around.

Normally no one touched my pile of books when

I left for lunch, but exceptions happened. Like then. It looked as if a preschooler sat on the table and threw books everywhere. Thank heavens the ladies at the front desk allowed me to leave my laptop and scanner with them. I thought about asking Mabel if she'd seen anything, but even with her glasses she was almost blind.

Still fuming, I started the process of re-stacking the books the way I wanted, the books I was most likely to refer to on top. As I moved one, I spotted a piece of paper folded in half. On the outside, in hand-printed block letters, it said "Treasure Hunt." Curious, I opened up the note. It read "Let them eat cake."

If that was the quality of the rest of the clues, the game would be over quickly. Still, it would distract me for a little while. I figured the next clue would be one of two places—and bibliographies were on the first floor, so that's where I started.

By the time I found the fourth clue, things got tougher. "Old Smokey"—did that refer to the old folk song, somewhere in the Smoky Mountains, or one of the singers who made the song famous? I finally found the next clue in the travel section in a book about Gatlinburg.

By now, I'd attracted the attention of Janine and a couple of the volunteers. As I found each clue, they spat out ideas on the meanings, and scurried around the library trying to help me find the next one. While the group of middle-aged and older women tried to figure out what "Hell's Half-Acre" was, Janine pulled me aside.

"Any idea who did this?" she asked quietly.

"I figured it was you or someone else who works here. But unless one of them," I waved a hand toward the group huddled together over a computer, "is an awfully good actor, that theory is shot all to hell."

"What bothers me most is that someone set this up and no one on my staff noticed," she admitted.

My heart caught for just a second when she called them her staff. How often had I dreamed of being in her position? "I didn't want to bring that up." Truthfully, it worried me too.

"Got it!" someone called from the magazine section where the library had an extensive collection of National Geographic's. "And it's the last clue!" So much for keeping quiet and not disturbing the other patrons. Janine shrugged her shoulders and we followed the crowd to find out where we would be sent next. The paper was thrust into my hands.

"I guess I get to read it," I said with a false grin. I made a show of opening the paper and folding it back again. "It said," and I paused dramatically and looked around "Jewel of the Nile."

"Too easy," said one of the volunteers. "It's an old movie. Do we have it in the DVD collection?" The group herded themselves off to find out.

I wasn't so sure. Maybe it referred to the actor who played the jewel, or the movie's soundtrack, or had nothing to do with the movie at all. "Does the library have any books on Egyptian jewelry?" I asked Janine, who had stayed behind with me.

She looked thoughtful. "I think we do. The 730's?"

"Or the 390's. Meet you back here."

I wanted to be the one to find the prize at the end of the game. The prize might be the identity of its creator. Or, if my hopes were fulfilled, I might find the actual person at the end.

I scanned the shelf, eying the books on jewelry, trying to find one just enough out of place to let me know it had been handled recently. Easier than trying to go through each book individually. One book stuck out half an inch further on the shelf than any other. A likely candidate although the title told me it was about U.S. art deco jewelry of the 1920's. When I rifled through the pages and came up empty-handed, I decided it was a decoy and returned it to its spot.

But when I spotted the book perfectly aligned with all the others, but out of order, my scalp tingled. The title made it even more likely this was the book I needed, "The Art of Modern Egyptian Jewelry." I glanced around, hoping to see who had set up the game. I'd convinced myself it was Eli, and he was hiding around a corner, waiting to present me with a bouquet. But as I opened the book, two pieces of paper fluttered out. No one appeared to congratulate me.

I picked up the folded papers and opened the

heavier one first. It read "Congratulations!" and attached was a gift certificate for Mama D's. The second one, taped shut, read "For your eyes only." I slipped it into my pants pocket before putting the book back on the shelf, in the correct spot. Then I walked out into the main floor waving the first piece of paper in the air.

"That was fun," Janine said later as I shelved the day's research materials and got ready to go.

"Except for the whole creep factor of not knowing who set it up."

"There is that," she sighed. "But it would be a good thing to add to the training program for our volunteers."

"Only if you could set it for after hours. Some of the more elderly patrons were upset by the commotion."

Janine started to laugh, but turned it into a cough. "You mean Mrs. Dean? She gets upset if someone accidentally closes a book too hard. I'm not worried about her. Will you help me?"

I nodded. "Let me know when you're ready. We can brainstorm over drinks."

It was hard waiting until I got home to pull the wrinkled paper out of my pocket and open it. It was the longest message of all. "Please meet me for supper tonight. Location: The Aldridge House. Time: Ten PM. Menu: Italian. Come alone."

I searched for any hidden clues in the unsigned note, a double meaning in the words, invisible ink, anything, and came up empty handed. I knew the risk I'd be taking if I went. I remembered Chief Sorenson's concern that I needed more skills to be able to protect myself. I tried to talk myself out of it, I really did.

At precisely ten o'clock I pulled into the driveway of the house. I'd debated what to wear, not knowing who I was going to meet, and settled for my best-fitting jeans and my favorite silky blue blouse. Not that anyone could see the blouse under my winter coat. In light of the situation, I settled for flats instead of heels because I might find myself in a situation where I needed to run. There wasn't another car in the driveway. Had I been stood up?

The front porch light was on, no other lights shone in the windows. I probably needed to buy a case of light bulbs for the interior. The door was locked, and after unlocking it, I opened it slowly. It was the perfect setup for an elaborate practical joke. I peeked inside and spotted what appeared to be the flickering of candles in the front room.

"Thanks for showing up so promptly. Please, come in and shut the door. We don't want anyone calling the police because they think someone has broken in. Wine, Harmony, or should I say, Martha?"

I gulped, and my mouth went dry. Wine sounded like a really, really good idea. "Harmony is fine, Orson." I looked around. "You went to a lot of work to set this up."

He'd cleaned a spot in the living room and arranged a picnic on a blanket on the floor. A few candles provided the lighting, and I spotted a small heater off to one side. And clearly, he'd hit Mama D's up for take-out because I could see containers of everything from salad to lasagna to cheesecake for dessert. Heavy paper plates and plastic silverware were neatly arranged at either end of the blanket.

He chuckled. "I had fun doing it. Between the damned dog that lives downstairs from you, and how busy your life has been the past few days, I needed to get creative. It was the only way I could get you alone."

"You found out a lot about me in just a couple of days." I rocked uneasily, heel to toe, and considered running.

"The receptionist at the newspaper office was most helpful. Once I figured out your real name, the rest came easy. You've made the news more than once."

Wasn't that the truth.

"They splashed your picture on the screen on one of the TV news reports. Made it easy for me to find you." He grinned. "The food's getting cold. Take off your coat and stay awhile."

Once I'd shrugged my coat off, I discovered the little heater did a good job of warming the room. I sat and picked up the glass of wine he'd poured for me, a nice Cabernet Sauvignon.

"Oh, before we get started," he said, grinning, before he pulled a knife from his belt and gently tossed it halfway between us. He cocked his head and looked at me expectantly.

I matched his smile as I took my cell phone out of my purse, turned it off, removed the battery, and set it down by his knife.

His smile got bigger as he pulled up his pant leg and took the second knife out of its case and placed it with the first.

I studied the collection and his face, then reached behind me. I'd left my blouse untucked for a reason. With a smooth motion, I pulled my Beretta from my belt, slid out the clip, ejected the bullet loaded in the chamber and laid everything on the blanket. Orson's eyes widened, narrowed and then returned to normal as he tracked each movement.

"You continue to astound me," he said, shaking his head. "Did you have that with you when we met? I didn't feel it, and I checked."

"No. But after getting shot at the other night, I decided it was time to even things up. I've been taking lessons and already had my permit."

His smile lit up his face. "I'm afraid I don't have anything to match that. If I can't dazzle you with my arsenal, I'll have to amaze you with my wit."

Chapter 30

It was not how I'd expected to spend my evening, sitting in a partially gutted house sharing a meal and pleasant conversation with a wanted man. Or maybe he wasn't wanted anymore because the fake Orson had somehow cleared his name. Trying to figure it out gave me a headache.

As entertaining as the man and his stories were, I kept expecting the other shoe to drop. Or knife, or something. I didn't believe he'd gone to all this work just to feed me. As I finished of the last bite of cheesecake and picked up my napkin to wipe my lips, he suddenly asked "Can you get your hands on that ring?"

I knew without asking which ring he was talking about. "You're not serious?" I sputtered. A small nod of his head told me that indeed, he wasn't joking.

"You know, I never touched it. And I have no

way of getting it out of the station's property room if that's where it is."

"Too bad," Orson said. "I heard of a party willing to pay a pretty penny for it. Ten years ago, I would have considered accepting the challenge, but no more."

"I'll pass the word along," I said. "The chief may want to move it somewhere more secure." That's all he needed, was for evidence to be stolen out from under his nose.

Orson raised his eyebrows. "Won't he ask how you found out?"

"He will, and I won't tell him." I emptied my wine glass. "He offered me a job with the department, but I won't accept it. I don't want to be under any obligation to reveal my sources. As it stands, I can always tell him I saw it on the internet in an underground forum and he has no way to prove me wrong."

"You won't do it in exchange for information to help clear Hennessey?"

It was my turn to arch an eyebrow. "I am fully aware that what I'm doing skirts the law sometimes," I said. "But I have my limitations. Actually stealing something would cross the line so far it would erase it. No, not even to clear Jake's name."

"Good. I hoped that would be your answer. I haven't misjudged you."

And I hoped he planned to share the information anyway.

"I haven't been able to find out who stole the

necklace in question." Orson emptied the last of the wine into his glass. "However, I'm pretty sure it was an inside job. And the person who did it forgot one rule of stealing something of that uniqueness and value. You need to have a buyer lined up first. Otherwise, all you can do is strip the individual stones out and sell them in small lots. When you do that, the profit margin goes way down and it's not worth the risk."

"I thought Stephen Sallis wanted it?"

"He did. But he didn't want to pay for it. In fact, he put out a contract for whoever had it."

"So when Jake gave me the fake necklace the thief seized the opportunity to plant false information to make it seem like Jake had stolen it," I said, thinking out loud. "And when things got too hot, and he had to ditch it, he somehow snuck into my apartment and stashed it. Then he dropped hints about the location to the right—or wrong—people."

"That sums it up nicely."

"But how does that tie into the ring?"

Orson frowned. "I haven't figured that out. I can't determine if the ring is stolen. If it was, it was from someone who didn't report it to the police. A collector, perhaps, who knew it was stolen when he or she acquired it years ago."

I noisily blew out a deep breath. "Still doesn't explain how it has anything to do with me."

"Or your friend Hennessey."

"Or my friend Hennessey," I agreed.

We put the remains of the feast in the dumpster out back, hidden under discarded construction materials. The temperature had dropped, and the cold seeped through my coat. "Do you have someplace to stay tonight?" I asked Orson.

"I'll be hitting the road," he answered. "I've been in town too long already."

"Afraid someone will begin to ask questions if you hang around?"

"Something like that. Besides, my work here is done."

"Your work?" I hadn't heard of any robberies in the last couple of days. Of course, I'd been too busy trying to avoid looking at news about me to read the paper thoroughly.

"As I told you, I don't like owing people," he said, as he watched me lock the door. I'd already checked to make sure the kitchen window was closed as securely as possible. That was how he'd gotten in. "And now I don't owe you."

I hesitated. What was the proper procedure for saying good-bye to someone like Orson? I considered giving him a hug, but opted to hold out my hand instead. "Thank you. It's been a pleasure meeting you."

Even though it was after midnight, I didn't want to go home. Orson, as interesting as he'd been, struck me as a lonely person. I felt that way sometimes. Lately, even when I was with friends, I felt alone and disconnected. It was hard keeping secrets and having no one to share them with. So I drove around town aimlessly for a while. Oak Hill traffic after midnight was so slow that the traffic lights at the minor intersections were set to flash yellow. I drove by The Towers more than once, but didn't spot a Charger on any of my trips. Eli must have gone home.

❋ ❋ ❋

They'd driven me out of the library, the all-too-perky reporter and her cameraman from a Pittsburgh station. Thank heavens, Janine had sternly informed them they were not allowed to film in the library, so they didn't get a sound bite to use for their newscast. While they waited for me out front, Janine took me out the staff entrance in the back and I escaped unseen. But I was afraid to go home, in case they'd staked it out too, so I was trying to find things to keep myself busy.

I made a trip to the garage to talk to Nikos, the owner. I didn't think he could repair the damage to Dolores, but figured he would suggest a good body shop.

He walked around her, sighing, shaking his head, muttering to himself and occasionally rubbing a spot of dirt from her body. Finally he squatted by the driver's door and ran his finger over the hole. "It's a shame," he said. "To have this fine piece of machinery abused like this."

"I didn't have much choice," I said testily, defending myself.

"Oh, not you. You did what you needed to do." He clucked his tongue. "This is something I can't fix. But I can recommend just the guy to help you out. I'll get you his information."

Then I met Will at the Aldridge house. His crew had finished and I needed to sign off on the paperwork. In my inexpert opinion, it looked as if they'd done a nice job, and I gladly paid. Luke, Joe and I could finally start serious work on the interior.

Next stop was at Jane's liquor store. Mornings were slow for her, so she had time to chat. We sat in her office in the back while she kept an eye on the front by watching the security camera. I laughed with her over the story that I'd pulled Jake out of a burning car with one hand while wielding a pistol in the other, all the while belting out the "Cop's" theme song at the top of my lungs. Inside, I died a little. No wonder people were staring at me.

With my special order of a variety of wheat beers from a small Colorado brewery tucked in the trunk, I tried to figure out what to do next. I considered checking in on Jake, but until I'd confirmed that Eli had left town, I didn't want to take the chance of running into him. The shooting range seemed as good of a place as any to burn a couple of hours.

Only one other person was practicing, so I had my pick of bays. Not wanting to bother the guy who'd gotten there first, I picked the one way at the other end. I loaded up my target, put on the rented eye and ear protection, and went to work.

I shouldn't have blamed it on the gun, but I was better than that. The bulls-eye remained as elusive as a unicorn. Frustrated, I tore down the old target and mounted a new one. As I sent it sailing down the lane, the target in the lane next to me followed. I hadn't even noticed that someone set up in that bay. Busy reloading the magazine, I half-watched as the person fired a quick six rounds, all center shots.

Damn, he was good. Or she. I didn't want to make assumptions. Gave me some motivation. I couldn't beat them, but I should be able to match their accomplishment.

I adjusted my stance, raised the gun, fired, and missed again. Okay, I'd hit the target, but in the upper left quadrant. After wiping my palms on my pants leg, I tried again. I didn't aim for center, but down and to the right. The second bullet hit the target close to where the first shot had gone.

I swore silently, knowing what was wrong, and not knowing how to correct it.

"You're anticipating the recoil and it's throwing your shot off," said a voice from the next booth. The ear muffs distorted the sound, but the voice seemed familiar. "Lean forward slightly before you fire the next round."

I'm sure he was just trying to be helpful, but I really wasn't in the mood. I wanted to be by myself and wallow in my self-pity. "Thanks," I muttered, not meaning it. I considered packing up my stuff and finding somewhere else to go. I'd never taken my suitcase out of the trunk, so I could go anywhere the wind blew me. Or, I could try again, hit the bulls-eye, and prove something to myself. Show him a thing or two in the process. I just needed to overcome the vision of Eric bleeding in the street that haunted me. Each time I pulled the trigger, it wasn't the target I saw, it was Eric's face when the first bullet hit him.

I needed something else to focus on. I brought the target to me, pulled a pen out of my purse, and sketched a couple bottles and tin cans on the paper. That should do it.

After sending the target back down the lane, I picked up the Berretta, and, with the safety on, bounced it between my hands to become comfortable holding it. Mr. Know-It-All next door chuckled when he noticed the change in my target. I'd show him.

My quarry was a bottle I'd drawn over the bulls-eye. I'd done this enough times that I should be able to perform the motions by instinct. I'd been over-thinking and over-analyzing. With a swift flow of movements, I released the safety, raised the gun, and fired. The bottle was toast.

If it had been a real bottle, glass shards would be flying everywhere. No, I didn't hit dead-center, but close enough. I steadied my breath and aimed for the one to the left. BAM! And in my imagination it was lying on the desert floor.

I missed the next one, but barely. A second attempt took it out. After reloading, I finished off the rest of the drawn targets. Yes! The girl was back.

"Good shooting," came from next door.

"Thanks."

"I'm glad to see you can take care of yourself."

Who the hell was this guy? Was Chief Sorenson over there? Had he tracked me here for a reason?

I set the Berretta on the counter and stepped backwards to look around the barrier between us.

Even with his back to me, I knew who it was. No, not the chief. Much worse. I wasn't prepared for this.

Eli.

I quickly moved back behind the separating wall and put both of my hands on the counter. The way my heart raced, I needed more than a deep breath to handle this, I needed a good stiff drink.

"I thought you'd be back in Florida by now," I said, making sure to keep my voice steady. "Your boss must be about ready to fire you."

"I'll be leaving this afternoon," Eli said after a long pause.

"So nice of you to drop by and say goodbye." I raised the Beretta and drilled a shot right in the middle of the target.

He matched my shot with one of his own. "So nice of you to let me know what you were up to."

I banged the now-empty magazine down on the counter, and re-filled it. "So nice of you to return my phone calls for the past week." A bullet went whizzing down the lane and struck almost the same spot as the last one.

"I'm glad I didn't." His own shot didn't make the middle of the target. I grinned. "Nobody wants to be broken up with by text or voice mail."

"It's hard to break up with someone who you think dropped off the face of the earth." Two shots left my gun in no time flat. I didn't pay attention to where they hit.

"It's hard to call someone when your phone is smashed to bits." His shots landed wildly off the bulls-eye.

"It's hard to believe someone who owns a whole damn company can't afford to buy a damn cell phone." The placement of my next bullet was perfectly on target.

"Maybe someone was stuck where they couldn't buy a cell phone." His answering shot was just as good.

"Maybe someone should have sent an email."

"Maybe someone didn't have an internet connection."

"Maybe someone should have picked up a landline and called. Or driven that fancy yellow car to where someone else worried about him."

"Maybe someone got snowed in and had to wait while that fancy yellow car got a new drive train."

I remember hearing about a big snow storm that hit several states south of us. Eli would have needed to drive through the area.

There was a long verbal silence, but a barrage of shots from two guns continued. Suddenly I was very, very tired. I brought the target up to my station and ripped the paper off the base. I turned to get a broom to clean up my spent shells and ran right into Eli's chest.

Chapter 31

Eli's suit jacket was off, and the sleeves of his tailored dark blue shirt rolled up. His pale blue eyes were half-closed, and his hands clasped behind his back. His shoulder holster was empty, and I assumed he'd left his gun on the counter in his bay.

"Maybe someone," he said, "was afraid because someone else was spending time with a different lover."

"Maybe someone else tried to do her ex-lover a favor and help him get his life straight."

"Maybe someone else fell back in love with her ex-lover. Why else would she kiss him?"

"Maybe because he'd almost gotten killed doing her a favor?"

"Jake almost got killed?" Eli asked, startled.

It may have been a slight exaggeration, but I ran with it.

"Yeah. I got tired of him trying to be my bodyguard, so I hooked him up to be a bodyguard for Lori. It was my money paying him too, although he doesn't know that, and if you ever tell him I'll deny it. Haven't you read the police reports?"

"No." He blinked. "How many police reports are we talking about?"

Hell, I'd lost track. "You read the ones about the dead guy at the house and the window being shot out." It seemed like it happened a year ago, not just a couple of weeks.

Eli nodded.

"Then there's the one about the guy who broke into my place and I took out with hair spray."

His mouth formed a tight line.

"Aaand one about Lori getting shot, and the one about the person who shot at Lori, Jake and I, and the one about the other night when Jake was being followed and I followed both of them, and he shot Jake and I shot him. And the one about a video that showed who murdered the guy they found at the house. And if you can hack the FBI systems, there's a few reports that even the local police don't know about." And a few things I hadn't told the FBI and I hoped they'd never find out.

Eli remained wordless for a good thirty seconds or more and I couldn't stand it.

"Oh, and Chief Sorenson offered me a consultant job with the force, but I turned him down. I don't want to reveal my sources."

"I've only been out of the loop for a week." He sounded as if someone had punched him in the stomach.

"In that week Lando and I tried to track you down every way we could figure out. He's hacked airline sites and called local hospitals. I've searched for reports of small airplanes crashing and tried to find out if there were any patients with amnesia that looked like you. Shoot, my suitcase is still in Dolores's trunk. I planned to hit the road and search for you. Although Lando still hasn't told me what kind of car you drive."

"It's an old Acura. I left it at the storage yard where I kept the Charger. I thought it would only take me two days to get here. I figured I'd bring Jake his car, he'd leave town and you'd be mine again."

"And then you saw me kissing him."

"Then I saw you kissing him. If that cop hadn't stopped me I would have been on my way back to Florida."

"I sent that officer after you. Well, I asked Chief Sorenson to send him. When I didn't see Jake's car last night, I figured you'd already left."

"I was going to. Then I called the office and didn't finish handling emergencies until late last night."

"But here you are today."

"I couldn't sleep last night, and I saw you driving by the hotel. I realized I couldn't leave without seeing you one more time and making sure you were all right. What were you doing out that late?"

I held my arms out to my side and avoided the question. "As you can see, I'm all right." Physically, anyway. Emotionally I was a wreck.

"I hoped you were looking for me." With one

hand, he started to reach for my cheek, but pulled it back. "And afraid you were looking for Jake."

"If I wanted Jake, all I had to do was go to his hotel room. I have the key."

Eli's body stiffened. "Why?"

"I took care of him when he was sick, remember?" Yeah, I'd nursed him back to health just to set him up for getting shot. Some friend I was. "But there's a trend here, and I don't like it."

"What are you talking about?"

"You don't trust me, Eli. To tell you the truth, I'm not sure I trust you either. You've been keeping secrets from me. What sort of relationship is that?"

I wasn't planning on saying those words. But when they came out of my mouth, I knew they were true.

Eli closed his eyes and sucked in air as though he couldn't fill his lungs. It looked like he was having a panic attack, and I reached out and gently laid my hand on his shoulder. "Eli?"

"I'm use to keeping secrets, Harmony." The words came out slowly as if he was forcing them out. "My entire adult life I've had to, first when I was in the Rangers and now with the business." He opened his eyes and I scanned his face, trying to read it, unsuccessfully. "Trust doesn't come easy to me."

"That's understandable." I moved my hand back to my side. Where did that leave us?

"I talked to Jake earlier this morning."

The sudden switch of topics threw me for a loop

and made me nervous, but I rolled with it. "How's he doing? I planned to go by and check up on him later. Maybe take him to lunch or something. I imagine he's tired of hanging around the hotel."

"He didn't tell me he'd been shot. We talked about you." Eli's face was expressionless.

I tried to play it cool, but my stomach quivered. "All good things, I hope."

Eli moved an inch closer to me. "He told me that he'd blown it with you, and it was up to me to restore the honor of the Hennessey name. That I'd be a fool to let you go and he'd do me bodily damage if I hurt you."

I didn't anticipate that.

"What I'm trying to say, Harmony," Eli said as he reached out and tucked a stray lock of hair behind my ear, "Is I'm sorry. Give me another chance. Please?"

The firing range didn't seem like the best place to continue the conversation, and it was lunchtime anyway. Going home wasn't an option because a phone call to Joe let me know the reporter was still hanging around. So off to Mama D's we went, with hopes of getting a quiet booth. The lunch rush should have been over. But I forgot it was Friday, and all the office workers in town go out to eat. That's the way it seemed, anyway.

Which meant Eli and I got seated at a table in the middle of everything. To make matters worse, people kept stopping by our table to check and make sure I was okay after my adventure. One group of diners hummed the chorus of "Bad Boys" as they walked by us on their way out. It didn't provide a very good background for a private discussion. In one respect, it worked to my advantage. I hadn't made up my mind what I wanted to happen. Did I want to give him another chance, or break my heart now and say goodbye so he wouldn't break it later?

By the end of the meal, Eli kept sneaking glances at his watch. At least, he thought he was being sneaky, and each time I pretended not to see. I decided to put us both out of misery.

"What time do you have to leave, Eli?" I asked, my heart falling into little pieces.

"My flight's at six."

Too damn soon. I did some rapid calculations. At the most, we had two hours left together. "You're welcome to hang out at my place for a while," I said. "I think we've worn out our welcome here. If you ask nicely, I might let you use my WiFi." I just hoped that pesky reporter had left.

He studied my face, as if searching for a hidden message, but I carefully maintained a blank expression. Not that my poker face would win any tournaments, but I didn't want to give away my real intentions. Of course, I wasn't sure what my plans were.

"That would be good," he said. "That way I can spend time with the folks tomorrow. I'm glad Lando didn't contact them any earlier than he did. And Monday, I suspect Darla will tie me to my chair until I get everything done she has lined up for me."

That gave me an idea. I wondered if I still had the ball of twine stashed in the closet. Or I could use a couple of my scarves.

"Tell me more about your company, Eli," I said while I put on a pot of coffee and he fired up his laptop. For some odd reason, the city decided to make urgent repairs to the street. It was closed to everyone but residents. Although, other than the bulldozer parked at one end, I didn't see any sign of real work going on. But the news station van was gone, and I doubted it was a coincidence.

He sat at the table waiting for his laptop to boot up and shrugged. "Not much to tell. While serving in the military, I realized the importance of security for government programs and played around with creating fixes for a couple of the programs we used. Came up with a few ideas for civilian use, but didn't start tackling them until I got out. Sold one program I developed to an established company, and it gave me enough money to start my own."

He smiled at me when I handed him a filled cup. "You want to hear what I did while I was stuck for four days in the worst possible motel in Nowheresville, USA?"

"What?"

"I wrote a new app for cell phones, to sound an alarm if someone tries to attach to your hotspot if you have one going. It's an idea that's been brewing in the back of my mind for some time, but I never had time to do anything with it. With no meetings to go to, no one to bother me, and without the temptation of the internet, I programmed it, start to finish. Haven't tested it yet, since my cell phone got smashed when it fell out of my pocket and under the wheels of the tow truck hauling the Charger away, but it will work, I'm sure of it."

The excitement in his eyes made me grin.

"I haven't checked if there's another product on the market that does the same thing," he continued. "But it doesn't matter. I'm not sure if I want to sell it." He looked at me sheepishly. "I did it again, didn't I?"

"Did what?"

"Got carried away talking about a dumb little program I created. Sorry about that."

I took the coffee cup out of his hands. "Do you know how happy you looked? It was kind of sexy." I leaned over and barely touched my lips to his.

"Sexy? Usually I get made fun of for being such a geek."

Our second kiss lasted longer. "Yes, sexy."

I gave a little shriek when he suddenly pulled me into his lap.

"Should I talk Python or Ruby," he asked. "Or are you a C++ type of girl?"

"I haven't the foggiest idea what you're rattling on about," I laughed. His mouth found a particularly sensitive spot on my neck. "But don't stop."

And, of course, his new phone rang.

Chapter 32

So did mine. Talk about a mood-buster. We exchanged glances, and since mine rarely rang, I shrugged and answered it while he reached for his. One of my authors was in a panic because she was up against a deadline and needed to verify the information I'd provided her about ancient Egypt. By the time I got off the call, Eli was engrossed in whatever emergency he'd been summoned to handle.

An hour and a half later, I brushed one hand along his cheek. "It's time, Eli. Why don't I take you to the airport? We can drop off the rental at the agency here." He'd gotten a rental car for his stay in town and the trip to the airport, and returning it locally would give us a little more time together.

"Let me send this email." He pressed a few keys, waited for the laptop to turn off, and closed the lid. "Are you going to let me drive Dolores?" he asked with an impish grin. "If not, I might as well take myself."

I swatted him lightly. "Aren't you the guy who broke the Charger?"

"I got lucky with that. I pulled onto a scenic side road a few miles earlier. I had to fight it to get to the side of the road safely If I'd been going full speed on the interstate, I'm not sure I would have been able to control it. It's at the garage getting a once over to make sure it doesn't have any other mechanical issues."

I shivered. Too many close calls. "In that case, I'll give you a chance. But I'll be watching you," I teased.

He stood and gave me a kiss. "Thanks, Buttercup."

That was new. I gave him a questioning look. "Buttercup? Where did that come from?"

He took a deep breath. "I was overseas, Small village, can't tell you where. It was the end of winter, and everything was brown and dead-looking. From a distance I saw a small patch of bright yellow. I thought it was a rag or something, but it was windy, and it wasn't blowing around like I expected. As I got closer, I figured out it was a bunch of little yellow flowers. Somebody told me they were buttercups." Eli reached out and stroked my cheek. "You're like that. A patch of brightness in my life."

Buttercup. Once I got done melting, I mulled it over in my mind. Yeah, I could live with it.

The trip to Pittsburgh went by too fast. Dolores, ever the lady, handled like a charm for Eli on the clear and dry roads. But the nagging knowledge that it would be too long before I saw him again destroyed the mood. That and the prickly feeling at the back of my skull.

It may have been because Eli kept checking the rear view mirror. "What's up?" I asked, turning around to see.

"Not sure. I keep seeing the same car. Two guys in it. They might just be traveling the same direction as us. I can't tell."

"Which car?"

"It's an older car, faded blue with body damage. I don't see it now."

I kept looking, but didn't spot it. "Maybe they took the last exit." I twisted back around to face forward.

Eli nodded, but he kept his eye on the road behind us until the turn-off for the airport. The traffic got heavier the closer we got to the airport, and if someone was following us, it would be far too easy for them to hide. Lots of cars were going the same way as us, but nothing to show they weren't just fellow travelers. The driver in front of us stayed a steady five mph under the speed limit, and the driver behind us kept looking for an opportunity to change lanes. When he finally got an opening, he didn't look our way as he passed us.

` At one of those "waiting for a plane to land" lots, Eli pulled off. "We're a few minutes early. I figured we'd say goodbye here. Once we get to the drop off lanes, they chase you off so fast it makes your head spin."

Been there, done that.

"Besides, I need to stretch before I stand in the security lines forever," he added.

Sounded like a good plan. Other people were out of their vehicles, walking around and talking on cell phones, or leaning against their cars and staring at the cloudy skies. More than one couple occupied their time with hugs and kisses. I needed a few of those myself.

We opened our doors simultaneously and I swung my legs around to get out of the car. As I stood, an arm suddenly draped itself across my shoulder. Even through my coat, I felt the pressure of a gun pressed into my side.

"Nice to see you again, Martha," a voice hissed in my ear.

Between the car door and the man's body pressed against mine, I had no room to maneuver. I stole a glance in Eli's direction and spotted another man standing close to him. Eli's hands clutched the top of the door frame, and he looked ready to explode. We were in trouble.

His gun was locked safely inside his luggage, and the Beretta stowed under my seat. The only weapon left was my meager set of self-defense skills. And I couldn't attempt anything if it meant putting Eli in danger. But then I remembered. Eli had been a

Ranger. Weren't they supposed to be some crazy kind of super soldier?

I took the lead. After all, I knew who these guys were. The one pretending to be Eli's best friend was Steve-Alexander. And the one standing close to me? Yeah, I recognized the voice.

"What do you want, Orson?" I asked loudly. Even if he was the fake Orson, I didn't have another name to call him.

He shoved the barrel of the gun deep in my side. If we got out of this alive, I'd have at least one bruise to show for it. "Keep your voice down," he said harshly. "Or you'll regret it."

Eli's eyes narrowed when he realized it wasn't a random robbery. "Right, because you'll shoot me with all these people around. In fact, I saw someone taking pictures of the car."

Steve-Alexander jerked his head. "She's right. This car attracts too much attention."

"Get them into ours," Orson ordered.

Steve reached out and grabbed the key out of Eli's hand. "I'll come back for this sweet little thing later."

No way would I be getting into their car. But I could try to drag this out, pump them for info, and get them to underestimate me at the same time. I hoped Eli would play along.

Orson grabbed my arm, twisted it, and pushed me in front of him. I let out a soft screech as if he hurt me, stifling the instinct to put my training to use. "What do you want?" I fake-sobbed.

"I want my ring back," he said "And you're my ticket to get it."

He was crazy, I decided, and that made him more dangerous. "Your ring?" I held up my right hand. On a whim, I'd put it on when getting dressed. "This is the only ring I have. Take it and let us go."

Orson roughly pulled the ring from my finger, barely glanced at it and tossed it to the pavement. It caught a stray beam of sunshine and glittered against the black surface. I hoped someone would find it and realize it was special. "That piece of junk isn't what I'm after." He pushed me again. "But I figure the police will swap the real ring for you. And your friend is a bonus."

"Matt has nothing to do with this. Let him go." I risked a glance at Eli, hoping he would understand. I didn't want our captors to know who he was.

Although Steve had Eli's arm twisted painfully behind his back, he gave me the slightest nod. I took it as encouragement and plunged ahead.

"You really don't think the police will trade that ring for me anyway, do you?"

"They'd better, if they don't want a dead body on their doorstep. Or should I say, another dead body?" His quiet laugh was vicious.

Another dead body? Did that mean he had something to do with Booker's death? The possibility made me shiver.

"Why did you try to plant it in my place anyway?"

"Easy. I'd report it as stolen, send an anonymous tip to the police where to find it, and either you or Hennessey would be in jail. And I bet if you were arrested he'd take the fall. Sweet, eh?"

Not in my book. "What do you want, for me to walk up to the police and demand the ring?"

"Even better. I have a bone to pick with your friend Hennessey. He gets the ring, gives it to me, I kill him, disappear, the police will find you and everybody's happy, right?"

Not by my definition of the word. "What did Jake do to you?"

"He messed up a deal I had. I was putting together a big job for Booker and he got there first." Orson shoved me against a faded blue, beat up old car. "Now shut up and get inside." As he reached to open the car door, he shifted the gun to his left hand, giving me the opportunity I'd been waiting for. I prayed that Eli would follow my lead.

I clasped my hands together, swiveled, and with all my strength, swung and screamed.

The worst I could do was attract attention as I got shot. The best I could do was break Orson's nose and expect the pain would make him drop the gun. I hoped for the best.

❋ ❋ ❋

"You missed your flight," I said. Eli and I sat on the curb, clutching foam cups of coffee that had miraculously appeared from somewhere. We sat side by side, shoulders touching, and watched the last ambulance take off, sirens silent. The police started removing their barricades.

"I'm going to get so much crap," he moaned.

Not as much crap as I'd already gotten. "Well, at least your cell phone's not broke." I tossed the rest of the coffee in my cup down my throat. With no trash barrel handy, I held on to the cup because I didn't want to litter. Not with all the law enforcement types around. "You can call someone and let them know. Who was going to pick you up at the airport?"

"Darla. She'll kill me."

"So she's first on your list. Or should you call your mother and then Darla?"

"Won't matter," he muttered glumly.

One of the Highway Patrol officers approached us. Exhausted, I didn't even look for his name tag. "We found this, ma'am. Is it yours?' He held out his hand and handed me a ring.

Somewhere I found the energy to smile. "Yes, thank you." I slipped it back onto my right hand. Surprisingly, it wasn't damaged. I'd expected it to have been run over and squashed by one of the many police vehicles.

There were a lot of them. Someone had called 911 before I screamed; realizing something weird was going down. By the time I'd swung at the fake Olson and Eli tackled Steve-Alexander, help was already on the way in the form of airport police. Although I hadn't made Olson drop his gun, I broke his nose before a couple of men in the lot joined the fracas. I had a few bruises, including a big one on my cheek where Olson connected with his fist, but was in relatively good shape. Especially compared to Olson, who had the fury of three big men pound him into the ground.

Eli fared worse than me. Steve-Alexander not only had a gun, but a knife. And while Eli got the gun away from him, the knife found its mark several times. Nothing deep or serious, and Eli refused an ambulance ride to the hospital once the paramedics cleaned and bandaged the wounds.

The airport police weren't the only ones who showed up, just the first, being the closest. But since the lot wasn't technically on airport property, and it wasn't technically in a city either, the Highway Patrol came to the rescue as well. And before it was over, lo and behold, the FBI in the form of Felton *and* Garza showed up. Frankly, I thought Garza seemed disappointed when he realized the Hennessey involved wasn't Jake.

The appearance of the feds did the trick and got Steve-Alexander talking. Both men maintained their right to silence until Felton waved his badge around and spouted off all the federal level charges the men faced. Then Steve was more than ready to rat out Claude Corsinski—AKA fake-Olson—in exchange for lesser charges.

"Are you sure you're all right?" Felton asked me for about the twenty-third time, coming and sitting down beside me.

"I'm in need of a long, hot bath, but other than that, I'm fine," I assured him yet again.

He took the cup out of my hands and handed it to Garza who had followed him. "This isn't the ending I expected."

"I hope it's the end." At least, it appeared all the bad guys were rounded up. Well, with the exception of the real Orson Wallington. I hoped he was hundreds of miles away. Felton didn't need to know about him.

"I'm still upset you weren't notified Thermopolis made bail."

Thermopolis. He meant Steve-Alexander. "I suppose it slipped through the cracks in all the excitement." Chief Sorensen would get an earful about it later.

Felton grunted. "Maybe. But you can rest easy, because I can't foresee a judge giving him bail again."

I hoped not. "I still don't understand how Corsinski was tied to Booker's murder."

"From what Thermopolis said, Judson paid Booker to become a partner in the business, but Booker cooked the books and claimed there was no profit to split." Judson was Eric's last name. "Corsinski was a regular supplier to the store Judson ran for Booker, and they worked up a scheme to take ownership between the two of them. But when the original plan didn't work, they resorted to killing him. Figured since Judson's name should be on the paperwork, it would be easy for Judson to take over."

"Obviously, they didn't count on Booker being married," Eli said.

"Nope. They thought he and your friend were divorced. When she was arrested for the murder, and the news came out they were still married, it complicated matters. They figured the easiest way to solve the issue was to kill her too."

Lucky for us Eric was incredibly bad at hitting his targets.

"Where did Thermopolis fit into their plans?"

Felton shrugged. "I think his story is pretty much on the mark. He was a bit player who got suckered into being part of a bigger con. Corsinski set up the thefts, arranged for book signings to use as a cover and he just carried them out. He wasn't all that good at it, from what we can determine."

Based on how badly Thermopolis had messed up breaking into my place that sounded about right. Although I was curious about it, I decided not to mention the ring. I didn't want to drag Jake into the discussion.

Garza must have read my mind. "I've been researching the ring Thermopolis had when he broke into your place," he said.

"Oh?" I asked casually.

"Yeah. The only thing I've been able to track down is a story about a ring in England in the 1800's. Something about a minor English lord who married for family duty, and, late in life, after he'd become a widower, found his childhood sweetheart and married her. What I can't find is anything to tell me what happened to the ring. No reports of it being lost or stolen or anything. I asked for help from Scotland Yard, but there's no way to tie the story back to a particular family, so we can't ask the heirs. It was their version of an urban legend."

The story varied from the one Jake had told, but that was the way of folk tales. I wondered what would happen to the ring, once it was no longer needed for evidence.

Felton gracefully rose to his feet. "We'll be in touch, Miss Duprie, if we need anything else. I suggest you take it easy the next few days. You may find yourself hurting in places you didn't expect."

"Of course." I didn't feel like moving yet, but now that the barricades were gone, traffic was flowing into the lot. Besides, it was getting late, the sun had set, and sitting in the cold wouldn't do me any good. I got up, not at all gracefully.

Felton hesitated, then held out his hand. "I want to thank you for the assistance you've given us."

"I won't say it's been a pleasure," I said, with as much of a smile as I could manage, taking his proffered hand. "I'm glad I could help. But I hope you understand when I say I don't want to do it again." So much for my dreams of being a PI.

He turned to Eli. "Take care of her, Hennessey. Try to keep her out of trouble."

Eli nodded. "Try is the operative word here. I haven't had much luck so far." He and Felton shared one of those mysterious glances that make up so much of male conversation. I took it to mean "What's a man supposed to do?" I'd get Eli for that later.

When Felton walked away, Garza didn't follow

him. "Give your friend Hennessey a message for me," he said. "The other Hennessey. Tell him he's not off the hook. I'll be keeping my eye on him, and when he messes up, he's mine."

"I'll pass the word along, Agent. Good night."

I shivered as the taillights of the agents' car disappeared down the road. "Cold, Harmony?" Eli asked, as he wrapped his arms around me. In that moment, all of my doubts about our relationship disappeared.

"Cold and tired."

"It doesn't matter which as long as it gives me an excuse to hold you."

I was afraid to lean against him, not sure where the cuts were on his body and how much he was hurting.

"Is it bad I don't want to drive home tonight?" I asked.

"After what we went through? I'm not sure it would be safe for either one of us to drive very far. Did you have something in mind?"

"Well, I never took my suitcase out of Dolores' trunk. How about we find a hotel with a whirlpool to spend the night in?"

His arms tightened. "We could order room service for supper," he breathed into my ear.

"Do you think there's a nice hotel nearby that doesn't offer free internet?"

"I doubt it, but I'll leave my laptop in the trunk."

"Yeah, and I'll put Betsy there too."

"Betsy?" He turned to examine my face. "Who's Betsy?"

"The Beretta. Her name came to me when I was wishing I could reach under the seat and grab her."

Eli's mouth twitched.

"Don't laugh," I pouted.

"Not even a chuckle?" he asked, using one finger to trace a line down my arm.

"Not even the tiniest hint of a chuckle."

I didn't remember seeing any wounds on his shoulders, so I wrapped my hands loosely around his neck.

"You know you don't have to treat me like I'll break," Eli said. "I've been injured worse than this."

"More secrets?"

"No, just stories I haven't had time to tell you yet," he said before barely touching his lips to mine. I wanted more, but he pulled away. "Tonight we can swap stories."

"Or," I said, pulling him back. "We can swap spit."

He laughed, but only for a second. "Like this?" he asked as our mouths touched again.

Before we left the lot, his phone rang. It was Darla, trying to find out where he was. She was at the Orlando airport, waiting for him. After giving her a short explanation of the afternoon's events, she agreed to arrange another flight for him and to text him the information. Then, it made sense for him to call his mother, and for me to call Luke and let him know I wouldn't be home and not to worry.

When we found the perfect hotel a few miles down the road, room service became a priority. While we waited for our twin dishes of Chicken Fettuccine Alfredo to arrive, I slipped into the bathroom to take an all-too-quick shower. I was putting my hair back into its traditional bun when Eli knocked.

"Food's here," he called through the door.

I cracked the door open and peeked out. "Are we alone?"

"Yes?" he answered, with a question in his voice.

I opened the door a little further. While I'd been in the shower, Eli had taken off his destroyed shirt and switched into a white t-shirt. A t-shirt that fit nicely, showing off his muscular chest. It made me feel better about what I was wearing.

For some reason, all those many days ago, I'd packed a silky red nightgown when I'd prepared to go find him. Thinking I might have to seduce him away from the beautiful temptress who'd kidnapped him. That's what I was wearing when I nervously pushed the bathroom door open the rest of the way.

Eli was removing the covers from our dishes when he saw me. He smiled and let them fall. I jumped a little when they clanged against the plates. "I don't know where that came from," The huskiness of his voice sent shivers down my spine. "But I approve. You're beautiful all the time,

Harmony, but now…" He smirked. "Too bad you won't get to wear it very long."

For an injured man, he moved fast. I didn't even have time to blush. In a second, he'd lifted me and carried me to the king sized bed. He laid me down gently, and started to take off his t-shirt.

"Wait," I said. Startled, he stopped in mid-pull. "Isn't there something you need to do first?" Besides, I wanted to be the one to do the honors of stripping his clothes off.

"The door is locked." He sat on the bed beside me. "And the do not disturb sign is posted." He reached into his pants pocket, pulled out a small foil package, and smiled as he showed it to me. "What else?"

I rolled away from him and grabbed my phone from the nightstand. With a flourish worthy of a game-show hostess, I held down the button to turn it off.

With a wide grin, he reached into his pocket again and pulled out his phone. He looked at me, then at it, then at me again, and copied my movements. The mellow sounds of a phone powering down never sounded so sweet. He took my phone from me, laid them both down on the dresser, and leaned close. "Anything else, Buttercup?"

"No," I whispered.

"I can think of one more thing." He lifted my head and started taking my hairpins out. After removing each one, he kissed me somewhere new. "I want your hair loose," he said. "I want to run my fingers through it, and I want to see it spread across the pillow. Do you have an issue with that?"

"No, just hurry."

He laughed. "We have all night, and I plan to use as much of it as I can." He stopped, mid-kiss. "There is one rule tonight."

"What's that?" I asked, propping myself up on my elbows. Were there other secrets he'd kept from me?

He gently pushed me back down. "The only name…" he said, running one finger down my nose, "… I want to hear coming from these gorgeous lips tonight…" the finger moved to my lips, "…is *mine*."

As his mouth replaced his fingers, I couldn't think of a single reason why that might be a problem.

The End (for now)

If you enjoyed Her Ladyship's Ring,
you might want to check out
Wolves' Pawn,
by P.J. MacLayne.

Dot McKenzie is a lone wolf-shifter on the run, using everything available to her to stay one step ahead of her pursuers. When she is offered a chance for friendship and safety with the Fairwood pack, she accepts.

Gavin Fairwood, reluctant heir to the Fairwood pack leadership, is content to let life happen while he waits. But old longings surface when he appoints himself Dot's protector…and becomes more than a friend.

But her presence puts the pack and her new friends at risk, and Dot must go into hiding again. When old enemies threaten the destruction of the Fairwood pack, it will take the combined efforts of Dot and Gavin to save it.

Can anything save their love and Dot's life when she becomes a pawn in a pack leader's deadly game?

Coming soon:
The Baron's Cufflinks
Oak Grove Mysteries 3